MISTERS & MOCHAS

BOOK 2 OF THE HIGH SCHOOL CLOWNS & COFFEE GROUNDS SERIES

BY A.J. MACEY

Cover: Moonstruck Cover Design and Photography
Editing: Personal Touch Editing
Formatting: Inked Imagination Author Services

This book is dedicated to...

My daughter, Evelyn Rose.
Run wild and follow your dreams.

WARNING

The High School Clowns & Coffee Grounds Series is a WhyChoose/Reverse Harem trilogy featuring MFMM meaning the female main character doesn't have to choose between her love interests.

This book contains references involving PTSD, sexual assault recollections, abuse, underage drinking, and other themes that some readers may find triggering.

BLURB

Emma's to-do list:
1- stay away from Brad
2- survive the ACT
3- make memories with my boys

Moving cross country a month into my senior year
was turning out to not be so bad despite all my initial
dramatics. I had made some awesome friends and even
got a great part-time gig at the coffee shop. Oh, let's not
forget to mention I got a boyfriend... three in fact, all of
who have made the not-so-awesome parts of my forced
relocation after my parents' divorce easier to handle.

But when our creepy classmate decides to press charges
against Jesse, the confrontation with my parents finally
comes to head, and my still-pestering ex from California
decides to take it up a notch- will we be able to deal with
all the stress, or will we end up in over our heads?

#TickedOffTuesday entries just got a whole lot longer,
but we can totally handle our senior year and make it to
graduation, right?

CONTENTS

Chapter 1

NOVEMBER 18TH

She stood in the storm, and when the wind did not blow her way, she adjusted her sails — Elizabeth Edwards
#IWillSurvive #BestFriendsEver #MotivationMonday

I stood in the parking lot, surrounded by Reid and Kingston, while Jesse grabbed his bag out of the back of Reid's Jeep. Sighing, I mentally prepared myself for the storm of questions I was sure I was about to get. Thankfully, it was almost Thanksgiving break.

Only *a week and three days of classes*. I tried to make that my mantra for this week. *Maybe if I say it enough times, it'll sink in.*

Eight days of questions, then I'd have a four-day weekend to spend with my boys.

"Ready?" Reid questioned. Jesse nodded before turning to Kingston and me. I sighed again and returned the gesture. Adjusting my backpack, I steeled myself to enter the school. *Maybe they hadn't heard about what happened,* I hoped—until we crossed the threshold.

They'd *definitely* heard about Jesse's arrest.

Stares from every single student shot our way, and hushed whispers buzzed around us as we walked past. I held my head high, despite wanting to curl into myself,

1

taking everything in stride because right now, all I cared about was Jesse knew we were here for him. Reaching down, I intertwined my fingers with his and squeezed lightly.

"Hey, Emma, boys," Zoey greeted with a bright smile, Aubrey and our other friends following suit as if there was nothing going on, and we totally weren't the entertainment for the entire student body of Arbor Ridge High School.

"Hey, Zo," I replied with a grateful smile. "How was your weekend?"

"Boring. Homework and cleaning to prep for Thanksgiving next week. You? Did you guys have a good time at Kingston's barbeque? That was this weekend, right?" Zoey continued to ask questions, looking over at Reid and Kingston, where they stood behind Jesse, the latter with his nose buried in a textbook as it always was before school. Kingston answered, content to play along and pretend it was a normal morning. I knocked my knee into hers with a tiny thank you. The bell rang, and we all headed to homeroom. Flashing me a wink, she headed down the hall with Kingston, Carter, and Jason. Reid and Aubrey broke away leaving Jesse, Brayden, and I at the table.

"Come on, babe," I said, nudging Jesse with my elbow as soon as his book was put away. Smiling, he pulled me into his muscled chest and pressed his lips to mine in a quick kiss. My heart sputtered as we walked to homeroom, Brayden chuckling at my dreamy grin before breaking away from us.

Homeroom passed quickly, Jesse and I content to study or read so we wouldn't have to look around us at all the curious, gossip-hungry gazes aimed our way. When the bell rang, I stuffed my notebook back in my bag, expecting Jesse to have taken off as usual, but when I looked up, I noticed him standing, patiently waiting.

"I don't want you to have to fend off any questions or shit by yourself," he murmured, answering my unspoken question. My confused expression smoothed out in understanding, and we walked down the hall toward my American History class. We almost made it before someone stepped in front of us. The newcomer had bleached blonde hair, styled into a buzz cut, and I had absolutely no idea who he was.

So much for this day going smoothly.

"If it isn't the delinquent and the slut," the boy sneered, looking from Jesse to me. My stomach flipped, my cheeks burning from the laughter of the surrounding students. Jesse stepped forward, half blocking me.

"Don't talk about her like that," Jesse ground out.

"Oooh, going to beat me up too, criminal?" the boy taunted. Pretending to cower, he mocked Jesse with a faux whimper. His fake fear only served to amp up the crowd slowing around us, stopping to watch the confrontation. Jesse took half a step forward, but I curled my hand around his arm, eager to avoid this escalating.

"He's not worth it, Jess," I murmured softly, glaring at the jerk who had started this. "Let's get to class." Jesse exhaled sharply, but followed me without argument, his hand intertwined with mine.

"Aww, called off by your bitch. Is she that good in bed, or are you just a coward?" the jerk called from behind us. *That's it.* My head whipped around.

"Go screw yourself, you're wasting air." Without further banter, I stormed down the hall, already over the day.

"Jeez, what took so long?" Reid asked, his shoulders

tensing as we drew nearer, taking in our hard gazes.

"Assholes trying to pick a fight," Jesse whispered. "Pretty sure this is just the beginning."

"Ugh," Reid groaned, his hand coming down his face, muffling the sound slightly before he looked at us. "You guys alright?"

"Yeah, I've heard worse," Jesse added. The bell cut him off, but before darting off to his class, he gave me one last kiss. Unfortunately, not even the sweet gesture could shake away the dark cloud rapidly descending over me.

"Come on, Cali girl," Reid said, wrapping his arm around my shoulders and directing me into the classroom.

It's going to be a long day.

I flopped ungracefully into my chair in my nutrition class, completely worn out and exhausted, even though it was only the third class of the day. Doodling in the corner of my notebook, I kept my head down and my eyes off of the people I heard whispering about me.

"Hey, Emma," Ashley greeted politely, her lips curled in a sympathetic smile.

Ever since the party from hell, the gossips had been less of a nuisance to me. Ashley and the twins running interference by sharing the truth of what had actually happened compared to spreading the rumors still zipping through the student body. So, while it had been a rough start with them, it turned out not so bad.

At least for right now.

"Hey," I responded quietly, unable to drum up much enthusiasm.

"How are you doing?" she asked in a whisper. "We heard about what happened in the hall earlier. Dylan is a huge ass who's always trying to get attention, so try not to let him bother you."

"So, that's his name," I muttered with a tired laugh. *Douchebag Dylan does have a nice ring to it.* "Thanks. I'm definitely trying to keep a positive attitude, but it's, uh, a struggle."

That's one way to describe it.

"I can imagine. Do you want us to try to control as much as we can?" one of the twins asked. I still hadn't figured out who was who, so I just flashed a grateful smile with a nod.

"That would be great, but let's do so before lunch when everyone's not hovering around me," I murmured. They agreed, all of us nailing down the details of where to meet before turning around to face the front of the classroom as Mrs. Sanders started her lecture.

At least there are a few people on my side.

"Let's go, Cali girl," Reid mumbled, dropping a kiss on the top of my head after we had packed up our backpacks and readied for lunch.

"Hold on," I pressed, steering him toward the top of the stairs. With nearly everyone rushing to get to the cafeteria, it was an easy spot to have privacy. When I neared the balcony, I stopped at the column we had decided on.

"What're we doing?" Reid asked, glancing around.

"Hopefully, doing damage control to the rumors going around," I explained, waving slightly to Ashley, Ivy, and Iris, who were coming down the hall toward us.

"Ah," Reid hummed, "very smart, Cali girl."

It was difficult to explain. Memories of what had happened at the party and Kingston's barbeque flashed through my mind as I recounted the details, but I had to shove all those feelings away. *You can do this, Em. It's what we need.* Ashley shook her head in disgust when I explained Brad and his family were more than likely going to fight us tooth and nail to see Jesse behind bars. As if on cue, I felt eyes on me. Glancing through the crowd, my gaze found the last person I wanted to see—Brad.

God, I hate those ugly boat shoes.

His cold, too bright eyes centered on me, and a devious Cheshire cat smile curled his lips. A shiver of fear worked its way up my spine as he took a bite of food off his fork, leisurely swirling his tongue around the metal tines. My appetite was lost, the feeling of Brad's hands and mouth on me completely ruining any thought of eating.

"Ugh, what a freaking creep," Right Twin exclaimed, her voice pulling my attention to those around me. They were all glaring at him, Reid more so than the girls, his arm curling around me possessively.

"I've always had a weird vibe from him and his snotty family," Left Twin agreed before looking to me. "Don't worry, we'll try to spread the truth."

"Seriously, thank you," I stated, unable to explain how much I appreciated their support. Feeling a small hint of relief, I curled into Reid's waiting arms.

"Come here, Cali girl, I got you."

"I know you do, babe," I mumbled, my words muffled by the press of my face against his chest. In his arms, I felt strong and safe.

Screw those jerks who think this situation is funny.

One day, they'll learn how much they screwed up by believing the wrong person. Until then?

I have my boys.

NOVEMBER 19TH

My dad proceeded to call me while I was in school and left a five second voicemail. This was like the eighth time I had talked to him since our move. I miss my dad, and whatever alien took him over can go back to its own planet.
#WhereIsMyDad #Abducted #TickedOffTuesday

"Bye, Babydoll," Kingston whispered, his lips brushing against the crest of my ear. "I'll text you." I blushed brightly as he started to leave, trailing after Reid and Jesse, who were climbing into the Jeep.

"Bye, King," I mumbled, my fingers brushing over my lips in a poor attempt to keep my giggle contained. He flashed me one more handsome smile before heading to the car.

"Emma!" my mother called from behind me, the garage door closing quickly. "Ah, good. Can you help me, please?" Nodding, I darted down the stairs and took two of her work bags as she pulled her small rolling file bag behind her.

"Wow, they're really keeping you busy, aren't they?" I joked, keeping my tone lighthearted when, in reality, I felt a chest deep ache, knowing I had basically been forgotten since flying to the middle of nowhere.

Or that my dad has barely talked to me.

Or that my boyfriend is facing assault charges.

Or that I know I have to sit down with Kingston's dad and recount every terrible detail from the party from hell.

"Yes, yes, they are. I have several contracts I'm working on and three major events I'm planning over the next month and a half," she explained breathlessly as we hauled her work stuff to the main floor and dropped it in her office. "You hungry? I'm going to make some sandwiches."

"Yes, please," I said, perking up.

Maybe she'll finally have dinner with me.

Settling into a chair at the table, I watched my mom flutter around the kitchen as she pulled out ingredients. We were both quiet, and while it wasn't necessarily an awkward silence, it was strained. *At least it is for me.* I was unsure of what to say or do. *How did my mom become a stranger in only a few months?*

"Stella Bell contacted me earlier today," she added randomly, and my heart thudded into my throat. I hadn't yet told her I was dating Kingston—let alone *three* boys—since she hadn't been around.

"Oh, yeah? What about?" I asked, keeping my tone curious but steady.

Well, as steady as I can when I get nervous.

"They're having a Thanksgiving get together next Thursday and asked if we wanted to come," she explained. My brows shot up. I had planned on going after Reid had basically whined today at lunch until I gave in. I mean, not that it was hard to convince me; I certainly didn't want to spend Thanksgiving alone.

"So, are you? Going, I mean. Kingston and the boys asked me today, and I planned on it, but I wasn't sure what your schedule was," I explained as my mom handed me a plate with a sandwich.

"I figured it would be good to get to know them and their parents a bit more."

"I think it's only going to be Kingston's parents. Reid's will be returning home from an international flight, and they're having their own family dinner on Saturday. Jesse's are working." Reid's part of the statement was true, but Jesse's? I had lied easily, hoping she wouldn't be able to tell I had no idea what his parents did or what they were doing for Thanksgiving.

"Well, that's a shame, but it would be nice to meet Stella and Kaleb," my mom replied simply before grabbing a soda out of the fridge and turning to leave the kitchen.

"Have some more work to do?" I called, my heart squeezing as she had turned to look at me.

"I have to input a bunch of information into the system for a meeting tomorrow with one of the clients. We can have dinner together tomorrow, how about that?" she compromised.

"Sounds great," I said, plastering a brittle smile on my face as she turned and walked into her office, my eyes filling as soon as she shut her office door.

Alone.

NOVEMBER 20TH

I proceeded to crush Reid's soul today when I told him that all Froot Loops are the same flavor.
#Oops #SorryBabe #MyBad #WeirdnessWednesday

"What's the plan tonight? I mean, other than studying, are we getting together after?" I asked, piling all the books I didn't need for studying and homework into my locker.

"Figured we can all go to the library or something, maybe Coffee Grounds and work on our stuff while you two study. If you want," Reid suggested.

"I'm good with that." Kingston agreed. "Get ahead on the last bit of reading for the test next week."

"Alright, studying, it is," I chuckled. "Let's go." We made

our way out into the emptying parking lot, content to stay silent as we walked to the Jeep.

"Can we stop by your place, Emma, and drop all our extra stuff off before we go? I could go for a pop," Reid asked as he looked to the back seat where Kingston and Jesse were buckling up.

"Works for me," Jesse responded, and Kingston nodded before smiling at me. My cheeks warming at his attention, I turned to face forward, watching the empty fields go by. With the weather change and Halloween finally over, the corn stalks had been cut down, leaving barren patches of land in their wake. It only took a few minutes until we were pulling in front of my house, my car sitting in the driveway since Reid had picked me up today.

The boys busied themselves with putting their bags in the basement, pulling out what they would need to study or work on as I made my way into the kitchen, my phone buzzing with a text before I could grab Reid his soda.

Mom: Had a last-minute snafu here at the office with one of the event's plans. Won't be home until late. Rain check on dinner?

My throat constricted, but I swiped the tears away and texted back, shoving my phone in my back pocket after turning it off. Opening the fridge, I came face to face with an empty appliance—nothing, not even a gallon of curdled milk on the shelves. Shoving the door shut, I scanned the cabinets and found only the butt of a loaf of bread left in its bag.

Just when I thought the week couldn't get any worse.

"Wow," Reid breathed as he looked over my shoulder. "Were you this low on groceries when we were here yesterday?"

"I don't know. I just had some water, and my mom made both of us a peanut butter sandwich when she got home," I mumbled, my lip finding its way in between my teeth, a nervous habit I'd never been able to break.

"Is your mom going to the store?" Jesse asked, looking in the freezer before the refrigerator. "Because there's literally nothing in here, Em."

"I, uh, don't know. I wrote out a list last week," I explained, pointing to the notepad as my cheeks bloomed in a wave of heat that had nothing to do with my boys being sweethearts. The warmth only grew as I noticed it was collecting dust.

"Let's hit the store before studying," Kingston suggested, looking at me with a sympathetic smile.

"Agreed. I don't want to know what Cali girl is like when she's hangry," Reid joked, squeezing me lightly. Despite the embarrassment flooding my system, I couldn't stop the smile that curled my lips. We made our way back out to Reid's Jeep, but before Reid could walk around to the driver's seat, I tugged on his sleeve.

"Thank you," I murmured, "for trying to help me feel better."

"Always, Cali girl." A wide smile appeared, his teeth bright against his olive skin and dark five o'clock shadow before he softly pressed his lips to mine. "Now, let's go get some food, maybe some treats, and we can blow off studying and watch some movies."

"Only if you wear your onesie," I teased, climbing into my seat. Reid's hazel eyes lit up.

"You got it."

Hopefully, the total doesn't come to more than what I have on me; otherwise, we'll be screwed.

Well, so much for that, I grumbled, staring at the total.

Forty dollars over the thirty I had with me, meaning I either had to magically make it appear in the next thirty seconds or put half of this back.

"Here you go," Reid handed over a wad of cash before I could pull out what I had in my wallet.

"Reid," I hissed under my breath, staring up at him in shock. He gave me a cocky smile but didn't say anything. "Seriously, you don't have to do that, babe."

"Just let us, Babydoll. We don't want you to stress more than you already are," Kingston explained softly, his hand rubbing my lower back in comforting circles. I sighed, biting my tongue as the cashier gave Reid his change. Jesse had taken the cart from the bagger and was waiting for us.

"So," Reid started, his tone holding a hint of something I couldn't identify, setting me on edge, my eyes narrowing on him as I waited. "Is there a reason your mom hasn't been to the store yet?"

"She's been really busy lately," I explained with a shrug, knowing it was a terrible excuse, but I didn't want to talk about it or be reminded how much my broken home hurt.

When they didn't say anything, I turned from loading up the last bag into the back and saw their shared gaze, thinned lips, and clenched jaws. I knew sooner or later, I would have to tell them just how much my life had started to fall apart.

Later, though, because there is no way in heck, I want to do it now.

I already have too much stress.

NOVEMBER 21ST

Something I learned while prepping for the ACT—only two
words in the English language contain all the vowels in order:
Facetiously and Abstemiously!
#TheMoreYouKnow #StudyingWithJesse #ThankfulThursday

"Want me to come in?" I questioned as I pulled up to
the rundown house. Jesse's shoulders tensed, his head
shaking violently as he glanced at me.

"No, stay here, it'll be real quick," he tried to reassure
me before practically sprinting into the little ramshackle
building. His behavior was odd—stiff and abrupt—but it
was Jesse, so it wasn't necessarily out of character, not to
mention the issues we'd struggled with the last few days,
so I let it go.

As I waited for him to return, I turned up the radio,
jamming out to this week's hottest hit, and before the song
even ended, Jesse beelined from the front door into the
passenger seat.

"Okay, go," he exclaimed breathlessly.

Taking his cue, I shifted from park to drive, making
our way to Coffee Grounds, our official/unofficial
study location. After the crap yesterday with my lack of
groceries, we had decided to push our studying to today.
Plus, Jesse said I had made a lot of progress and could do
with a day or two off. The longer we drove, the more Jesse
seemed to relax, but even when I pulled into the lot, he
still was antsier than usual.

"Hey, you okay?" I asked quietly as we sank into one of
the open tables.

"Yeah," he murmured, his tone laced with a hint of steel

in his attempt to not have me push. Narrowing my eyes, I debated whether to keep questioning, but he opened his mouth, content to focus on me instead. "How are you feeling? After everything with Dylan and the other students?"

"Ugh," I groaned, slumping in my chair at the thought of what had been happening during lunch and in the halls. "Irritated. It's over, though, at least for now."

"I don't get why they feel the need to be all up in our business, but it's really starting to be a nuisance," Jesse bit out, angry on my behalf at how the rest of the kids were behaving

"Yeah, it is," I mumbled, my lips curling into a frown as I looked at my ACT study book, my motivation to actually study diminishing after the crappy week I'd had.

"Want to do something else?" Jesse murmured, his fingers coming to brush the back of my hand ever so lightly. "You've been making a lot of progress, and if you're not in the mindset for studying, it won't be much help."

"What do you suggest?" I asked, glancing over at him and shutting the book. Jesse hummed slightly, glancing over his shoulder.

"We could get some coffee, maybe go see what else the strip mall on the other side of the parking lot has. You know... if you wanted..." he trailed off, shrugging his shoulders. My lip curled up, the little butterflies soaring at his suggestion.

"I'd love that, Jess," I assured. "Want anything to eat?" I asked, starting to get up before Jesse hopped up.

"You sit, I'll get it. Your usual, right?"

"Yes, please, and a plain bagel with cream cheese." Nodding, he pecked my cheek and stepped into the quickly growing line. I could feel my cheek burning and my smile growing at Jesse's sweet gesture.

"Here you go, Em," Jesse stated as he set down my cup and plate, the scent of toasted bread filling my nose.

"Thank you," I exclaimed, carefully smearing the cream cheese on the bagel, so I didn't burn my fingers. "What did you get?" I asked before stuffing a bite into my mouth.

"A mocha latte and a cream cheese Danish," he explained, taking a bite. "It's pretty good, want a bite?" I shook my head when he offered it out, pointing to my own bagel.

"This massive thing will fill me up. Besides, that's yours, enjoy it," I teased. "So, other than all the crap with the other students, how's my Jesse doing?"

"*Your* Jesse, huh?" His lips quirked up, and even with his deep skin tone, I saw the tiniest flush of pink as he looked at me. "It's going, just making it through the school days until we get to graduation."

"Oooh, so you're one of those focused on getting out of high school," I hummed. "But yeah, same here. I was thinking of doing something different with my hair. Thoughts?" I asked, randomly letting my nerves get to me when I realized I was basically on a date with Jesse. "Did you know the average person has around one hundred thousand to one hundred and fifty thousand hairs on their head?"

Stop talking, Emma.

"I didn't know that," Jesse replied, his lips smashed together to keep his laughter contained. "What were you thinking of doing with it?"

"I'm not sure, maybe change the color? The burgundy maroon is almost faded out. I could cut it or add some highlights?" I rambled.

"I like how it is, but if you want to do something, I think

anything will look good on you, Em. I'm pretty partial to the pink coloring you had, though."

I perked up, Jesse's gentle, honeyed voice music to my ears in the quickly growing conversation in Coffee Grounds as the post-work crowd came in for a quick pick-me-up.

"Maybe I'll do that, then," I added. "I was pretty partial to it too."

"You ready to go?" Jesse asked after I finished my last bite and chugged the last of my coffee. Nodding, I got up and followed Jesse to the trash can. The air held a bite, the warmth from the coffee shop's interior seeping away as we walked hand in hand across the parking lot to the strip mall.

It looked to be new construction, the stone face smooth and modern, the signs for each store popping against the tan. We stayed silent as we leisurely looked between the different storefronts until one caught my eye.

"What about this?" I asked, pointing to the bright colored sign, *Painting and Co.*

"You want to do a painting class? I thought you didn't like drawing," Jesse countered, looking at the schedule posted in the window. "Looks like they have one starting in about ten minutes."

"I like drawing, I just suck at it. Painting, though, I haven't done that since middle school art class, so what do you say? Up for something new, Mr. Bookworm?" I teased, pulling a laugh from Jesse. Smirking at me, he held open the door with a challenging glint in his dark chocolate gaze.

"Welcome to Painting and Co! Our class will begin here shortly. Have you two been here before?" the young woman at the front desk asked cheerfully. Shaking our heads, we stepped up, signing in and paying the class fee. "You two are all set, and all the needed supplies are set up at the easels, so feel free to pick any of the open chairs."

Excitement had me antsy as I breathed in the scent of art supplies and sank onto one of the open stools. Jesse seemed hesitant as he plopped down at the easel across from me, his gaze darting around the space curiously. I opened my mouth to ask him if he'd done a lot of art stuff when the instructor started the class.

Glancing to my left, I tried my best to follow along with the steps, and by the end, I was pretty proud of my painting. The vintage blue-green of the truck stood out from the fall leaves behind it, and when the instructor said we could put a phrase or family name on the tailgate and something fun on the license plate, I smirked.

I painted 'For Jesse' on the back of the truck, followed by a 'LUVEM' on the license plate, then signed my initials in the bottom corner. *Aww, how cute!*

"You all done, Em?" Jesse murmured, glancing over the canvas at me, his eyes lighting up.

"I'll show you mine if you show me yours," I teased. "On the count of three?" He nodded. Counting down, I grabbed the back of my painting to turn toward him. "One, two, three."

Holy crap!

Jesse sure can paint.

"Wow," I breathed, staring wide-eyed at his canvas. It was the same painting, but the colors flowed together, the painting more lifelike than mine. "You totally could be an artist, Jesse, that's amazing."

"Really?" His head tilted as his brows furrowed, his eyes looking to his canvas. "You don't think it looks bad?"

"Psh, of course not. It's better than mine," I exclaimed

with a laugh.

"I love yours, and I love the truck dedication," he murmured with a wide, white-toothed smile. Glancing at his once more, I saw he had done something similar with 'My Em' on the truck and 'BSTGF' on the license plate.

"Aww," I cooed, my heart skipping a beat at the sweet gesture. "I love it, Jess." Leaning around the easels, I pressed my lips to his, happy we decided to come here.

Maybe I can get him to paint me something else.

I would love to have a little gallery of just Jesse's artwork.

CHAPTER 2

NOVEMBER 26TH

I seem to be a Brad magnet... Bradnet? Where I go, he follows.
What did I ever do to this creep?
#BoatshoeBrad #CreeperAlert #TickedOffTuesday

It had been a while since I had been called to see my
counselor, Ms. Rogers, but I found myself wandering the
empty halls toward her office with a call slip clutched in
my hands. I had just reached the main floor and turned
the corner to walk the last bit across the entryway to the
door when a pair of ice-cold, predatory eyes found mine,
a cruel smile curling his lips as he stepped in front of me.
My heart thudded painfully in my chest, but I didn't cower
away, my fingers tightening into fists as anger poured
through me.

"Hello, Em," Brad murmured softly. My teeth ground at
the way Jesse's nickname was twisted by his slimy tone.

"Don't call me that," I hissed, trying to step around him,
but just like in the bathroom at the party, he stepped in
front of me and blocked my escape.

"Why not? Oh," he hummed and nodded, "that's right,
that's Jesse Parker's nickname for you. How about
Babydoll or Cali girl? Are those any better?" His was tone
was low, taunting as he took a half step closer.

"Back off," I exclaimed, "or I'll scream."

"Maybe I want to hear you scream," he challenged. A shiver worked down my spine, and try as I might, I couldn't stop the shudder that radiated through me, and Brad's eyes lit up.

"Mr. Warland," Ms. Rogers called out, her tone sharp as she glared at him. "Don't you have somewhere else to be? Somewhere that isn't harassing another student?"

"Oh, of course, Mimi," he smarted, a sickly-sweet smile taking over his face. "I didn't mean to make Em late for anything." My lips pursed at his words, but it seemed Ms. Rogers wasn't fazed by his fake persona.

"I'll see you later."

"Yeah, freaking right, creep," I ground out under my breath as he walked away. Huffing in rage, I nearly stomped to where Ms. Rogers waited, my anger fueled by the adrenaline pumping through me. We didn't speak as we made our way to her office, the door closing behind us, the only thing allowing me to calm.

"Are you alright, Emma?" she asked softly, her hand coming to rub my shoulder blade in comforting circles. It was odd at first, but the motion helped the anxiety building within me slow.

"Uh, yeah," I mumbled, finally deflating. "A bit shook up, but I'm okay."

"Just remember, you can come to me whenever you need. I won't make you talk about it if you don't want, but my door is always open if you need some place to escape to," she offered with a friendly smile.

"Thank you." I knew my smile was brittle, but for the life of me, I couldn't make it any wider—flashes of Brad's hands on me keeping that dark cloud on my shoulders.

"Before we get into why I called you in, do you want me

to file a student conduct complaint against Mr. Warland?" She must have read my confused expression because she continued. "There are different reasons we can file one on behalf of a student, one being harassment. Mr. Warland purposely stopping you, making you uncomfortable, and not allowing you to make it to your destination all seem like valid reasons to do so."

"Uh, I don't want to stir up any more trouble," I started staying.

"This wouldn't just be for the school's documentation, it's also for legal matters, so it's formally documented, and proper action can be taken if the behaviors continue," she explained, her eyes holding a knowing glint that conveyed what her words didn't.

It might help save Jesse and solidify my case against Brad.

"So, would you like to hold off, or would you like to file the complaint?" she asked softly, no judgment in her question.

At least I have one ally at this school besides my guys and my friends.

"Yeah, let's file the complaint," I murmured, still feeling rattled from the confrontation, but I knew, in the end, it would be best for Jesse and me. She gave me an encouraging smile, patting my shoulder as she grabbed a notepad and jotting down some thoughts before turning to me.

"I will file that after you head back to class. The reason I called you in is to check how studying is going with Mr. Parker and see if you're feeling more confident to take a practice ACT next month," she explained.

While I was thankful she wouldn't press me, I couldn't bring myself to drum up much enthusiasm for the current topic of conversation.

Stupid test anxiety. Stupid Brad.

"Studying is going well, and we're still meeting most Wednesdays," I explained, "I think I'll be ready, but maybe we can make it a bit later in December? Would there be enough time to schedule the actual test for January if we do that?"

"We can definitely do it later in the month. It might be a bit close, but we can schedule later in January for your actual test, so we have enough time to get your results back. After the January slot, we will have one more chance in mid-February. That will be the last to make the cut off for fall semester for both UNO and UNL," she explained, jotting down notes on her pad of paper. I nodded, ignoring the worry flooding my stomach at the deadline.

Well, if worse comes to worst, I could just go for the spring semester.

Maybe I could work extra hours for a few months and save up some money.

It was a sucky backup plan, but it was a plan, nonetheless.

"I know you said you had scheduled visits, but I can't remember if that was this upcoming weekend or the weekend after," she stated, looking through her notes.

"Next weekend, the seventh and eighth," I explained. "We're waiting until Reid's lacrosse season is done, and his last game is this Saturday." Ms. Rogers smiled brightly as she looked at me.

"That's good. Are you going to watch it? My nephew plays in middle school. I have to say it's a pretty interesting sport to watch." As if she spoke a different language, my brain stopped working.

Why haven't I gone to watch Reid play? Guilt started to settle in, despite visions of my work schedule flashing in my mind, hours at Coffee Grounds filling the slots when he usually had games.

What kind of girlfriend am I?

One that will surprise him at the last game!

Thank goodness I have a later shift this Saturday.

"I will be this time, but I usually work Saturday mornings," I explained, feeling a little less terrible now that I had plans to go.

"Oh, where? I don't think we talked much about that," she said, perking up at the easy conversation flowing between us. The more we talked, the more I felt my adrenaline slowing, and my smile growing more and more genuine.

"Coffee Grounds. I usually work a couple nights a week, then at least one day on the weekends, depending on scheduling."

"Have you considered using a marketing degree for running a business like that or expanding to a management position? That is if you're still planning on getting a business degree in marketing," she offered. She must have seen my eyebrows raise in surprise because she chuckled. "Yeah, thinking really far into the future can sometimes be on the back burner, but keep that in mind when you visit. It's always good to be aware of what you're thinking of doing after college while you visit."

"I'll definitely do that," I stated excitedly.

I may have walked into this office in a terrible mood, but I definitely left with a bright smile and hope for the future for the first time in several weeks.

This might work out after all.

NOVEMBER 27TH

America consumes almost 50% of the world's chocolate, but after the day I've had, I may have to increase that statistic
#AlmostTheWeekend #CantComeSoonEnough
#WeirdnessWednesday

"So, what's the plan today?" I asked.

Thank goodness it's almost the weekend. No more stares, no more whispers, and no more Brad—at least for four days.

"We're officially out as soon the bell rings, and I don't want to think about anything to do with school, homework, or work," Reid responded with a shudder, his words muffled due to the large bit of food he had just stuffed in his mouth.

How this boy has never choked never ceases to amaze me.

"Don't you guys have studying?" Kingston asked, waving between Jesse and me. It had taken a bit of time, but the fact I needed tutoring to pass the ACT was finally something I was able to talk about with them without feeling bad or ashamed. Last week had been the first time we openly discussed it.

"Oh, duh, I forgot it was Wednesday—"

"Miss Clark, would you come with me, please?" a familiar hard voice bit out behind me, cutting Reid off. Glancing over my shoulder, the food in my stomach turned to lead as I came eye to eye with Mr. Derosa, the assistant principal, who seemed to hate me.

Why? I have no freaking clue.

"Uh, yeah," I muttered, standing up and throwing my bag onto my shoulder.

"I can take this," Kingston stated, grabbing my tray. I flashed him a grateful smile before taking a deep breath. When I couldn't stall any longer, I turned and followed Mr. Derosa, purposely ignoring the many nosy and hostile stares following me. My heart thudded in my chest as he held open his office door, his stern frown and harsh glare making me want to cower, but I strode in and took a seat in one of the two chairs facing the desk, my head held high.

His office was bland, nothing on the walls except a clock and empty whiteboard that looked to have never been used. His desk was tidy, only holding a computer and a small TV next to it. Security camera footage from around the school rotated randomly through the blocked sections on the screen.

"Miss Clark," he started, his gruff words making me jump in my seat. "Do you know why I called you in here today?"

"Nope," I stated quietly.

"Well, it has come to my attention, Ms. Rogers' has filed a student conduct complaint against Brad Warland for harassment."

My blood ran cold, seeing the raised brow and pursed lips on Mr. Derosa's judgmental face. *Well, I guess I know where this is going. Don't back down, Em, even though you know, it'll fall on deaf ears.*

"That's because he was," I challenged. Apparently, that was the wrong thing to say. His eyes hardened, and he smashed a button on his keyboard roughly, turning the screen so I could see.

"According to this, it looks like you had no problem having a conversation with Mr. Warland," he countered smugly. I watched the video and Brad's opportunistic sneer when he saw me coming down the hall. It had been a coincidence we were in the same place together, but he didn't let the opportunity slip by him as he stepped up to me, towering over me. I could see the agitation and fear on my face, my lips thinned, and my eyes wide as I crushed the call slip in my hand. It was only a few moments before Ms. Rogers was dealing with Brad, but it was long enough, even a day later, I felt my skin crawl.

"Well, as you could clearly see, he stepped out in front of—"

"I don't want your excuses, Miss Clark. I just want you to remember, you will not cause trouble in my school," he barked, cutting me off.

"*I* wasn't!" I exclaimed, anger radiating through my veins as my stomach burned with acid at being accused of doing something I hadn't done.

"Enough! You will stay out of trouble, or I will do more than just call you into my office," he shouted. His face was beet red, his chest heaving as he glared at me, and I couldn't stop myself from jumping at his harsh tone.

"Can I go to class now?" I murmured, my throat and eyes suddenly burning with the urge to cry as the haunting sound of the class bell rang through his abysmal office. I would rather face the entire collective of nosy students with a tear-tracked face than sit here being berated by Mr. Derosa.

He didn't speak, choosing to wave a hand dismissively toward the door. Gathering my bag from the floor, I made my way out into the hallway, pleasantly surprised to find it was empty of students. *I must have missed the first bell with Mr. Derosa's freaking yelling.* I was angry and wanted to do nothing, just sit in my car for the rest of the day, but I took another calming breath and turned to go to trig.

Time to pull up those big girl pants and be responsible.

Kingston must have told Mrs. Hazel what was going on because when I walked in late, she glanced at me with a sympathetic smile and a head tilt to my seat.

Then again, it might be the fact I look like I'm about to cry.

Kingston nudged his notebook closer to me, so I could read what he had scribbled on it.

You okay?

I gave him a quick grin, trying to ease the worry I saw in his warm brown eyes, but when it didn't ease, I jotted a note back. It was slow going, so I didn't get in trouble with the teacher. She had been lenient with me coming in late, but I didn't want to push my luck, getting caught passing notes in class.

Mr. Derosa just being himself. Claimed I started that confrontation with Brad in the hall yesterday I told you guys about. Said I need to stay out of trouble, or he'll get me in trouble.

Kingston's hands curled tightly into fists as he read my note, and a few tense moments passed while I watched my sweet, laidback boyfriend glare harshly at the paper and take a few calming breaths. With a shake of his head, he seemed to let go of his anger, and turned back to the paper, a small smile breaking through the last remnants of tension.

Want to go on our date? Get away from all the stress for a little while? Just you and me? How about tonight after school? Jesse explained you guys don't have plans.

My heart fluttered, my cheeks flaring in a rush of heat at the way his small smile widened into his usual gorgeous grin. I nodded slightly, happy butterflies and a wave of hope replacing the anger. Finally, able to focus, I tuned into Mrs. Hazel's pretest lecture, ready to pay attention.

I may have sucked at the ACT, but I can totally rock this trig test.

Right?

♥ ♥ ♥

"I'm seriously so freaking nervous," I murmured, my mind going a thousand miles a second as my body buzzed with jittery excitement. Throughout the rest of the day, I had been able to keep the sensation at bay, but now that the final bell had rung, everything I had held back came pouring through me with a vengeance.

"First solo date with Kingston?" Aubrey asked, her hands going up to tighten her loosening ponytail. I nodded, my fingers fiddling with my backpack straps as we walked through the halls.

"I've known Kingston since I was little, and I've never seen him as smitten as he is with you. All three of them, actually," she said with a tiny shrug. "I'm sure he'll have something fun planned for you guys."

"I know," I groaned. "It's just... my last boyfriend wasn't sweet or caring, and we never did anything like actually going on dates. I mean, we went out, but it was usually with our friends. I'm not sure I know what to do on a *real* date, like a romantic one. Well, Jesse and I had an impromptu date last week when we had coffee, but not an actual, pre-planned *date* date," I rambled nervously.

"Sounds like you totally upgraded then," Aubrey teased. I laughed, nodding as I looked at her.

"Upgraded is an understatement. I mean, freaking look at this! Even after almost three months, he still won't leave me alone." I pulled out my phone, showing her the long, long string of texts I got over the time since my forced relocation. Even when I didn't respond, he *still* tried.

You would think by now he would have given up!

"Holy cow, he really needs to learn to back off," she exclaimed, her eyes wide as she scrolled. "Yeah, definitely upgraded," she nodded, handing my phone back as we pushed the front doors open. Kingston waited near his car, a bright smile forming as we walked toward the lot.

"Good luck! I want all the details this weekend, so don't forget to text me." With a wave, she broke away from me toward Zoey, who was waiting over by their cars. Taking a deep breath and giving myself a quick pep talk, I walked to where Kingston waited.

"Ow, ow!" Reid hollered with a whistle from several cars down the line. His antics had my face burning as students looked at Kingston and me, but I couldn't stop the giggle that bubbled out at his ridiculousness. "Have fun."

"Hey, Babydoll, ready?" Kingston questioned, opening the passenger door for me. When I went to take my bag off to put it at my feet, he snatched it from my hands with a smirk. "I got this."

"Alright." Sinking into the warm car, the seat was still chilly through my jeans, sweater, and coat, but quickly dissipating.

Kingston was quick, placing my bag in the trunk and climbing into the driver's seat. The drug-addled butterflies continued to flutter in my stomach as he reached across the center console, wrapping his hand around mine. We didn't talk as we drove to wherever he was taking us, my eyes darting around, trying to figure it out.

"Are you cold?" His question surprised me, making me shake my head quickly and look at him with a scrunched expression. He must have seen the confusion. "You're shaking like a leaf, Babydoll. What's up?"

"Uh," I stuttered, "I may be a bit nervous."

"Why?" he asked, his expression full of genuine curiosity.

"I haven't really been on a proper date before," I mumbled under my breath, my lip worrying between my teeth as I glanced at him. His shocked face melted into a warm laugh.

"Me either, so hopefully, I did okay." Before I could reassure him, I knew he had, he pulled the car into a parking lot, and my attention was immediately redirected.

"Roller skating?" I perked up, excitement overshadowing the nerves. Once Kingston parked, he shrugged, two pink patches blooming on his cheeks in a bashful blush. "I love roller skating. I'm not that great, though, so I'll try not to fall all over you," I explained as I climbed out of the car and gave him an excited hug.

"That's what you have me for. I'll hold your hand the whole time," he whispered, his whiskers rubbing against my temple. Kingston's side was warm, his coat soft against my cheek as I curled into him.

"I wouldn't expect any less," I murmured, squeezing his trim waist as we stepped up to the counter. Kingston, unsurprisingly, paid for our tickets, and we got our skates before making our way over to one of the empty couches.

"Ready?" I asked as soon as my second skate was tied snugly around my ankle. Standing with ease, despite being on wheels, Kingston held his hands out to help me up. I wobbled slightly, but his steady grip kept me from falling on my butt.

Because that would be embarrassing, and no one wants to

see that.

"Just go slowly, Babydoll," he instructed, rolling backward toward the rink. "I'll be here to catch you, and if you do fall, we'll just get back up." I nodded, my heart warming at the 'we.'

It was a rocky start, my legs unsteady underneath me as we made our way around the rink. Kingston's hand never left mine, and after a few laps, I was finally able to move comfortably from one foot to the other.

Stopping though... that might be a problem.

We didn't talk, the music and the lights accompanying the rhythmic sway as we moved together. Stress, worry, and every negative emotion I had been feeling melted with each circle we skated. When Kingston switched hands, I glanced at him in confusion, surprised to see a very Reid-like mischievous glint in his eyes.

"Wow," I breathed as he effortlessly transitioned from skating next to me to facing me, skating backward with ease. "Show off," I teased.

"Maybe I can teach you sometime," he offered, the white in his plaid button-up glowing slightly under the black lights on the ceiling. "But you seem to be doing well. You never give yourself nearly enough credit, Emma."

"Eh," I didn't argue, shrugging at his statement. "You never seem to either," I countered with a smile. "This is a pretty amazing date."

"Well, it isn't over yet," he murmured, his eyes sparkling as he rotated back to face forward. "One more song, then we can go to the next part."

"*Parts*, huh? Just how many parts does this first date have?"

"You'll just have to wait and see, Babydoll," he stated happily, ducking down and pressing his lips to mine softly.

"Reid will be so pissed if I don't get a photo of us."

"Of course, he will." I laughed as I pictured Reid's reaction. Pulling out his phone, Kingston turned the camera to face us. I literally squealed as I leaned into him, my hand coming to rest on his chest as we coasted. "Send that to me?"

"You got it," he smiled. "But first, let's enjoy this skate."

Speechless by Dan and Shay started, the seductive notes filtering through space, and my stomach started to flip for a different reason than its normal butterflies. A spark of heat built as I felt Kingston's eyes on me, tracing over the planes of my face as we continued around the rink.

"You're so beautiful," he murmured, almost too low, I didn't hear it. Looking up at him, my heart thundered in my chest as a swell of emotions built, I wasn't used to. Nervous about making a fool of myself, I opened my mouth to compliment him back when I ended up doing just that.

"Did you know the feeling of butterflies in your stomach is because of a rush of adrenaline?" I explained. *Smooth, Emma.* Kingston didn't give me an odd look or say anything along the lines of 'why are you so weird?' only smiled, seemingly happy I randomly spouted facts, even at the worst times.

"Did you know slight physical contact like holding hands can help alleviate physical pain and help with stress?" he asked, squeezing my hand. "Ready to go to the next part of our date?"

More time with my sweet boyfriend?
Heck, yes.

"Where are we?" I questioned, glancing around the

parking lot. There were a few other cars in front of the different shops, but with the cold weather, not many were out today. There was an open area with heaters, tables, chairs, and benches. The surrounding shops hosted food, drinks, and shopping. There was a giant Christmas tree in the middle of the space, the lights flickering in the quickly setting sun. I quirked a brow at it, but seeing as how tomorrow was Thanksgiving, I didn't think too much about how they had *already* decorated for Christmas.

"I figured we could warm up before next part of our date," Kingston explained, placing his hand against my back, directing me toward the hot chocolate and cider stand.

"What can I get for you kids?" a rotund woman asked cheerfully, leaning forward, so her arms were resting against the window.

"Hot chocolate for me, no marshmallows," Kingston ordered, looking to me.

"Hot chocolate for me with marshmallows, please." I was nearly bouncing with excitement.

"You got it," she exclaimed with a wave of her hand.

"Having fun?" Kingston asked, pulling me into his chest. I nodded as I wrapped my arms around his shoulders.

"You know what would be even better? If there was some snow. It's been ages since I've seen snow."

"It is supposed to snow in the next couple weeks, so we'll be buried under a foot of snow soon enough, Babydoll. Maybe we can all go ice skating. Reid loves to go each year," Kingston explained, the call of our order interrupting any further details. He grabbed our cups and directed me to one of the two-person tables under a heater. The hot chocolate was smooth—cinnamon, spice, and a hint of sweetness swirled together. The delicious concoction was topped off with giant marshmallows, slowly melting in the hot liquid.

Just like with skating, we were content to enjoy each other's company in silence, focusing on our drinks and holding hands as we watched a few people flit in and out of the space.

"So, are you excited for Thanksgiving tomorrow?" Kingston asked, leaning forward to rest both elbows on the tabletop.

"Yeah, I think it'll be good to just chill," I explained with a smile. "What are you most excited about for it?"

"Spending time with my family and the people who matter most. Although homemade hot chocolate is a definite plus. Speaking of food, what's your least favorite?" Kingston questioned, his lips quirking up at his change of topic.

"Onions. I think they're so gross," I gagged, just the thought of them making me sick. "What about you?"

"Mustard, no idea why since I don't mind it cooked into things, like spicy brown mustard, but on a burger or a hot dog? Nope," he said with a head shake. Giggling, I leaned forward onto my elbows, loving the light-hearted feeling of the night. It was a welcome change after so much drama and stress lately.

"What's one movie you love but never told the other two about?" I continued our questions, curious about Kingston, about who my laid-back, sweet boyfriend was away from Reid and Jesse.

"*Sixteen Candles*," Kingston admitted after some thinking, "though I would tell the guys, it's just never come up. You?"

"Well, seeing as how I've only been around for a few months, I'm sure there's a lot of movies you guys don't

34

know I love, so..." I trailed off, dragging out the last word several syllables as I thought. "The Lizzie McGuire Movie. It's cheesy and fun, and I have the songs memorized."

"You would, Babydoll," Kingston laughed. "I'm not surprised at all to hear that. Let me guess? You binged on the series reruns?"

"I've got them on DVD," I exclaimed proudly, not caring it was a cheesy show. If Kingston wanted to be with me, he got to be with all of me—silliness and all.

The sun had set as we laughed, the Christmas lights decorating the shopping center blazing brightly, lighting the space in a soft romantic glow.

"Ready? Now that it's dark, we can go to the last part of our date," Kingston explained. Even in the low light and chilly wind, I saw his cheeks tint in another bashful blush. *He's so sweet.* Nodding, I got up, tossing my empty cup into the trash can, and followed Kingston to his car.

"So, you going to let it be a surprise, or are you going to tell me?" I asked, glancing out the window in excitement. He chuckled, grabbing hold of my hand over the center console.

"Ready?" he asked, turning down a street. I looked over at him in confusion when he didn't stop.

"Ready for what?"

"Look," he tilted his head to the other side of the street.

"Oooh, pretty!" My nose was practically pressed against the glass.

Large homes, yards, and trees were decorated in lights, the street glowing in an array of white and colored lights. Some even had blow-up decorations or scenes in the front yard. I gasped as we turned down another street to see a house playing music, the lights flashing and animated to the beat.

"The annual neighborhood lights display always starts Thanksgiving week, and I figured we should see them. Maybe I could convince you to help us decorate our house on Sunday. I know my mom has been pestering me to get your help," Kingston explained as we continued through the streets, one hand holding mine while the other turned the wheel.

"I would love to. I don't have anything going on." Bringing the car around the final bend, we looked around in wonder, enjoying the beauty of the lights and each other's company before he finally pulled into a fairly empty parking lot back at the shop. Only this time, he parked in the back, away from the other cars.

"So, how did I do for my first time?" he asked. Even though he seemed relaxed, I could see the worry in his eyes.

"It was absolutely perfect. It's only missing one thing," I murmured, leaning over the console.

"Yeah? What's that?" he whispered, the brush of his fingers over my cheek, leaving a trail of goosebumps.

"A first date kiss."

Without hesitation, Kingston closed the distance between us. He was growing more and more confident each time we found ourselves alone. His lips moved smoothly against mine before his tongue darted out. A flutter of something built in my belly, the heat flaring in my veins before moving to the crest of my thighs. Kingston's hand cupped the back of my head as he deepened our kiss, his other squeezing my hand gently. Tongues tangled and teeth nipped lightly as our makeout session heated, and before long, I was buzzing with nerves and desire, the latter making my core slick.

A ringing brought us out of our kissing, my heart racing,

startled by my phone. Digging into my coat pocket, I pulled out the irritating device and saw my mom's name flash on the screen. I flushed in a wave of embarrassment as if I had been caught doing something I shouldn't even though she couldn't actually see me.

"Hey, Mom," I greeted, glancing over at Kingston, who was chuckling at my wide eyes.

"Hey, sweetie. I'm finally on my way home and going to pick up some takeout. Want anything?" I could hear the sound of the radio playing softly in the background.

"Yeah, where from?" She rattled off the place, and I gave her my order before we hopped off the call. It had been short but long enough to essentially ruin the moment.

"Need to head home for dinner?" Kingston asked, his thumb rubbing the back of my hand. I nodded, buckling my seatbelt as we pulled out of the lot. It may have ended abruptly, but it was an amazing date, and I went to bed with one thing echoing through my mind.

I can't wait for our next one.

Sitting at the kitchen table, flipping through one of my well-loved paperbacks, I was waiting for my mom to get home. As soon as the door to the garage opened, the scent of Chinese filled the house, and my stomach grumbled.

"Hey, sweetie, here's dinner," my mom huffed breathlessly as she placed the large bag on the counter, her work bag balanced precariously on her shoulder. "I'm going to drop this off in the office, then we can figure out whose food is whose."

"Alright, Mom," I nodded, getting up and pulling out silverware and plates, making sure to grab the stack of napkins that had collected on the counter. It wasn't long before my mom stepped back into the kitchen and started digging around in the bag.

"Ah, here we go, here's your bourbon chicken with rice, no onions," my mom stated, setting several takeout containers on the counter. "With lo mein and eggrolls for me."

"Going to eat out here?" I asked, unable to stop the hope filling my question. *Please,* please, *eat dinner with me.*

"I figured I would. I don't have any work to finish up tonight with it being the holidays. I'll probably head to bed soon, so I can get up early for tomorrow," my mom replied, sitting across from me.

Yes! Dinner with my mom.

Only took two months to happen.

We sat in silence for a while, too busy stuffing our faces with delicious food to talk, but I couldn't complain, my mind struggling to come up with something to talk about. Thankfully, my mom took the lead after our eating started to slow.

"How's school going? Looking forward to the break?" My mom's eyes centered on me, her gaze tired and dark circles slowly growing more prominent under her eyes.

I can see why she wanted to go to bed early; it looks as if she never sleeps. She needs a vacation.

"It's going. Doing well in all my classes and none of my teachers turned into a terror," I explained, stabbing the last piece of chicken with my fork. "My English teacher is a bit of a stickler, but that's it. As for break, I'm looking forward to no homework for a few days."

"That's good, I'm glad you're doing well," my mom praised, making my heart surge. It had been forever since I had heard something even remotely positive from her, and I realized how much I missed it. "How are your friends?"

"They're good, doing the same as me, trying to get through homework and everything to enjoy our downtime." I tried to muster up the courage to tell her about Reid, Jesse, and Kingston, but my mouth wouldn't work, the words dancing right on the tip of my tongue but refusing to come out. A mix of fear and worry at the thought of telling her and what her potential reaction could be turned my food into a lead weight.

As soon as I decided to tell her about us later, my mind flicked to the grocery fiasco the other day, but the same thing happened, the words refused to come out, my mind not wanting to ruin our night.

"Good." My mom tried to say something else, but a large yawn cut off whatever it was.

"Go to bed, Mom," I huffed with a smile. "I'm actually really tired, too, and we have a big day tomorrow."

"Oh, joy," my mom prodded in jest, her lips quirking up. "Alright, sweetie, you win. I'll go to bed so long as you do. I love you."

"I love you too, Mom," I murmured as she wrapped me in a soft hug, her soft rose perfume familiar, reminding me of home, but before my eyes could water, I shoved back the unwanted memory of my broken family.

At least I got to have dinner with my mom.

Positive thoughts, Emma.

Chapter 3

NOVEMBER 28TH

Friends, family, my mom, everything I could hope for this year. Stella's desserts are definitely an extra cherry on top. Get it?
#DessertPun #TurkeyDay #ThankfulThursday

Emma, darling," Stella called out as she opened the door, her welcoming smile turning to my mom next. "You must be Erin, it is wonderful to finally meet you. I'm Stella Bell, Kingston's mom."

"Thank you for inviting us, your house is beautiful." My mom's eyes darted around the space in wonder at the fall decorations. The room was covered in burnt oranges and reds and smelled better than any Thanksgiving I'd ever had before.

"Thank you, you're too sweet. I'll give you a tour if you'd like. Emma, the boys are down in the basement, playing video games if you'd like to join them," Stella added. I dipped my head in thanks and made my way around the corner to the basement door.

"Hello, Emma," Kaleb greeted cheerfully with a brief wave, his attention focused on the several dishes scattered across the stove and counter, stirring or watching.

"Hey, Mr. Bell," I responded as I opened the door. He looked over at me with a brow raise.

41

"How many times do I have to tell you to call me Kaleb?" he chastised lightly. I smiled and shrugged as I started down the carpeted stairs.

"Probably at least five more times," I called over my shoulder. His jovial laugh followed me as I rushed down the stairs and around the half wall that separated the steps from the open area of the basement.

I had been down in the lowest level at Kingston's once or twice, but most of the time, we chose to spend time at my house since I lived closer to school. I glanced around, taking in the vaguely familiar space. There were four doors, two open to show a finished bathroom and a guest bedroom while the other two were closed. If I remembered correctly, one was a home gym while the last was a storage room. The basement walls were a soft creamy off-white, complementing the neutral gray carpet. The large sectional, bright turquoise with yellow and gray accent pillows tossed around the plush cushions, caught my eye, along with the matching yellow rug on the ground beneath the industrial metal and glass coffee table. A projector was attached to the opposite side of the room, pointing at the white screen secured to the wall, a matching shelving unit beneath holding an array of movies and video games.

"Cali girl!" Reid called from his spot on the couch, jumping up and hopping over the back of the furniture, scooping me into his arms. My breath left my lungs in a whoosh as he picked me up and spun me around, my arms circling around his shoulders. Butterflies erupted in my stomach as Reid dipped me, kissing me deeply before standing me back upright.

"Hi, Reid," I chuckled, knowing my face was bright red. *Well, it's worth it to see the twinkle in his eyes and that gorgeous smile.*

"Wait, I thought you were King's girlfriend?" Killian, Kingston's little brother, asked in confusion, his arm propped on the back of the couch as he looked at us.

"She is," Kingston answered, coming around to greet me.

Reid let go, rolling back over the back of the couch, his black curls flopping as he haphazardly sprawled across the bright cushions.

"Hey, Babydoll. You look pretty today," he murmured, wrapping me up more calmly than Reid before giving me a soft, ardent kiss.

"You look pretty handsome yourself," I added with a giggle.

A nudge on my side pulled my attention from Kingston. Jesse waited next to me, deciding whether or not to make a move, but after a split-second hesitation, he stepped forward, intertwining our fingers. His kiss wasn't as extravagant as Reid's or passionate as Kingston's, but feeling his lips on my cheek in a sweet kiss made my heart warm.

"Hi, Em," he mumbled under his breath, squeezing my hand lightly before moving back to his spot on the couch.

"Wait... I'm so confused," Killian huffed, glancing at us with a frown.

"We're all dating Emma," Kingston explained simply. "Not that complicated."

"You're not jealous?" Kill glanced around them in shock. "Never mind, I don't really care."

"Yeah, just focus on your homework and the game. You can worry about girls next year when you're a freshman," Reid joked. Killian rolled his eyes, shifting his focus back to the tv as the countdown started in their game. My guys jumped back onto the couch at Killian's signal. Shucking my coat over the spare chair in the corner, I sank onto the couch between Reid and Kingston.

"This is the basement, the kids tend to come down here and hang out," I heard Stella explain.

"Hi, Ms. Clark!" Reid hollered over his shoulder, his attention never wavering from their racing game. My mom chuckled as she took in the space.

"This is my youngest son, Killian," Stella introduced. "He would have manners if he wasn't busy." She thumped his shoulder lightly when he didn't respond.

"Ow, sorry. Hi," he exclaimed, leaning away from her as he redirected his car back onto the racetrack.

"That's quite alright," my mom countered with a laugh. My heart felt full, seeing my mom not focused on work. "Do you need any help with anything?"

"You're our guest, you don't need to do anything..." Stella's statement faded as they made their way back up the stairs.

"Ugh," Reid groaned, dramatically slumping down into the couch when he lost. "Here, Cali girl, you play. Let's see if you have racing skills to accompany those zombie killing ones."

I smirked and took the controller, but as we were about to start, Kaleb called down the stairs that everything was ready.

"Guess you'll just have to wait to see if I can keep up," I teased Reid as I stood up.

He laughed, curling me under his arm in a side hug before nearly sprinting up the stairs after Killian, shouting, "Time for turkey!"

He's such a clown.

Following at a calmer pace, Kingston, Jesse, and I made our way out of the basement, heading in the direction of the succulent aromas that swirled in the air. The biggest turkey I'd ever seen sat on the end of the table nearest Kaleb, the table surface covered with a ham and a huge spread of sides and. I salivated with anticipation but held the drool in check as we all sat in our seats around the table. My mom sat on my right with Kingston on my left, his warm brown eyes glancing at me every so often as we passed the food around, filling our plates until they overflowed.

It's still not the same as it was.

I shoved the negative thoughts away and enjoyed the sentimental moment. A sliver of me missed my dad and the conversations we would have in the moments he was home from the vineyard, but then the heartache of being forgotten smothered that ache and replaced it with anger at the realization he hadn't called me today.

You know what? If he wants to forget me, I'll enjoy my time with the people who care.

"You okay?" Kingston murmured.

Guess sitting in silence doesn't hide the dark cloud very well, does it? I smiled, trying my best to not let it look brittle or fake, knowing Kingston saw right through it. *He always pays such close attention to me. Can't keep anything from him.* He opened his mouth to say something but was cut off.

"Oh, Emma, Kingston told me you work at Coffee Grounds," Stella said, turning her attention from my mom to me with a cheery grin. "How's that going? Are you planning to work there after graduation?"

"I love it, my coworkers and boss are really cool. Depending on where I end up going to college, possibly," I answered honestly. Until that point, I hadn't thought that far ahead. "I'll know more after visiting UNO and UNL next

45

weekend."

"That's good. Are you excited about it? This is your first college visit, isn't it?"

"Yes, to both your questions," I said with a smile, the first genuine one since sitting down to eat. "It'll be fun to see a different part of the state and a new city."

"It's so hard to remember you and your mother are so new to the area. You fit in perfectly with these three," she teased, her fork pointing to Reid, Jesse, and Kingston. With that, her attention shifted to my mom.

"How are you enjoying Nebraska, Erin?" As soon as the conversation was directed away from me, I tuned it out, focusing on eating the last bit of my food.

As everyone was finishing their dinner, Stella asked, "Is everyone ready for dessert?" glancing around the table. "Kingston, dear, would you grab the cheesecake and other desserts from the fridge and freezer?" He nodded, nudging my leg slightly.

"Want to help me, Emma?"

Getting up, I nodded silently, following Kingston to the kitchen. As soon as the door was kicked almost closed, he turned to me and pulled me into his chest.

"What's going on, Babydoll? You've been quiet all supper."

My sweet Kingston. I felt my chest warm as I wrapped my arms around his trim waist, his orange and cinnamon scent filling my nose as I buried my face into his chest.

"Emma?" he prompted, so I took a steeling breath and faced what I had been trying to ignore all day.

"It's the first family holiday I've had without both of my parents, and I miss my dad, but at the same time, I'm angry as heck because he's barely talked to me since we left. It was like, when my parents divorced, he forgot I even existed." I purposely left off that my mom had done the same thing, knowing I would have to confront her, eventually.

But right now, I'm going to focus on the feeling of my boyfriend's arms around me.

"I'm sorry, Babydoll. I know it doesn't mean much, but I'm happy you're here today." Looking up at him, I smiled, and just like we did last weekend, I popped up onto my toes and met him halfway. While his kiss was still hesitant, his thumbs rubbed my lower back in comforting swipes. Unscented Chapstick coated his lips, and his short beard tickled my skin. Feeling brazen, I nibbled his lower lip, and his arms tightened around me.

"Emma." My mom's voice shocked me out of my butterfly-fluttering-girly-giggling haze.

"Oh." I whipped around, my cheeks no longer flushing from excitement but embarrassment as I saw her raised brow raise and frown. "Uh," I said lamely, unable to figure out what to say. Picking up on my discomfort, Kingston's fingers rubbed my back.

"I didn't know you two were dating," she exclaimed. "Do I need to give you the talk? Birds, bees, condoms, and STDs?"

"Oh my God, Mom, no," I exclaimed, my tone frantic. "Please, don't."

"Alright then, just remember what I'll do if you do something you shouldn't. I came out to tell you I was called in for an emergency meeting with the boss, something about a last-minute event being thrown for Christmas."

"Oh, uh, alright." I plastered a smile on my face, darting forward to give her a quick hug, squeezing a little harder than normal. "Happy Thanksgiving, Mom."

"Happy Thanksgiving to you too, sweetie," she murmured, hugging me tightly. "Stella said you can stay here tonight since you and your friends are going Black Friday shopping, but when you go to sleep, I expect you to stay in a separate room from Kingston." I didn't have to look up to know she was eyeing him over my shoulder before I pulled back. "I love you."

"I love you too, Mom. See you tomorrow." As she turned and walked away, my eyes watered, but I shoved back the wave of sadness that washed over me and tried to focus on being *thankful* she even came.

"Alright, load me up," I exclaimed, faking to heck and back the pep in my voice. Kingston flashed me a skeptical look with narrowed eyes but didn't ask me what was wrong, knowing I didn't want to talk about it. Once we had the desserts pulled out of the fridge, we quickly made our way back to the dining room.

We placed the cakes and pies on the table, then took our seats again. After getting two mugs of hot cocoa, Jesse moved over to where my mom had been sitting, placing one in front of me. I inhaled the sweet scent before taking a sip, letting the warmth coat me from within, erasing the emptiness my mom's abrupt exit had left me with. I felt him squeeze my leg under the table, flashing me an adorable wink when I looked up at him. Out of all of them, he knew what it was to feel abandoned by a parent. I let out a heavy breath as I squeezed his leg in return. *Alone in this together.*

"Ah, perfect!" Stella added with a bright smile before giving her signature mom glare to Reid. "Reid, one piece of everything until everyone else gets their fill."

"Aw, man," he whined, but the curl of his lips gave away he wasn't actually upset being told to hold back from feeding his sweet tooth.

"Here you go, Emma," Kaleb said with a smile, sliding a plate of pumpkin pie in front of me with a giant dollop of whipped cream on the side.

"Thanks, Mr. Bell," I murmured, having lost the reprieve Jesse and the hot cocoa had given me. Suddenly, the barely closed wound of my father's self-imposed absence was ripped open again by Kaleb's sweet, fatherly ways. It wasn't his fault, but it hurt all the same. I took another sip of my hot chocolate as I pushed the longing of past holidays further away.

I'm here with my boys. I'm not alone. I am blessed. I am thankful.

"Four more times," he teased, going over to the counter where they had hot cocoa in a crock pot and refilling his mug.

"Four more times for what?" Reid asked around his mouthful of cheesecake. Stella popped him, making Reid laugh.

It's so nice how they treat everyone like family.

"I told her to call me Kaleb and asked how many more times she would call me Mr. Bell. Her response?"

"Five more times," Kingston finished with a smile.

"Typical Cali girl," Reid teased when he had finally finished his bite.

"Emma, can you come help me for a second?" Stella called from the front hall.

"Want some more hot cocoa while you do that, Em?" Jesse asked me quietly, grabbing my mug.

"Yes, please." Getting up, I went to where I'd heard Stella, her upper body digging through the front closet. "What's up?"

"Quick question," she murmured, shifting out of the way

so I could see what she was talking about. "How do these look as presents for the boys?"

"You're asking me?" I was surprised, shocked even, she had thought to ask me what to get them. I mean, I had spent *a lot* of time with them since moving to the middle of freaking nowhere, but I had only been here a couple months.

"Of course, you're their girlfriend, so I figured you would know what they want," she stated simply, casually dropping the girlfriend bomb like it wasn't a big deal. She must have read the panicked expression on my face because she waved her hand in the air.

"Don't worry, Emma darling, Kaleb and I aren't concerned about the four of you. I mean, we had our concerns at first, but we sat down and talked about it. We realized we trust the four of you, and if you're not hurting anyone, why wouldn't we support you? We want you kids to be happy. So," she exclaimed excitedly, "do these look good? I wanted to ask when they were all distracted by sugary deliciousness. Nothing puts those boys in a food coma like cake, pie, and ice cream."

I looked into the box, scanning the items. It was easy enough to figure out which present was for which of my guys—a new pair of boots in the style King always wore, this pair a rich, warm brown leather, a stack of new paperbacks that just screamed Jesse, and finally a hat, a pair of socks, and a shirt, all with weird patterns or phrases on them for Reid.

"I think they're perfect," I murmured. "They're going to love them. I'm hoping to get some shopping done over the next couple weeks," I explained as Stella packed the box back up and tucked it away under a pile of coats.

"Well, if you want someone to go with you, you know

where to find me."

My brain whirled in confusion. Did I eat so much, I was too tired and full to understand what she'd said? Or was her offer just too good for my quickly growing cynicism to handle? Either way, I stood there with my head tilted and face scrunched up.

"Oh, don't give me that. Your mom has been really busy, and you can't very well take the boys Christmas shopping with you, so if you want someone to go with you—"

She didn't get a chance to finish her sentence, my body moving on its own as I curled my arms around her tiny waist and buried my face in her soft sweater. Stella didn't say anything, just folded her arms around me as she cooed softly while the tears I had been trying so hard to hold back finally leaked out.

"Thank you," I mumbled against her shoulder.

"You don't have to thank me, Emma. You're a part of the family, and that's what family does."

Not my family...

The movie was wrapping up, all of us lounging on the couch in the basement for the majority of the evening until Killian finally called it quits and headed up to bed over a half hour ago. I was bundled up in a large blanket between Kingston and Reid, my body slowly lulled into a relaxed state, but I couldn't seem to take a quick nap before our plans. My mind was just too worked up about my mom.

"What's up, Cali girl?" Reid murmured, his hand finding my leg under the blanket. "You just tensed up."

"It's nothing," I tried to reassure him, but based on the cocked brow and frown, I didn't manage. "Uh, my mom knows about me dating Kingston. She walked in on us getting the desserts in the garage, but when I tried to tell her about all of us... I froze," I mumbled, feeling worse the longer I went on. "I tried last night, too, when we were eating, but I couldn't seem to make the words come out."

"Did you forget to close the door again, King?" Reid teased. "You really need to learn how to do that, so people stop walking in on you two making out."

"Ha ha, very funny," Kingston deadpanned, but I could feel his shoulders shaking as he held back his laugh.

"But for real, Cali girl. It's alright, I haven't told my parents yet," Reid confided. "I don't think they'll necessarily be okay with it, but that isn't going to stop me. We know you're not ashamed of us, right guys?" Reid asked, Jesse and Kingston both nodding as they looked at me with soft smiles and understanding expressions.

What did I do to deserve such sweethearts?

"So, don't worry or feel like we're pressuring you to tell your mom. Or anyone, for that matter. Okay? Just do it when you're ready," Reid leaned forward, pressing a kiss to my lips with a smile. A buzzing in my pocket pulled my attention away from Reid's kiss, irritation filling me as I glanced at who it was.

"What's up, Babydoll?" I heard Kingston ask, his question trailing off when he noticed who was texting me. "Is that Tyler? Like ex-boyfriend Tyler?"

"Ugh, yes," I groaned, swiping the text away, so I didn't have to look at it. "He doesn't leave me alone. I've just decided to stop responding, hoping he'll back off."

"Let me see," Reid demanded, his hand coming out. I cocked a brow at his gruff tone, and he grimaced. "Sorry, Cali girl. Can I please see it?"

"Much better," I murmured, handing over my phone after

I plugged in the passcode.

"What a douche," Jesse muttered under his breath as he watched Reid scroll, my normally cheerful boyfriend's jaw clenched as he read through.

"Can I text him? He clearly doesn't respect what you want," Reid bit out, passing my phone to Kingston's waiting palm.

"Reid, I don't want you spending the rest of our holiday weekend fighting with my ex because he's a stupid jerk," I huffed. "Please, boys," I pleaded when they all started to argue.

"If he continues, we're figuring out a plan, alright?" Reid compromised, clearly unhappy, I wouldn't let them go full steam ahead in their fight against Turdtastic Tyler.

"Deal, I just want to enjoy our time together, that's all," I pouted, leaning forward to kiss him again. Reid sighed, pecking me as I heard Kingston and Jesse's sigh as well, all of them quickly deflating.

"Okay, okay," Jesse muttered, "just stop pouting."

"You win, Babydoll," Kingston teased, his fingers tracing circles on my back. Reid glanced at the front of my phone, a smile appearing as he glanced at me.

"Enough about that, it's nearing our time to head out, and you know what that means?"

"Black Friday shopping?" I replied with a grin, his hazel eyes lighting up in excitement.

"SHOPPING TIME!" he hollered, throwing his arms in the air with a weird little dance before jumping off the couch and bounding up the stairs, leaving the rest of us laughing.

Such a clown.

A cute clown, but still.

CHAPTER 4

Factoid about Black Friday—it's the busiest day of the year for plumbers.
#WhoKnew #BlackFridayShopping #FunnyFriday

I'm so freaking excited," Aubrey squealed, her breath puffing out in front of her in the cold winter air. Her exuberant cheer had the people in front and behind us in line to the mall looking at us, laughing at her bright smile and excited dance.

"I would never have guessed," Jason teased with a smirk. Aubrey scoffed, elbowing him in the side, but even with the bite to the air, I saw her cheeks darken at his prodding. *I think someone has a crush*. I knew she liked someone but hadn't told us who yet.

"Only a few more minutes!" Zoey added from where she stood next to Aubrey, fueling each other's excitement. "Are you ready, Emma?"

"Yes, it's been a long time since I've done Black Friday shopping," I explained, a shiver wracking through my body as a chilly breeze whipped around us. Reid, being the observant man he is, wrapped his arms around my shoulders and pulled me into his chest. As soon as I was settled against Reid, Jesse's fingers squeezed mine, the heat from his coat pocket, where our entwined hands were, seeping into my chilled body.

"I'm ready to pick up that new gaming system," Brayden added, looking around the group. "We all got our plans ready?" A round of yeses went up, all of our gazes turning toward the front doors as workers neared. A thrill uncurled, adrenaline buzzing through me as Reid and Jesse let me go. I stepped up to Zoey and Aubrey, grabbing hold of them so we wouldn't lose each other in the crowd.

"Meet back up at the water fountain in two hours," I instructed, my face hurting from my wide smile. "Ready."

"Set," Carter added, bouncing on his toes.

And as soon as the door was open, Reid shouted, "Go!"

Clutching each other like our lives depended on it, Zoey, Aubrey, and I darted to the edge of the crowd, intending to hit the department store. As soon as we were in the proper department, we split up.

"What about this?" Aubrey called, holding up a plum-colored sweater. "Oh! With this?" She held up a denim jacket, but I had to crinkle my nose at the weirdness of the cut when she put it on.

"Here, try this one." I held out a slightly lighter one, the fit better for her lean shape. She switched it out and squealed.

"It's perfect! I'm going to look for a pair of skinny jeans and maybe a pair of shoes. Oooh or a scarf!" Chuckling, she darted away, her straight chestnut hair the only thing visible as she swerved around the stacks.

I continued to browse over the next hour, content not to spend any of my money on myself since I had everything I needed. Besides, getting something good for my boys would be worth more than another CD or something for me. *These might be cute for Zoey.* She was eyeing items that would look good with the muted yellow scarf and tan purse I pulled off the rack.

"Hey, Cali girl," Reid's effervescent voice startled me, causing me to yelp and jump. "Sorry, I didn't mean to startle you."

"Jeez, give a girl a heart attack," I teased, my hand pressing the scarf to my chest to calm my racing heart. Reid grimaced, his hand rubbing the back of his neck. "What happened to getting gaming stuff and all things electronic?"

"I got what I wanted," he stated, holding up a bag. "Kingston and Jesse went with Carter to look at books, and Brayden and Jason are looking at shoes. I didn't really care about either, so I figured I could help you pick out some stuff." His cheeks tinted pink as he shrugged.

"I would love your help, babe. Right now, though, I'm just picking some stuff out for Zoey. So, after I show her these?" I asked, showing him the two accessories still clutched in my hands.

"You rang?" Zoey's said right behind me, and once again, I jumped and yelped. Flashing them a half-hearted glare at their chuckles, I passed over the two items. Her brown eyes lit up, and she exclaimed, "They're so pretty! I love them." Shooting forward, she wrapped me in a bear hug with a mumbled "You're the best" before making her way to the dressing room.

"You're so cute, Cali girl," Reid teased, curling me under his arm. "Come on, show me what you want."

"You're not getting me anything," I challenged, my fingers trailing over several soft sweaters displayed on their hangers. "But I don't mind wandering around with you."

"Good because you're stuck with me," he murmured, his

lips pressing to my temple. "Well, at least until breakfast, then pancakes have me for a short while. Don't worry, though, you'll get me back." His joke had me laughing, the butterflies erupting as I felt him smiling against my hair.

I think I could share him with pancakes.

But only if he shares me with French toast.

"Oh God, so freaking full," Reid whined, pushing his plate away as he slouched in his seat with a groan.

"You're so dramatic," Jesse countered with a shake of his head, but his lips quirked up as he watched Reid clutch his stomach with a pathetic grimace.

"Yeah, but if he wasn't, he wouldn't be Reid," Kingston added, taking a sip of his milkshake. Jesse conceded his point with a head tilt and nod.

"What's the plan now?" I asked, also pushing my plate away. As much as Reid was being a dork, I had to agree on the front of being super full.

"Go sleep off the food coma from supper and our middle of the night breakfast," Reid explained, his face scrunching up. "What would you call that? Supfast or breapper?"

"Brinner?" I added with a shrug. "Breakfast and dinner."

"Fourth meal," Kingston continued the ridiculous conversation.

"But we're not at Taco Bell, that's their thing," Jesse argued, "I like brinner." His shy smile and the fact he agreed with me had those butterfly wings flapping in my belly on overdrive. I loved the little ways he let me know I mattered to him.

"Brinner it is! But right now, all I care about is flopping into bed and not moving," Reid stated. "You're working at eleven, right, Cali girl?" I nodded, pulling cash out and moving to pay my bill at the counter when Reid snatched the receipts and shoved them into Kingston's outstretched hand. I half glared, but I had learned several times ago, there was nothing to say when they wanted to pay, so I let it go.

The drive back to Kingston's was quiet, a late-night radio talk show filling the silence as we all digested our food. I thought everyone might have been asleep, but when we walked in, Stella and Kaleb were cuddled up on the couch, watching a movie. They just waved, content to let us go to Kingston's room to sleep.

This was the first time I had been in here since the barbeque, and this time, my mind was clear enough to look around. *Jesse is safe and sound with us, no need to be nervous this time.* Kingston had a large, king-sized bed, covered in a blue plaid comforter and matching sheets. On the far wall, in the large open space, was a futon that looked well-loved. A TV hung on the wall next to it, and the door open to the left revealed a messy, walk-in closet. On the carpet, there was a large, blue rug, matching his sheets. While the room was massive, it felt homey and warm, with the signature scent of orange and cinnamon permeating the space.

"Got some pajamas, Babydoll?"

I nodded, realizing there was only the bed and futon for the four of us.

"Where am I sleeping?" I murmured, glancing at Kingston, who smiled.

"You, me, and Reid will be on the bed, and Jesse will take the futon as usual," he explained.

Why does he always take the futon? I wondered, my brows dipping unconsciously. Noticing the look on my face, King's smile softened, but he gave his head an imperceptible shake. *Okay, then. Guess I'll just focus on getting ready for bed.*

"Goodnight, Em," Jesse said when I came back out, cupping my jaw and giving me a soft kiss.

"Goodnight, Jesse," I murmured, my lip tucking between my teeth as I stared up into his dark brown eyes, loving the way they lit up as he looked at me.

"Come on, Cali girl, let's get some sleep," Reid gently suggested, hooking an arm around my waist and hoisting me up onto his shoulder. I squealed at the jarring movement, but I couldn't help but laugh as he flopped me down on the soft mattress.

"Good thing I wasn't super full anymore, otherwise that could have been bad." I threw him a smirk and a raised brow, but he wasn't fazed, waving me off as Kingston and he crawled onto their respective sides.

"I don't think a bit of Emma throw-up would frighten me," he countered.

I cringed, the thought of vomiting, making me groan. I hated throwing up.

Nice job, Em. Totally romantic thoughts to put in your boyfriends' heads right before a cuddle session.

"Okay, let's get some sleep," Kingston directed, turning off the lamp as he talked. "Emma has exactly seven and a half hours until work. Got your alarm set?" I hummed an affirmative, hunkering down in bed. "Alright, night, everyone. Sleep tight, Babydoll."

"Goodnight, Cali girl," Reid mumbled, kissing my shoulder as he curled around my back.

"Night, guys," I whispered. My hand reached out until it brushed across Kingston's soft t-shirt. As soon as it touched him, a hand curled around mine, bringing it to his lips, his whiskers coarse and rough against my skin, but the sensation helped lull me into a dreamless sleep.

A loud thud and a half strangled, muffled shout jolted me upright from my cocoon in a sleepy panic. Reid and Kingston were both out of bed before I even realized what was happening. The moonlight was the only illumination in the space, but it was enough to see Jesse hunkered down in front of the futon, his hands up around his head and torso. The others didn't approach him, their hands open and up as they talked softly.

"Jesse, it's okay, you're at Kingston's," Reid started. His voice gave Jesse pause, and his arms dropped slightly. My heart shattered as I saw Jesse's wide, frightened gaze.

"Yeah, you're in my room, on the futon," Kingston continued, taking half a step closer, kneeling down in the process. "Emma's here, do you want to talk to her?" Kingston and Reid looked over at me.

Unsure what to do or say, I sputtered out the first thing that popped into my head.

"Did you know a giraffe only needs one-point-nine hours of sleep, whereas a brown bat needs upward of twenty hours a day?"

"Em?" Jesse's voice cracked, confusion lacing his single-worded question as his arms dropped down. "Is that you?"

"Yeah, Jess, it's me," I said softly. *This has definitely happened before. Reid and Kingston are handling this far too well for it to be the first time.* Reid and Kingston continued moving forward at a slow and steady pace, neither making physical contact with Jesse.

"You back?" Reid asked when they reached him. Jesse nodded, a hand running down his face as he sighed.

"Sorry," he mumbled, his shoulders sagging as he looked

at them.

"You don't have to apologize," Kingston reassured. "Was it the usual nightmare?" Jesse nodded again, glancing at me with a frown. Not wanting him to think I was afraid or put off, I climbed out of the middle of the bed and padded around to where they were all collected on the rug. Kneeling down, I gave Jesse a reassuring smile.

"You alright?" he asked, his hand coming forward to push a strand of hair out of my eyes I hadn't even noticed. I nodded, grabbing his hand and pressing a lingering kiss to his palm.

"I should be asking you that," I asked with a light tone. He huffed out a single laugh, not bothering to counter what I said.

"Cali girl, why don't you sleep with Jesse on the futon," Reid suggested, rubbing my back encouragingly. "We can unfold it to make room for both of you."

"No—" Jesse tried to object, but I cut him off.

"That's a great idea, babe"—I flashed a smile at Reid—"I would love to."

Reid smirked and moved to expand the bed, happy to let me cut off Jesse's potential argument. Kingston chuckled, helping Jesse up off the carpet before dropping a kiss on top of my head.

"Come on, Jess, let's get some sleep." I offered my hand, waiting for him to choose to come with me. After staring at me for a few moments, his fingers curled around my palm and squeezed, following me to the futon. As we walked over to the now expanded bed, I glanced at Reid and Kingston, my brow raising discreetly in question. Of course, neither answered me, only grimacing with head shakes small enough, they didn't catch Jesse's attention. Grinding my teeth, I let it go, focusing on helping Jesse get a good night's sleep.

Well, as good as he can get after something like that.

As he had when he stayed the night in my room, Jesse curled around me, his arm coming to rest over my chest as his nose pressed into my shoulder and neck. It was only a minute until I started to drift off once more, a soft whisper following me into sleep.

"Thank you, Em."

After a few hours of sleep, following Jesse's nightmare, I found myself bustling around. Coffee Grounds was busy with customers, the cold wave bringing in loads of people wanting a hot drink or a pumpkin spiced treat to get them through the day. Lyla and I worked in tandem, taking and filling orders, stocking the counters as needed, taking only a few brief moments to chill between the large groups of people.

Finally, after about four hours of non-stop rushing, the crowd slowed, and we were able to breathe. Lyla leaned against the chest-high bartop, her head propped on her hand as she wiped the top with a rag. I echoed her tired stance, slouching against the counter behind the register. My feet throbbed, and I was tired, but Lyla stuck out her tongue at me, distracting me long enough, I didn't swirl into negative thoughts.

"So, you're extra quiet today, anything on your mind?" Lyla asked, giving me narrowed eyes and propping her fist on her hip. I gave a soft chuckle.

Should've known she'd pick up on it as soon as my thoughts went south.

"Not much," I tried to say, but Lyla's brows rising sharply told me she didn't believe a word I said. "Just thinking about Thanksgiving. My mom and I went over to Kingston's and celebrated it there."

"Was it awkward? Your mom and your boyfriends?" Lyla questioned.

"Eh," I hummed, shrugging awkwardly as I struggled to explain what was on my mind. "It wasn't weird, necessarily, because my mom doesn't know about the three of us. She walked in on me kissing Kingston, so she definitely knows about him. No, my thing was she keeps getting called away for work stuff, and I don't know... I'm lonely, and I miss her, and the fact she left Thanksgiving for work just bothers me, I guess," I trailed off, realizing I was rambling.

"Ugh, that's the worst. My dad used to be like that when I was growing up, always gone for work trips. He finally retired, but that was after all of us had grown up. Not that I'd trade it for anything, mind you, but still," she explained, her hand rolling in the air animatedly. "On the positive, though, you got to spend a little time with her, and Christmas is coming up, so you'll get even more time soon."

I tried to look on the bright side, mustering a smile. Lyla was right, I got to spend some time with her, and focusing on good over bad was the best thing to do.

Now, if this happens again at Christmas, that'll be a whole other issue.

"How'd you get to be so smart?" I teased with a laugh. "You always seem to know just what to say."

"Been there, done that, I guess," she shrugged, her cheeks tinting pink. "I know what it's like to need someone's fresh perspective on things, and sometimes, that's the best way to get clarity on the shit going on in your life," she explained, her voice lacking its usual boisterous enthusiasm. Grabbing a second rag, I bumped shoulders with her as I came around the counter to help wipe down the tables. Lyla laughed, straightening as she finished wiping down the counter.

"You know I'm here for you too, Ly," I added.

"Yeah, you're pretty cool, you know... for a high schooler," she teased, her signature smile returning to her freckled face.

"So, how was your Thanksgiving?" I asked now that our deeper conversation was finished.

"It was good! All twenty thousand of my family members were there, but thankfully, there weren't any family fist fights," she explained, moving to the table next to me. "Although Rick ended up making a fool of himself."

"Tell me, tell me," I egged her on, curiosity burning as she laughed.

"Well, since it's such a big get together, we usually have our holidays at my aunt and uncle's property because they have a large barn they use for events. You know, weddings and stuff, so it's big enough to fit all of us. Well, the food was all lined up on one end of the room on a large buffet line, and Rick, if you haven't noticed, is a bit clumsy, which is why being manager here instead of a barista is a good fit. So, he was walking along, actually paying attention to his surroundings, or so he says, and ends up tripping."

"Oh God," I laughed, having an idea of where this was going.

"Ended up falling and face planting right into one of the extra pies. It was the pumpkin pie... covered in whip cream... it got everywhere, including up his nose." She was laughing so hard, she had to pause to catch her breath. I could totally picture it—redhead Rick and his pale, freckled face, covered in whip cream and orange pumpkin pie—and I lost it. Rick's deadpan laugh radiated through the room, only making my own laughter worse as tears streamed down my face.

"Ha ha, yes, *so* very funny. At least I didn't spill my glass of hot cider on myself, *Lyla*," he called out, smirking in triumph. Their back and forth familial banter made me laugh harder until I was barely standing, the table I was leaning against the only thing keeping me upright.

Who needs siblings when I have these two?

CHAPTER 5

NOVEMBER 30TH

Today, I will drink some orange juice. According to WebMD, high levels of vitamin C are said to physiologically reduce your stress levels.
#AllTheStressReduction #GimmeOJ #StressfreeSaturday

Knowing the weather was going to be chilly, lower than it was most of the time in Cali, I bundled up in a thick sweater, sweatshirt, and coat. I also grabbed my knit hat and scarf, gloves, and a blanket to make sure I wouldn't freeze. Running up the stairs, I poked my head into my mom's office.

"I'm heading to watch Reid's last lacrosse game," I informed, pulling my hat over my hair. "Then, I have work this evening."

"Going with your friends?" she questioned, her eyes darting between her file on her desk and her computer screen.

"Nope, just me."

"Kingston isn't going? Is he alright with you going to watch his best friend's game without him?" She looked at me with a sharp brow raise.

"Uh, yeah, Reid's my friend too, and that isn't going to stop just because I'm dating Kingston," I explained, my stomach dropping. She hummed skeptically.

"Alright then, have fun. Let me know where you are throughout the day," she stated, turning back to her work. As I darted down the stairs and out to my car, I couldn't help feeling a twinge of bitterness, she was just now asking me to check in when it wasn't like she'd cared any other time in the last few years since I got a car and a phone.

Doesn't matter, I thought, hopping into my car. *It's time to go surprise Reid.*

"Holy crap, it is so freaking cold here!" I hissed under my breath, wrapping the blanket around me tighter. The stands weren't full, but there were more people here than I had anticipated, most of them were bundled up like I was. A blanket was definitely a good idea. I made sure to sit in one of the first rows, hoping Reid would be able to see me. After a few more minutes of fiddling around on my phone, the teams came out onto the field.

As expected, Reid was focused on the game and his teammates as they warmed up and got started. I'd never watched a lacrosse game, so at that point, I was just watching them run around the field. Granted, I'd seen enough football, I was able to hazard a guess what was happening, so as soon as the crowd started to cheer for our team, I did too.

"Yeah! Go, Reid! Woo!" I screamed obnoxiously loud, catching the eyes of several people around me, but I waved my arm when he looked over. His confused frown split into a bright smile when he realized it was me. I could see the happiness that lit his face even from halfway across the field.

No, Emma! No happy dances. Keep those toes curled.

Over the next hour, I kept my eyes peeled to Reid's '21' jersey as he played or rested, finding myself really enjoying the game despite my teeth chattering. The final score was called, and I jumped up along with the others who had come to the game and celebrated our win. Even though Reid had played pretty much the entire game, he sprinted to the building I assumed held the locker rooms, taking the lead and running ahead of his still-celebrating teammates. It only took a few minutes until my phone was buzzing in my hand.

Reid: I'll be out in a bit<3

Emma: I'm not going anywhere, babe.

Reid: You're perfect!

Excited, giddy, and away from the other spectators, I did a little squeal, my lip tucked between my teeth. As promised, Reid came back out onto the field only a few minutes later, hair damp and changed into a pair of sweats and a hoodie. Darting down the sideline, he vaulted over the fence, separating the stands from the turf.

"Cali girl!" he exclaimed, panting from exertion. "I didn't know you were coming today."

"I wanted it to be a surprise," I explained, shrugging, "I figured I didn't have a chance to go to any of your games, and since this was the last one, I would... I don't know..."

"Surprise me?" he finished with a smile. My cheeks burned, the signature tingling as my skin blushed under his attention.

"Yeah. Want to grab some coffee before I have to head to work? I have another two hours, but I wasn't sure when the guys were expecting you," I rambled, continuing to pepper him with questions as I bundled the blanket up and stuffed it under my arm.

"I'd love to get coffee, but before I go to Kingston's, I need to change. Want to come over for a bit while I do that? It'll only take a second," Reid explained, his arm going over my shoulder. "Don't worry, it's not sweat, I showered."

"I assumed, seeing your soaking wet hair, but that sounds great. I can finally be nosy and see what Reid Hughes' room looks like. Is it dark and broody? Oh! It's pink, isn't it? That's why you love my room so much, huh?" I teased as we walked up the stone steps to the parking lot.

"You know it, Cali girl," he exclaimed proudly before losing it in a fit of laughter. "Meet you there?"

"That'd be great." Reid hurried around me, opening the driver's side door of my car, signaling me to have a seat with an exaggerated arm wave. I couldn't stop the grin that curled my lips as I climbed in and buckled up, trying not to shiver at the biting chill of the seat.

Hey, it's better than being outside in the Nebraska winter wind.

Fifteen minutes later, we pulled up to Reid's home, a modern single-story house that looked relatively new. The exterior was dark, almost black, while the trim was a light gray. The lines were sharp, standing out against the large tree in the front yard, I knew would have been lush and bright if it wasn't winter. Reid pulled into the third space in the drive as I pulled up to the curb.

"Come on, Cali girl." Reid tilted his head as he got out, wanting me to follow. As we walked up to the garage keypad, Reid hopped up, looking into the small semi-circle windows at the top. "Looks like my parents are still here. They should be heading to work soon, though. Hopefully, they won't pester you with questions."

"Seeing how your mom zoomed from one topic to the next when I first met her, I don't foresee that happening," I murmured. Reid grimaced but didn't argue.

The interior of Reid's house was just as modern as the exterior with sleek lines and a contrasting monochromatic color scheme. The mud room was also a laundry room, its black cabinets, white stone countertops, and gray-washed wood flooring matching the kitchen we walked into. The only color in the room were the flowers on the table and a couple of paintings on the walls.

"Is that you, Reid?" I heard his mom call as we stepped deeper into the kitchen.

"Yeah, Ma," he shouted back, chucking the duffel on his shoulder into the corner of the mud room. "Cali girl is here too, just so you know. Going to change before we head to King's."

"You don't have to yell, I'm right here," she chastised playfully, coming around a corner that led to what looked to be a hall. "Nice to see you again, Emma. How have you been? We didn't get much of a chance to talk last time we saw each other. Come"—she waved me to follow her to the counter—"would you like something to drink? Coffee, tea, hot chocolate?" She zoomed from one topic to the next, barely taking a breath as I stood there awkwardly.

"Hot chocolate sounds great," I said, my fingers fiddling with the hem of my sweater. Reid's mom—Faith, if I remembered correctly—busied herself, pulling mugs from cabinets and milk from the fridge. She looked the same as when I'd first seen her, only this time, her dark brown hair was tied in a smooth ponytail instead of a messy bun. She was dressed in the dark blue uniform I recognized from the airline where I knew she worked as a flight attendant, the red patterned silky ascot tied around her neck, bringing a stark contrast to the deep suit skirt.

"Have a seat, dear, no need to stand there." She waved toward the barstools under the counter. Doing as she asked, I sank into the wooden stool. "So, how has school been?"

"It's been great," I lied with faux cheer. "Having a lot of fun with my friends. Classes are good."

"Faith," Reid's dad, Micah, called out. "Are you almost ready to go?" His voice was deep and gravelly, rumbling down the hall as he stepped into the kitchen. "Oh, I didn't realize Reid had a guest." He wore his pilot's uniform, his black curls cut shorter than the last time I saw him. His lips curled down slightly as he glanced at me.

"This is Emma, Reid's friend, remember, honey? We met her that night at the store," Faith stated brightly, unfazed by his irritated tone. "Here you go, one cup of hot chocolate for you and one for Reid whenever he's finished. If you'll excuse us, we need to get to work." She flashed me a cheerful smile before moving around the island and throwing on her coat. "We're heading out, Reid. I'll let you know when we land in New York. Bye, Emma."

Wow, does she always move at a thousand miles an hour? I stared at the now closed garage door, alone in the silent kitchen. Getting up, I grabbed the two piping hot mugs and started down the hall, following the noise coming from one of the far doors that was partially open.

"Babe?" I called, glancing in the room. Reid's toned back flexed, his olive skin bared with only a pair of light wash jeans hanging low on his hips. My mouth went dry as he turned. His torso was muscled, the slight hint of a six-pack cutting his stomach.

"You can come in, Cali girl. I don't bite," he teased, digging through his drawer. Swallowing the lump that formed in my throat, seeing Reid half naked in a house where we were alone, I inched into his room.

I forced my gaze away, glancing around the room in an attempt to not melt into a puddle of heat on his floor. His walls were filled with posters, most science themed, including space, a periodic table, and some things I didn't recognize. Some posters were of different bands I knew Reid liked. There were so many, it took a while to realize his walls were a pale green that matched his green sheets. His bed was tucked into the corner, the black comforter bunched up. I had expected it to be messy, but there wasn't as much spread around his room as I anticipated, only a couple pieces of clothing that seemed to have missed the hamper and a small pile of glasses and empty soda cans.

"Aww, look at that cute blush." Reid's cooing pulled me from being nosy and back to him. My eyes inadvertently widened at his still-exposed chest. He glanced down, a cocksure smile taking over his face. "Does Cali girl like what she sees?" he murmured, stepping closer. Tucking my lower lip between my teeth, I shrugged.

"Maybe," I muttered, my eyes glued to his warm skin as he stopped in front of me.

"I would hope you like it, I mean, I *am* your boyfriend," he teased, tilting his head down so he could look me in the eyes. "You don't have to be uncomfortable, Emma. We don't have to do anything, and I do, in fact, plan on putting on a shirt."

I half-heartedly glared before chuckling. *I still feel like these nerves are going to make me combust, but he always knows how to make me feel comfortable again.*

"Ha ha," I deadpanned. "I'm not uncomfortable. I mean... I'm a bit nervous, but I'm not uncomfortable with you without a shirt on," I rambled. "Did you know your earlobes line up with your nipples or that the average size of people's nipples are the size of a ladybug?" I huffed, rubbing my face to help calm my thoughts. "Sorry," I mumbled on the other side of my hands.

"Cali girl,"—Reid pulled my hands away from my face and held them together, bringing them to his lips for a soft kiss—"you can feel whatever you need to feel; I just don't want you to be uncomfortable around me. Or nervous, but I get that may take some time. Don't think I forgot what you said during your birthday Q and A about never wanting to do stuff back in Cali but feeling differently here."

"I know, and I don't want you to think I don't like seeing all of this," I emphasized, looking at his chest. "I'm just weird."

"You're perfect, Cali girl, nervousness and all," he murmured, leaning forward until his lips barely brushed mine, not moving forward or try to deepen the kiss, giving me the chance to do it.

With a surge of confidence, I kissed him back, tentatively brushing my tongue against his lips. Before it could go further, Reid pulled back, giving me a soft grin.

"See? Not so bad, but I am getting cold, so I'm going to put a shirt on now." His abrupt change of topics made me laugh as I reached over and grabbed the hot cocoa mugs.

"Here, your mom made these for us." I held it out after Reid tossed on a long sleeve shirt.

"Perfect, we'll drink this, then head to Coffee Grounds. I want you to myself for a little while longer," he explained, sinking onto his bed with a pat next to him.

Can't say I didn't want that too, I thought, sinking next to him.

I'll always take more time with my clown.

Once our hot chocolate was gone, Reid and I headed out, and fifteen minutes later, we pulled into the shop's lot. It was busy since it was the middle of Saturday, but thankfully, Lyla was working, as usual, her red hair fluttering as she moved from one end of the counter to the other, working alongside one of the other part-time employees; I couldn't remember her name. *Note to self, look at her name tag when you get closer.*

"Hey, I'm going to go to the bathroom real quick, can you get me a..." Reid trailed off as he looked at the board. "Peppermint mocha?" I nodded, begrudgingly accepting the ten-dollar bill he placed in my hand, knowing he would be upset if I didn't. I ordered quickly before glancing discreetly at the name tag of the other worker, focusing on committing her name to memory—*Rebecca*, I repeated as I stepped off to the side. Apparently, I hadn't been looking where I was shifting to because a man bumped into me.

"Oh, sorry!" I squeaked, trying to shift out of the way so he would have more room to pass.

"It's alright," the man stated, his voice deep and gruff. Glancing up, I was met with an older man with graying black hair, ebony skin, and sharp eyes. "Are you okay?" I nodded, unsure of what to say. "Good, though, maybe next time, look where you're walking, hmm?"

"Yeah, sorry about that." I cringed. He smiled with a slight nod and a "Don't worry about it" before walking out of the crowded shop. I spent the next few minutes waiting for Reid and our drinks, running through the scenario. I could have sworn he wasn't there when I'd moved over, but maybe I really wasn't paying attention to my surroundings.

"Hey, Cali girl," Reid's effervescent voice pulled me from my wandering thoughts just in time for Lyla to call out our names.

"Thanks, Lyla, I'll be heading back shortly to change," I called with a wave as Reid stepped forward to get our drinks, handing mine to me as we sat at one of the few open tables. "Ha, she drew curlicues on yours."

"What?" Reid questioned, glancing at the side with a laugh. "What's yours say?"

"Emma Bean," I read, chuckling at the little heart next to it. "She's such a dork."

"Very true, but life would be boring without the weirdos in the world," Reid half shouted while striking a gallant pose with his arms, nearly smacking someone in the process. "Oops, sorry!" The person just shook their head with a chuckle and continued walking.

"Yeah, yeah, you're the weirdest of them all, babe," I sputtered through my laughter.

But I wouldn't have it any other way.

DECEMBER 1ST

Decorating at Kingston's resulted in a race to see who could wrap a person in wrapping paper the fastest. I ended up being the person turned into a human present.
#ButWeWonThough #Joyful #SundayFunday

Mom was sleeping in, her light snores resonating through the upstairs. For whatever reason, I hadn't slept well, so I found myself up early, the sun barely peeking over the horizon as I buttered my toast. *What do I want to do until I head over to Kingston's?* Sinking onto the cold wooden chair at the table, my mind was calm as I watched the pinky orange of the sunrise.

Oh, I could update all my photos. I had so many pictures since coming here, I hadn't updated my albums. *Maybe I could write in my diary; it's been a while since I've made a dedicated post.* With those ideas in mind, I finished my breakfast and darted down the stairs. Digging my laptop out from under a pile of papers from school, I got comfortable on my bed.

It was soothing, transferring photos and organizing them into folders, my mind running on autopilot, and before I knew it, my photos were sorted and ready to be printed. Now, which ones did I want to have in my photo album, and which did I want to keep digital only...

"Oh, I like that one," I muttered to myself, selecting a few from my Halloween birthday and a couple from the pumpkin patch. "That's adorable," I whispered when I found one from when Reid stayed the night. It was when I stumbled across a photo of the four of us before the party from hell, I realized as much as I had been ignoring the problem, I had a long road ahead of me.

I was smiling happily between my boys, oblivious to what was to come only a couple hours later. A sense of disconnect wound through my chest as I looked at the photo, my mind replaying the night as if I was an outsider looking in. My body cold and numb as I was carried back into the bathroom, I didn't feel Brad's hands or mouth on my skin despite knowing I should. The echo in my mind of Brad's scream as Jesse hit and kicked him had me shaking my head.

What is going on with me?

"You need some self-care, Emma," I told myself. "It's

been too long since you sat down to journal." Pulling up a blank page in my computer notes app, I started a new diary entry. It had been a while since I'd done this, so I sat down and just wrote out what was on my mind. No fun hashtags or little snippets of my day, just me and real-life talk.

December 1st
#SundayFunday

I have been in the middle of freaking nowhere, Nebraska, since early September, and at first, I thought it would suck, but surprisingly, it's grown on me.

That could totally be because of the guys I spend most of my time with or my job I really enjoy, but either way, I'm finding myself genuinely happy here, instead of to sulking like I thought I would be.

It's not all rainbows and sparkles, though. Some stuff has happened, and I found myself having nightmares a couple of nights a week while feeling jumpy and on edge when I'm at school because I know Brad is around. When I'm not at school, it's not a problem unless I'm going to a party. And let's be real, I haven't done that since what I've dubbed "the party from hell."

I'm starting to wonder if I should talk to someone about it. I know I have to talk to Kingston's dad for the courts, but thinking about doing that scares the living daylights out of me, so I don't even know if I can talk to someone else about it.

Maybe I'll ask Lyla. She always seems to have a level head about everything. Or if it continues being a problem, I'll talk to Ms. Rogers or maybe try to pin down my mom to tell her. Is it terrible I still haven't told her about what happened? I mean, I feel bad, but it's so hard when the little time I get with her, she's ALWAYS working, and I just want to enjoy the rare free moments we get together. Who wants to focus on depressing thoughts during that time? Not this girl, that's for sure.

I think I'm going to try meditation or maybe focus on doing a bit more journaling or doing things I enjoy, to help balance out that creepy feeling I get when I'm at school. You know, when I was in California, I would have had a dozen or so people to talk to, people I THOUGHT were my friends. But being here, around real people, I've realized just how fake everyone in Cali was. Their concern about my 'problems' or what I was dealing with wasn't because they actually cared, but because it was something to talk about, gossip for the rumor mill. I can't believe I was ever actually friends with them, or I ever wanted to be like them. I thought I would miss them when I moved, and while it hurt at first when they basically forgot me, I wouldn't know what to say anymore if they called or what we could talk about. But you know what? Good riddance to fake friendships.

Well, I think that's it, I mean, other than the stuff I wrote in my last post about my dad and mom both being absent in my life. That's still going strong. Hopefully, it'll be different next time I write a journal post, but I'm not going to hold my breath.

Positive note, though. I'm about to go help Kingston, the boys, and King's family decorate their house and tree. King said we're having cinnamon rolls with chili. How weird is that? I don't know what kind of crazy place I moved too, but that's probably the weirdest thing I've heard of so far, closely followed by pig races at the pumpkin patches.

Okay, I'm going to hop off and take a bath with a bath bomb, soak up the aromatherapy, and relax before going to King's. I'll be back, you know, whenever.

With that, I logged off and got my bath ready.

If things get any more stressful, I'm going to pick up more bath bombs.

But for real, who actually *needs a reason for more bath bombs?*

Chapter 6

DECEMBER 6TH

Stumbled across this gem of a joke this morning before school- Why do seagulls fly over the sea? Because if they flew over the bay, they'd be bagels!
#TerribleJoke #OfCourseILaughedBecauseImMe #FunnyFriday

"Freedom!" Reid shouted, his arms flinging wide into the air as he ran to his Jeep. Several other students around him whooped and hollered, cheering with excitement that it was finally the weekend. As much as I shook my head at his ridiculousness, I couldn't help but agree.

It had been a long week of quizzes, essays, and a bunch of homework. We were nearing finals for this quarter, and every single teacher was piling on the course work, so we would be free to study the next week and a half before exams. On top of the increased schoolwork, I continued to be a Bradnet, attracting his creepy gaze wherever I went. The only positive from the whole thing was it solidified my urge to talk to Kaleb when we got a chance.

"Em?" Jesse asked, his words quiet as his fingers brushed the back of my hand. "You slowed down." Only then did I realize I had stopped walking.

"Sorry, got lost in thought. Let's go," I stated, walking again. "We still hitting Kingston's first to grab everything?"

"That's the plan." Kingston nodded, having slowed when

I did. "You have your stuff, right?"

"Got it in the trunk," I nodded, hitching a thumb over my shoulder as we reached our cars. "I'll meet you guys there." Climbing into my car, I pulled out, following Reid's muddy Jeep. I was sad I had missed out on their most recent mudding adventure last week but wasn't too upset since the boys promised to take me when the snow was melting, and the trails were the best for it.

Thankfully, it only took twenty minutes, even in the post-school traffic, to get to Kingston's house, and soon enough, I was parked off to the side, away from possibly blocking his parents' cars while we were gone. A whip of cold air swirled around me, making me pull my hat down tighter on my head and shove my hands into my pockets as soon as I had my duffel pulled from the back.

"Ah, boys, Emma!" Stella hollered. "Before you go, I made some cookies and snacks for you all to take. Come and get them." Tossing my bag in the back of Reid's Jeep, I followed my boys into the house.

"Emma, darling," she murmured, pulling me off to the side as the others filed into the kitchen. "Kaleb and I need to talk to you before you go. It's about everything with the Warlands."

My stomach flopped, a sinking feeling filling my chest as I nodded and let her direct me to the office door off the front entry that was normally closed.

"Emma, it's good to see you again," Kaleb greeted, his smile forced as he looked over at me from his desk. "Unfortunately, it's not good news. Jesse's trial date came in, which I've already talked to him about. It's set for January 27th. I'm not sure if you two had talked about it or not, and it may seem like quite a while, but I need to start preparing his defense, meaning I'll need to—"

"Talk to me about everything," I mumbled, shifting from one foot to the other as I crossed my arms tightly. "I understand. Uh, when do you want to do that?"

"We can start after you're back from your trip. I don't want any of you to worry about it while you're visiting colleges," Kaleb reassured. "Would Monday work? Kingston will be helping at the firm, and I figured it might be helpful to have him there." Stella's hand came to my back, rubbing my shoulder blades in a soothing attempt to calm me.

"Uh, yeah, I think so."

"So, Monday?" Kaleb paused to double check, waiting for a sign I agreed. After I nodded, he continued, "Alright, that's what we'll plan on. Take the weekend to relax, have fun. Be safe." Kaleb emphasized the last statement, and I immediately groaned, my cheeks flaring in a wave of heat. "Oh, Emma, I didn't mean like *that*. But on that topic, be safe with that too."

"Kaleb," Stella chastised playfully, "don't embarrass her." Kaleb just laughed and turned back to his bookshelf, scanning for something among the spines.

"Call if you need anything," Stella stated as the guys finally followed, hands full of treats and a cooler for the drive.

"I thought it was only an hour?" I asked, pointing to the haul of goodies.

"We're going to take backroads. Takes about an hour and a half to two hours," Reid explained. "Besides, have you ever known me to turn down a cookie?"

I rolled my eyes and waved to Stella as we headed back out into the cold.

"Let us know when you're there!" Stella hollered after us. We gave a collective agreement and climbed in the car.

It only took a few minutes before they started chatting, their voices lulling me into a dreamless sleep.

My boys...

"Em," Jesse's gentle voice roused me, his warm hand on my shoulder, waking me from my deep rest. "Em, love, we're here."

"Already?" I mumbled, my voice thick with exhaustion as I sat up. My right shoulder was cold and stiff from leaning against the door and window during my nap, and try as I might, I couldn't shake the last of the sleep from my body.

"You were out before we even left Kingston's driveway, Cali girl," Reid explained, pulling on his coat in the driver's seat.

"Look outside, Babydoll," Kingston prompted. Glancing back at him in confusion, I saw the excited glint in his warm brown eyes. Wondering why he was so excited, I shifted to face forward and finally processed what was happening outside the Jeep.

"Snow!" I squealed, throwing open the door and hopping out.

The icy chill immediately shook the rest of the sleep from my body, joy flowing through me as the white flakes drifted through the air. It coated the sidewalks and grass, melting against my palm as I held it out. Doing a little dance, I stuck my tongue out and did the one thing I'd wanted to do my whole life — catch a snowflake on my tongue like in the movies.

There wasn't anything super special about catching frozen water on your tongue, but at that moment, nothing could dim the happiness that filled me. It was the first time in the last few weeks I felt light as if nothing could bring me down. When Kingston's arms circle around me, I let out a contented sigh.

"I love seeing you so happy, Babydoll," he murmured, pressing a cheek to the top of my head. "But it's cold, and you don't have a coat on, so let's head inside. It's supposed to snow on and off for the next couple days, so we'll have plenty of time to play in it."

"This it, Cali girl?" Reid called out, holding out my duffel. When I stepped over to take it, he shouldered the bag, flashing me an impish grin.

"You know I can carry that, right?" I challenged, taking my coat from Jesse. "Thanks, Jess."

"No problem, Em." He gave me a handsome smile and headed inside with Kingston.

"I know you can, but that doesn't mean I want you to. Don't you know that's what chivalry is?" Reid countered as I stepped back so he could close the back of the Jeep.

"So, you're a knight now?" I laughed.

"Of course, milady," he said valiantly before bowing as low as he could with two bags on his back. Shaking my head at his silliness, I let him open the door for me when he waved an arm in front of me to stop me from doing so myself. "What did I say about chivalry, miss?" he chastised playfully.

"Sorry, *sir*," I emphasized with an eye roll, but I couldn't hide the curl of my lips. Kingston and Jesse were waiting for us in the lobby, room key in hand. The heat of the hotel quickly warmed my chilled bones, subduing the last of the shivers I didn't realize I had. "We all good?"

"Yup, top floor, too. King bed and a pull-out couch," Kingston explained, leading us toward the elevator. By the time we reached our room, I was sweaty and hot in my winter coat, so as soon as the door was open, I shucked the thick garment over the back of the desk chair. It was a standard hotel room with a king-sized bed, wooden desk with a rolling chair, TV on top of a wood cabinet, and a couch. The bathroom was simple, off to the side when you first came in, right by the small closet. It smelled like fresh linens and air freshener, and the carpet was soft against my feet as I kicked off my boots.

"So, now what shall we do?" Reid asked dramatically as he flopped onto the bed face first, the end of his question muffled by the thick comforter.

"Hm…" Kingston trailed off, shrugging.

"We could, uh…." I struggled to come up with an answer as I sat next to Reid.

"Oh," Reid exclaimed, flipping over, his curls flopping out against the white of the bedding. "We could ask more questions! Like we did at Cali girl's birthday."

"I'm cool with that. We could put some music on and eat some cookies and snacks if you three didn't eat them all," I suggested, looking into the tins Jesse had put on the bed, pleasantly surprised to see a good chunk of the treats still there.

"Okay, so this time, how about we just ask a question, then everyone has to answer? That way, no one has to dig out paper to write it out," Kingston offered, getting situated in the office chair while Jesse sank onto the pull-out couch. Reid finally propped himself up, his arm pressed against my side and back as he leaned his weight back onto his hand.

"Alright then," I laughed, "I'll go first. In the spirit of the holidays, what is something you want for Christmas?"

"Oooh, right in for the hard questions, Cali girl," Reid teased before humming in thought. "I think going to the planetarium show at UNO would be fun. Well, when it's a nice night out and not snowing, obviously." I tucked the statement away in the back of my mind to keep as an option for Christmas present for Reid.

"Some fuzzy socks," Kingston stated, making me look at him with a cocked brow. He shrugged. "I love fuzzy socks, don't knock them until you try them."

"I'm not knocking them, I love fuzzy things too. I just didn't peg you as someone who liked them," I explained.

"Just a day to relax, play video games, and spend time with my favorite people," Jesse murmured with a soft smile, his eyes sparkling as he looked at me. A girly giggle bubbled out of me without warning, my cheeks burning as the guys chuckled at me. Groaning, I dropped my face in my hands so they wouldn't see how pink I knew my face was getting.

"Told you that little giggle is adorable," Kingston stated simply, and, being the mature person I was, I dropped my hands and stuck my tongue out at him, only making him laugh harder.

"You pick a question," I directed with a wave at King so he would stop teasing me. *Though if* I'm *honest, I have to admit, I love it.* Not that I would tell him that.

"But you didn't answer your question," Jesse pointed out, nudging my leg with his fingers.

"Ugh, fine," I playfully huffed, already embarrassed about what I was about to say. "I already got what I wanted. I wanted snow. Although I want to play in it, like build a snowman or go sledding. Oh! Do they have carriage rides like in the movies?"

"Yes, Cali girl, they do. Maybe if we have time this weekend, we can go on one," Reid offered.

"If you could live during another time or decade, what would you pick?" Kingston asked, quickly answering his own question. "Honestly, I really like right now, but if I had to pick, I think the eighties with the uptick in technology. I think it would be really cool to see the evolution of the computer and phones."

"Twenties," I piped in. "Well, the good part of the twenties, swing dancing and art deco. I could do without the Great Depression."

"The Civil Rights Movement," Jesse said. "Being able to make such an impact on history would be amazing." I smiled at his sentimentality. I knew if Jesse grew up in that time, he would proudly be right alongside everyone at sit-ins or protests.

"That's a hard one," Reid thought aloud. "I honestly don't know. I think I'd want to travel to a bunch of different times—ancient Egypt, fall of the Roman Empire, the first flight from the Wright brothers."

"Your turn," Kingston directed to Reid.

"Do you want kids?" My brows rose at the intense question, but Reid looked at me unapologetically, his lips curling slightly. "What, Cali girl? Call me curious."

"Yes," I stated simply, "I don't know how many, though. Do you?" I directed at him.

"Yeah." He beamed before glancing at Kingston, who rolled his eyes and nodded. All of our eyes turned to Jesse, who looked lost in thought before shrugging.

"I'm not sure, haven't given it much thought." There was a note in his voice that drew my brows down, but I didn't get a chance to ponder it because he started talking. "Favorite flavor of ice cream?"

"Oh God," I exclaimed, "I have no idea. I love ice cream, so it really depends on my mood." Reid nodded his agreement with a 'what she said.'

"Mint chocolate chip is my top, but I love anything with

chocolate in it," Kingston explained.

"What about you?" I asked Jesse, noting that he hadn't responded.

"Vanilla, mainly because I like mixing stuff in it. Candy or other toppings," he answered, glancing from me to Reid, catching my attention.

What are these three up to?

"I have another one!" Reid exclaimed. When he didn't ask it right away, I turned away from Jesse and looked over at Reid, gasping at what was in his hand.

A trio of white roses tied with a burgundy ribbon was held out to me.

"Will you go to winter formal with us, Emma Brooke?" he murmured.

"Oh my gosh, yes!" I squealed, taking the roses and smelling them, my cheeks hurting from how wide my smile was. "You guys totally planned this whole question thing just to ask that, didn't you?"

"Maybe," Kingston teased with a matching smile. "But we're happy you said yes."

"Of course, I said yes. You guys are my boyfriends," I countered as I got up, grabbing one of the glasses near the coffee maker and heading into the bathroom. Filling up the glass, I placed the roses in the makeshift vase and brought it back out.

"Holy shit, I just got super hungry," Reid exclaimed, his stomach rumbling loud enough to make my brows shoot up my forehead. "Anyone else hungry? For actual food, not cookies and chips?"

"Yeah, I could definitely eat," Jesse admitted. Kingston nodded, and three gazes landed on me. As soon as food was mentioned, I felt my stomach start to grumble, and the guys laughed at my unspoken agreement.

"What's around here?" I asked, moving around Kingston in the office chair to peer over Jesse's shoulder as he searched on his phone. "Oh, that looks good!"

"Pizza and subs? It's takeout only if we're good with that?" he asked, glancing over at me. The scent of mint and a flare of heat on my cheeks washed over me as I immediately realized how close our lips were, only a breath's distance apart. I wanted to press my lips against his, but I held back, irrationally worried about the other two being in the room. Nodding, I smashed my lips together, so I wouldn't spout some ridiculous fact and embarrass myself. *I need air.* Quickly becoming overwhelmed with the tingling building in my core, I shuffled back a bit and sat on the couch next to Jesse instead of practically sitting in his lap.

"Sounds good," Kingston agreed, standing and grabbing his coat. "It's probably going to be a wait since it's Friday night. Jesse, want to come with me?"

"Sure, I could stretch my legs after being in the car for two hours, then sitting around here."

"But you sit for eight hours a day at school, then another hour or two for studying," Reid teased. Jesse scoffed, pulling on his hoodie and coat.

"And I hate it then, too," Jesse countered. "We'll be back, Em. Message us what you want." Leaning down, Jesse did something I hadn't expected.

He kissed me hard and without hesitation, his warm palm cupping my jaw. My toes curled, and the butterflies erupted as he straightened. Jesse was so different here. My quiet and gentle boyfriend was more open, his eyes bright as he smiled freely. *I never realized how shadowed they normally are.* The difference was as clear as day, and I found myself loving this Jesse even more.

The L-word so casually filling my head had my stomach knotting and fear icing my veins. *Holy crap, when did that happen?* I started to panic, but my swirling thoughts were held at bay when Kingston dropped a quick kiss on the top of my head.

"So, what do you want to have them pick up?" Reid asked. The topic of food helped me focus on something other than such overwhelming realizations.

"Hamburger pizza?" I asked, moving to sit next to him again. Reid's smile widened as he texted what I wanted, but the smile confused me.

"You're becoming a real Nebraskan," he answered my unspoken question. "Now, all we need to get you to do is to call it pop and not soda."

"Not going to happen," I countered with a sassy brow raise. I opened my mouth to continue, but Reid darted forward, wrapping his arms around my waist and rolling on top of me, instantly distracting me.

"Alone at last," he murmured, his soft tone thick with heat as he stared down at me. His hazel eyes were half-lidded, and every plane of his body pressing into mine set my blood pumping. "Would it be un-knightly if I kissed the hell out of you right now?"

"I certainly wouldn't be opposed," I whispered, wrapping my arms around his neck.

Smirking, he dipped his head, kissing me fiercely before taking my hat off. There were no soft movements, no nervousness this time around, just my funny clown and me, tangled together as our lips locked and bodies pressed together. My skin buzzed as his tongue ran over the seam of my lips, begging for entrance.

Opening, he swept in, tasting every piece of me. An urge built, and a gush of slickness soaked my core. Brushing my fingers against his neck and into his soft hair, I felt him harden against my hip and belly. A hint of nervousness threaded with the excitement at what we were doing—making out in an empty hotel room while we waited for my other two boyfriends to return—but his hand cupping my rib cage and barely brushing against my chest pushed those thoughts away.

Holy crap! He ran his heated palm up, cupping the curve of my boob. A moan escaped me before I could stop it, my heart thudding in my chest as I lost myself in Reid. Taking a shuddering breath, I slid my hands down Reid's muscled back until my fingertips brushed the sliver of skin between his shirt and jeans. His breath caught as I ran my nails around his hips, and he pulled away from me, so I could reach between us. I knew our time would be cut short soon, but a part of me wasn't ready to stop.

The decision was made for me when the doorknob rattled before my fingers had barely brushed against the hardened bulge that strained behind his jeans. The sudden noise brought us both down to reality as we rolled away from each other, breathing heavy through swollen lips. Before Kingston and Jesse opened the door, Reid covered me quickly, searing me with one more breath-hitching kiss. His intense gaze promised more—much, much more.

Well, the next time, we were alone.

"Hope everyone's dressed!" Kingston hollered out in a teasing tone, my cheeks immediately burning in embarrassment. "Well, you two sure look a bit more rumpled than before we left." No jealousy colored Kingston's statement, and Jesse chuckled behind him as they set the food on the desk. I tried to smile, but all I could think of at that moment was I had just been making out with Reid, and my other two boyfriends *knew* exactly what we had been doing.

Have they... talked about stuff like this? I shifted to get a slice of the pizza. If they had, I felt I should have been angry, but I couldn't bring myself to be.

Because right now? All I wanted was some hamburger pizza and a cold shower.

Chapter 7

A tinkling alarm stirred me from my restful sleep.
Reaching over, I tried to grab my phone, but when my
fingers hit empty air, I cracked my eyes open.

"This is not where I fell asleep last night," I mumbled,
realizing I was curled up with Jesse on the pull-out couch.
Heat from his toned body pressed into me as he held me
tightly, his breath brushing against my shoulder blades
where he had buried his face against my back.

"He started to toss and turn," Kingston responded
sleepily, the alarm silenced. "And when he started to make
noise, you got up."

"Mumbling about how he's not allowed to be upset
on our weekend away as you stumbled over to him,"
Reid added, his smile appearing in the darkened room.
"Leaving us two to have to cuddle all night."

"I sleepwalked over here? I'm surprised I didn't injure
myself," I grumbled, stretching out and waking Jesse in the
process.

"You ran into something along the way," Reid laughed.

"Probably will have a pretty good bruise on your leg based on your long string of expletives."

"Ugh," I groaned, feeling the stiffness in my right thigh before the ache settled in. "So, our tour's at nine, and it's,"—I glanced over at the clock—"seven. Who's up for breakfast?"

"Oh, I am!" Reid said, his arm waving in the air enthusiastically. Kingston's hand followed, albeit more calmly, while Jesse gave a sleepy huff of agreement.

"Let me get ready, and we can hit up the cafe near here." Shuffling to sitting, I slowly made my way to standing. Peeking outside, I squealed loudly. "So much snow!"

"How much?" Jesse asked, his question muffled. Glancing over at him, I saw his face pressing into his pillow, one eye centered on me.

"A couple of inches, I think. I mean, I'm not exactly the best to be guessing these kinds of things. California born and bred, remember?" I teased. Jesse's honeyed laugh mixed with Kingston's chuckle and Reid's snort. "Okay, for real this time, I'm going to get ready. I'm starving." With that, we all turned our limited morning energy to getting dressed and socially acceptable. After a half-hour of shuffling around, we made our way out into the cold winter air.

White flakes swirled, drifting leisurely to the ground. A sense of excitement and joy filled me as we walked, our boots crunching on the snow. Here, in a different city with my boys, I didn't have to deal with Brad, Jesse's trial, or the ACT. It was just me and them, planning for the future. My cheeks started to ache from my smile, the sting of an ice-cold breeze whipping around us, making my pale skin redden.

"You enjoying yourself, Cali girl?" Reid asked as he

skipped ahead. "That's a mighty big smile for someone who's used to the coast."

"I've decided I love snow. Wherever I end up, it must have snow," I declared, jutting my chin out in a challenge when Reid turned to look back at us.

"Oh, is that so?" He hummed at the end of his question, an eyebrow raising. Bending down, he scooped up a handful of snow and packed it between his cupped palms. Narrowing my eyes on him, I watched skeptically until he cocked an arm back and tossed it at me.

"Ah!" I shrieked, curling just in time for the projectile to hit my side. "I'm unarmed! That's so not knightly, babe," I called out in between my laughter. Running behind Jesse, I scooped up my own snow. Trying my best, I shaped a deformed ball and launched it over Jesse's shoulder at Reid. "Aha!" I shouted when it hit him in the stomach, nearly crying with laughter when a second snowball smacked Reid in the face.

"You're supposed to be on my side, dude," Reid countered to Kingston, who looked innocent as if he hadn't just chucked a snowball at his best friend.

"This is it, the end." Reid pretended to stumble to the ground. "Stabbed in the back by my own friend, the betrayal tastes of bitter defeat and death."

"You're so ridiculous. I don't know how we go anywhere with you and not attract everyone's attention." Jesse shook his head, smiling down at Reid, who was fully laid out on the snow-covered grass.

"Let them watch. I don't do this for them, I do this because being weird is in my nature. It's in my DNA," Reid stated proudly. "Life would be so dull without the weirdos and clowns."

"And you're the biggest clown of them all. Now, let's get

breakfast." Kingston held out a hand, pulling Reid up, then helped him dust off the snow stuck to the back of his coat.

"I like this look on you, Em," Jesse whispered, leaning into me as he grabbed my hand.

"What look?" I asked, looking down at my outfit. "This is the same thing I usually wear."

"Happy, Em. I like seeing you happy."

My cheeked burned for a completely different reason than the winter weather. Warmth curled through me, the butterflies fluttering, and I nibbled on my lip.

"It looks pretty danged good on you too, Jess," I murmured, a hint of giddiness lacing my tone. Squeezing my hand, he smiled before turning to Kingston, who asked him a question. It wasn't just the snow or the weekend away that was making me happy. Well... not the only thing making me happy right now.

My boys made me happy.

"Welcome to the University of Nebraska-Lincoln!" our tour guide greeted brightly. "I'm Mark, a resident adviser in one of the dorms, and I work in the office part-time. Before we start the tour, are there any questions?"

"How big is the school?" Kingston asked. There were students scattered around the campus, but not many, most more than likely not having classes on Saturday.

"Physically, it's a little over eight hundred and fifty acres, whereas the undergrad student population is around twenty thousand. There are over one hundred and fifty majors to choose from." Mark continued, listing facts and stats about different buildings and classes as we walked the grounds. While I listened, I focused on the area around me. I knew when we set up the tour, it was an older campus, but some buildings looked to be updated, others under construction.

"So, you have to live on campus freshman year?" I heard Reid ask, catching my attention.

"Any unmarried students under nineteen and taking more than six credit hours a semester, yes," he explained. "There are a few exceptions, such as commuting from home, being married, or living in one of the Greek houses."

"Fraternity and sorority?" Reid continued, our guide nodding and rattling off about how the Greek life worked on campus. I tuned that out, not caring about sororities at the moment.

Maybe after I know I'll be able to get in, but not right now.

"So, what is everyone thinking for majors? Or are you guys going to choose when you get into college?" Mark inquired.

"Pre-law," Kingston stated. "My dad has a firm."

"Very cool. UNL would be a good choice. It has not only a pre-law program but graduate law as well."

"Thinking science-oriented, although I'm not too sure on what yet," Reid explained. "I'll probably decide after starting."

"Haven't decided yet." Jesse's response was short, his words clipped as he stiffened. My brows furrowed at his sudden change in demeanor, but I let it go, feeling Mark's eyes on me expectantly.

"Business, marketing, or management more than likely," I mumbled with an awkward smile.

"Oh, if that's the case, you'll love Professor Halloway. She's one of the business professors, one of my favorites," Mark rattled off. Plastering a smile on my face, I nodded, tucking the information away, but after seeing Jesse tense up, I found myself unable to focus.

We continued our tour—the main buildings, student center, library, and dorms. By the end of the two hours, my face was freezing, and I wanted to curl up with a cup of coffee or hot chocolate by a fire or at least be inside for more than a few minutes to see the lobby. Picking up on my quickly descending mood, Kingston asked Mark if there was somewhere we could get a hot drink and hang out before going to lunch.

With a location and a lot of extra ideas of things to do in mind, we turned and headed off campus to a local tea and coffee shop. The shop smelled of freshly brewed grounds and steeping leaves, with a fire roaring in a large stone fireplace in the corner of the room. Heat permeated my goosebump-covered body and soothed the bone-deep shivering. Kingston directed me, his hand on my lower back, nudging me toward a cluster of empty leather chairs and couch.

"So, Babydoll, how did you like it?" Kingston asked, sitting down on the cushion next to me, his arm going over my shoulders as he pulled me into his warm chest. "See yourself going to college here?"

"It was nice. I think once I pass the ACT and have a bit more of a solid idea I'll be able to get in, I'll be a bit more comfortable in terms of plans after graduation. But yeah, I definitely think I could. What about you?" I murmured, looking up into his warm brown eyes centered on me.

"I think so. I love their law program, and it's close enough to home and the firm, I would be able to see my parents and brother and still help out every so often."

"What do you guys think about the living on campus part?" Reid asked, handing Kingston his drink while Jesse passed mine over. I gave him a grateful smile and took a tentative sip.

"It might be an adjustment, but I don't think I'd have too many issues. It's only for freshman year and will give us a chance to get to know the area. We can get an apartment sophomore year when we're all nineteen," Kingston responded before taking a drink of his coffee.

"I've never lived with anyone other than my parents, so having a roommate might be interesting, but I don't think it'd be bad. You considering joining a frat?" I questioned, glancing around the group, but my gaze focused more on Reid than the other two boys.

"Why are you looking at me?" he questioned with a head tilt. "Do I scream frat boy to you?"

"No, but you're pretty social. I wasn't sure if that was something you'd want to do." I shrugged, hoping he wouldn't take me asking the wrong way. It was only when his lips started to twitch, I realized he was faking his offense. Flashing him a half-hearted glare, I took another sip of my hot chocolate.

"I liked it," Jesse added with a shrug, "but I haven't spent much time outside of our hometown, so going somewhere else seems like it'd be fun."

I tried to look at him, having noticed tension growing in his shoulders during the visit, but in the shop's dim lighting, I couldn't tell if he was upset. He didn't *sound* upset, so I settled in and got comfortable. We fell into a companionable silence when a violinist started to play in the opposite corner, the holiday tune flowing through the space, relaxing me into Kingston's embrace.

"So, what do we want to do for the rest of the afternoon?" I asked after our drinks were long gone, and the space had started to fill up.

"They have ice skating down in the Haymarket," Reid offered, scrolling on his phone quickly. "Has a lot of places to eat, and it's only a couple blocks if we want to walk."

"I'm terrible at ice skating," I warned, glancing at Kingston. "Worse than roller skating, but I'm totally down. Is it outside?"

"Yeah, I think so." Reid stood, holding out my coat for me as Kingston and Jesse took the empty cups to the dirty container bins. I felt my cheeks warm at the sweet gesture. "Ready, Cali girl? Think your warm coastal blood can handle being out in the snow for a couple hours?"

"Ha ha," I huffed, unable to stop the grin that spread across my face as I turned to face Reid. "I hope so, but we'll see. Never know,"—I shrugged—"might need someone to help keep me warm."

"I think I know the perfect man for the job," he murmured, his tone sinfully smooth as his hazel eyes glimmered.

"Okay, enough flirting. You two have hogged her," Jesse butted in with a cocky smile. "My turn." Reid and Kingston rolled their eyes, but much to my surprise didn't argue as Jesse snatched my hand, intertwining our fingers. My heart skipped a beat as we walked down the road, Jesse's thumb rubbing my hand and the way he gazed at me every so often, making the little butterflies flare.

"What?" I whispered. Brushing my cheeks, I felt tingles under the fabric of my gloves. "You keep looking at me."

"You're pretty, it's hard to not look at you, Em," he responded, his tone confident as he leaned over, kissing me on the cheek. Before pulling away, he whispered, his lips brushing against the curve of my jaw, "I can't get enough of that gorgeous smile."

"I think I like this more assertive, confident Jesse," I murmured, nibbling on my lips as my cheek buzzed where I swore I could still feel his lips.

"Yeah? Maybe I'll bring him out more, just for you," he teased.

"Okay, lovebirds, time for skating!" Reid hollered, darting forward and curling his arms around me and Jesse in a tight hug before nearly skipping to the front door Kingston held open.

"I also suck at skating, in case that'll help you feel any better," Jesse added as we got our skates, sitting down to lace them up.

I chuckled but couldn't deny it *did* help. No one wants to be the only one slipping and sliding all over the ice. *Maybe we can learn together. It'll be nice being able to learn something with him for a change, instead of me being the pupil.*

"Don't worry, I'll hold your guys' hands until you get the hang of it," Reid offered. Jesse raised a brow and shook his head, causing Reid to exclaim, "What? If I offer it to Cali girl, I'm going to offer it to you too, dude. Don't hate on the bro-love I have for you."

"You're ridiculous," Jesse laughed, "I appreciate the thought, but just focus on Em."

"Really? No 'love you too'?" Reid hollered after Jesse as he made his way outside onto the ice with Kingston. Jesse's honeyed laugh reached my ears, followed by a quick 'Yeah, yeah love you too.'

"Ready?" I asked, nerves building in my stomach as I wobbled on the skates' thin blades. "This is going to be a disaster."

"It'll be alright, and if you fall, we'll help you up," Reid offered with a smile, his playfulness toned down as he cupped my face. Rubbing my cheeks a couple of times with his gloved hands, he kissed me deeply, taking my breath away before helping me into the frozen rink.

It was slow and rough for a few circles around the rink, but after the fourth pass, I was finally able to go more than a few feet without stumbling or falling. Reid kept his promise, holding my hand the whole time as we started to glide smoothly around the edge of the ice. Jesse was wobbling a bit but only fell once, Kingston staying near him to help him up.

Once I had it down enough to move somewhat confidently, skating was relaxing. I was enjoying the cold icy air brushing across my face as I seamlessly shifted from one foot to the other. Reid was content to stay silent next to me, the tips of his curls, poking out from under his hat, flaring in the breeze.

"Having fun?" Kingston's smooth voice reached me, his fingers intertwining with my free hand. Jesse seemed to have gotten his balance, easily skating around us with a wave, his tongue sticking out at Reid as he passed.

"Yeah, this is amazing," I said, my cheeks numb as I talked, the cold air finally taking its toll. "But I think my face is frozen."

"Yeah, not surprising, the wind chill today is pretty cold. You up for dinner soon? We've been here for,"—Kingston checked his phone—"over an hour already."

My brows shot up in surprise. *Apparently, skating in circles is meditative enough to make time pass quickly.*

"Hey, Jesse!" Reid shouted. My third boyfriend glanced over his shoulder as he coasted to a stop at the edge of the rink. "Ready for food?"

"Yeah, starving," Jesse agreed. We quickly made our way off the ice, changing our skates out for winter boots. Not even the crowded, bustling sidewalks could dim my mood, and I knew if I could feel my cheeks, they would be aching from my smile.

"Oooh," I squealed, pointing as a horse-drawn carriage pulled up down the street, letting off its current passengers. "Can we do that after food?"

"Want to do it now? Food will still be there after," Jesse offered.

"You sure?" I asked, glancing around them. They all nodded, looking at me with such caring expressions, I felt my chest constrict, warmth and that pesky "L" word building within me.

"It's not every day you get to ride in a horse-carriage like in the movies," Jesse stated with a shrug, and I beamed.

They are the sweetest guys I've ever met, nothing at all like Tyler.

At the thought of my persistent ex, I wanted to roll my eyes. He had been immature, rude, and childish. My boys, though, were thoughtful and caring and wanted to make me as happy as I wanted to make them.

They say I'm perfect, but I think they're pretty perfect too.

DECEMBER 8TH

The snow's pretty to look at and so romantic. The driving part, though? Well, wish me luck.
#ImGoingToCrash #CaliGirlIsRight #NOTSundayFunday

"Holy crap, I am so not going to drive well in the snow," I squeaked, hopping out of the Jeep as if it was on fire. "That was terrifying."

"It's not that bad, Cali girl, I had control the whole time," Reid countered, following at a much more mellow pace.

"Except when you spun out on the ice a couple of blocks ago," Jesse argued, coming to stand next to me.

"Or when you slid through a stop sign back in Lincoln," Kingston added with a laugh.

"Had control *almost* the whole time," Reid amended his statement. "But we made it to UNO safely, didn't we?"

"Yeah, yeah, babe. Let's just not do any more driving for a few hours to give my adrenaline time to settle," I teased as he wrapped his arm around me. "Let's get this tour going. I want to play in the snow."

"Who said we're playing in the snow?" Reid prodded, poking my side, "Huh?"

"Well, why else would you have a couple of sleds in the back? Yeah, don't think I didn't see those yesterday." I gave him a bright smile, happy to know he had thought about the weather before we left.

"Alright, I confess, we're going sledding after the tour." I did a little skip hop as we walked to express my excitement, making the boys laugh.

The tour was similar to the day before, the only difference, more of the buildings were newer, and it seemed like the buildings were closer together. It was a bit easier to pay attention to this one; our guide was entertaining, prepared with anecdotes, facts, and other random tidbits as we walked.

"How are the science labs here? And the planetarium?" Reid questioned at the end of our tour.

"If you want, I can take you to see them. I work in the science department as one of the teaching assistants," the older woman shared, her eyes crinkling with her bright smile.

"Is that cool, Cali girl?" Reid asked, glancing over to see that I was shivering.

"I can go with you while she and Jesse check out the student center or library," Kingston offered, nudging

Jesse's shoulder.

"Yeah, that sounds good," I agreed. "I want you to be able to see what you want, babe."

"Thanks, Cali girl. You two have fun. Don't do anything too crazy," Reid whispered the end of his teasing statement, giving me a quick kiss before walking away with our tour guide and Kingston.

"So, where do you want to spend our time together?" I asked, curling my fingers around Jesse's palm. He hummed, glancing between the library and the student center, then directed us toward the library. "Ah, how did I know the studious Jesse Parker would pick books," I murmured, bumping his shoulder playfully. "Which section do you want to see?"

"I want to see what you like," he stated simply, nudging me back. "Take me to the books you like to read." My brows rose at the request, but I didn't argue as we wandered through the stacks, the scent of books surrounding us as I found the novels I knew I would pick up to read. "Fantasy, romance, and mystery, huh?" Jesse whispered, looking over my shoulder at the books I had picked up to glance at.

"I like escaping. Life can be hard, boring, but these? You get to go wherever for a while," I mumbled, embarrassment flooding me as I shrugged, realizing how silly that sounded out loud.

"I think so, too." Jesse's voice was much closer than I anticipated, his lips brushing against the curve of my ear as he curled his strong arms around my waist. "Maybe we can pick a book when we get back to school and read it together?"

"I'd love that," I agreed, putting the books on the shelf and turning in his arms.

Jesse's eyes were half-lidded, focused on my face before dipping to my lips. Wrapping my arms around his shoulders, I leaned in, kissing him. It was soft, chaste compared to my makeout sessions with Reid and Kingston, but as soon as I started to pull back, Jesse followed, trapping me against the shelf. Jesse's sweet kisses contrasted deliciously to his shifting hands, rubbing back and forth until his fingers caressed the curve of my butt.

My heart raced as our tongues brushed, and he nipped at my bottom lip, sucking it into his mouth. Confident Jesse's ability to completely take my breath away made me feel inexperienced and fumbling, but he didn't laugh or stop, letting the moment happen. So, I did too, losing myself in the feeling of his lips and his hands cupping my curves tightly until a gush of wetness surged in my core, and a pulse of desire shot through me.

"Cough cough." The fake coughing startled me, and I glared as soon as I saw who was smirking at the end of the aisle.

Reid and Kingston both struggled to keep their laughing contained as they watched us.

"We leave for ten minutes, and here you are, making out," Reid chastised playfully. "Though I can't say I wouldn't do the same."

"Don't embarrass her, dude," Jesse challenged before glancing down at me. His eyes were bright, his dark cheeks holding a slight flush as he smiled. "We actually looked at books for a bit, so fuck off," he added, the last of his statement directed at Reid as they both laughed.

"Ready for sledding?" Kingston asked me as we walked through the library. At the reminder of our afternoon activity, I perked up with a nod. "Let's grab the sleds.

There's a good hill across the main street."

It only took a few minutes to grab the two sleds and walk to the base of the hill. *A good hill? This thing is massive!* It had three flatter parts at different heights, the littlest of the kids sledding with their parents on the smallest curve while the older kids and adults were sledding from the second tier and the top of the hill.

"Race you!" Reid shouted before taking off up the hill, Kingston and Jesse following close behind. The all ended up winded and bent over near the top of the incline.

"I win!" I shouted, having walked most of the way. While they used up their energy, I'd sprinted the last fifteen feet to pass the three tired boys.

"How did you win? You were walking!" Reid puffed out between pants, struggling to laugh and shout back.

"Slow and steady wins the race," I teased. "I want to ride on that one." I pointed to the thin black and silver sled.

"Do you know how to sled?" Jesse asked as he flopped on the snow next to me. I waved a hand and harrumphed.

"You hold on and try not to fall off," I explained. "I think I can do that. Well, as long as I don't crash or go over a ramp some kids made." I got situated on the sled, my heels digging into the snow on either side as I grabbed onto the handles.

"This is Cali girl's first sledding run," Reid explained. Looking over in confusion, I found him recording me. "Good luck!" I shook my head but laughed as I picked up my feet and kicked off.

The thin sled picked up as I laughed and squealed as I raced down the hill. Adrenaline filled me as I finally reached the bottom, the buzz of wanting to go again and again growing as I hopped up and did a dance to the sound of Reid and the boys whooping and hollering from the top of the hill.

Yeah, I could totally get used to this.
Nebraska definitely isn't so bad.

"How was it, sweetie?" my mom called out as soon as I walked through the door. Trudging up the stairs, exhaustion weighed down my arms and legs until it was hard to move without stumbling into things.

"It was good," I said, looking into her room to find her getting ready for bed. "Early morning?"

"You know how it goes, always with the Monday morning breakfast meetings," she huffed with a tiny eye roll. "You think they would understand early on Mondays isn't the best time to have a team meeting, but what do I know?" I smiled, knowing exactly how my mom could be in the mornings. If there was a lack of coffee, it would be dangerous for everyone.

"At least there's coffee," I added. My mom's enthusiastic nod made me laugh, but another wave of fatigue pushed down on me. "I'm actually really tired. We went sledding, so I'm going to sleep. Apparently, my Cali body isn't used to tromping around in snow and running up hills."

"Alright, sweetie. Sleep well." Giving me a small hug, my mom squeezed lightly before crawling into bed.

"You, too. Night, Mom." I made my way slowly back down the stairs, being careful not to trip on my unsteady legs. Taking off my coat, I collapsed on the bed, grabbing Mr. Fritz in the process, but when my eyes closed, I couldn't fall asleep. *Ugh.* My mind was whirling with everything I knew I would have to do tomorrow. Not only school, where I would possibly face Brad and Dylan and get to hear a bunch of whispers about me. I also had to go over everything with Kaleb.

Exhaustion continued to push down on me, and my eyes started to ache, so flipping over onto my back, I counted to five, inhaling deeply before exhaling just as slowly. The meditative breathing took longer than usual to settle my mind, but finally, after another ten minutes, I started to drift off.

Hopefully, there won't be any sleepwalking this time; my poor noodle legs would never be able to keep up.

Chapter 8

"Three things cannot long be hidden: the sun, the moon, the truth."- Buddha
#TruthWinsEverytime #BoatShoeBradIsGoingDown
#MotivationMonday

"H ey, Emma." The scent of paper in Kaleb's law office strong, nearly suffocating me as I tried to smile. It was finally time to do the one thing I had been dreading since getting back from our weekend away.

Recounting what happened with Brad at the party from hell.

Awesome.

"We'll be in here," Kaleb directed me. "Would you like Kingston with you? If you don't, he'll be working right outside the room, where you can see him." Swallowing, I looked at my boyfriend. Kingston's gaze was tight, but I appreciated his attempt to give me a reassuring smile.

"I think I should be okay. If it gets to be too much, then maybe." It would be that much harder to talk about it if Kingston was there, listening to what happened. Kaleb nodded in understanding and held the glass door open. He left the blinds on the door's window open, allowing me to easily see Kingston.

"Alright, to begin, do you have any questions?" Kaleb

started, sitting in the chair across the table. Shaking my head, I swallowed the acid that had started to build in my throat. "I'll explain a bit about what to expect. I don't say this to scare you, but unfortunately, your testimony is the one keeping Jesse from going to jail. We're unsure at the moment if he'll be tried as an adult, but I would rather be prepared, so that's how I'm mounting his defense."

"Okay," I whispered, the sickening feeling swirling in my stomach, worsening at the gravity of what I was trying to do.

"The prosecutor and I had a preliminary hearing with the judge last week. The Warland's lawyer presented their probable cause for the charges against Jesse and a motion for a trial since I'd advised him not to take the plea deal currently on the table."

"Why not?" I asked.

"What they offered is worse than what I think he would get if the judge is presented with why he went after Brad," Kaleb stated, his tone clipped in anger. "Now that the prelim hearing is over, we have time to prepare our cases, meaning both the prosecutor, Steve Corsian, and I will be able to interview witnesses, and as much as I hope they won't want to talk to you, I know that it's highly likely they will at some point. When that happens, don't say anything other than you want your lawyer."

"But I don't have a lawyer," I countered. Kaleb looked questioningly, his lips curled downward slightly, and his brows drawn together.

"I'm your lawyer, Emma," he explained. "Since you're considered an adult in the Nebraska legal system, they can talk to you without notifying your parents, but I highly advise, and I cannot emphasize this enough, do not say anything until I'm there. Even then, follow my lead on what to say and not to say, alright?" His grave tone put me on edge, but I didn't say anything as I tucked the information in 'Emma's do not freaking forget' file in my head.

"What do you mean in the legal system? Am I not considered an adult normally?" I murmured, my brain latching onto that statement after committing the rest to memory.

"Well, in Nebraska, for state-regulated bills, such as signing contracts or getting loans, the legal age is nineteen. That doesn't apply to federally-regulated laws, such as age to buy cigarettes or the federal and state legal systems. So, while you can't go get a loan for a house or get an apartment, you can still be questioned by the police and the courts without your parents' consent." I mumbled a 'got it,' my throat tightening as Kaleb continued with his original explanation.

"It will be a bench trial, meaning only be the judge will hear the case, and I can almost guarantee, you'll be called to testify."

His explanation sent me farther into a state of panic, but Jesse's bright smile flitted through my thoughts, helping me shove the nerves back.

This isn't about you.

This is about Jesse's future.

About making sure Brad can't do this to someone else.

With that in mind, I sat up straighter, ready to tell him what I knew.

"I think that's everything. When we get a bit closer, I'll go over what both you and Jesse should expect at the trial. I don't want to overwhelm you now. Well, any more than I already have," Kaleb tried to tease; his grin was small, but the effort was appreciated. "Ready?" Taking a deep breath,

I nodded. The motion was slight, but the truth was, I just wanted to get this over with.

"It was Saturday, October 13th. Reid, Kingston, and Jesse picked me up from my house. We went straight to the party," I explained quietly, giving him time to take notes as I went through the night. I was doing okay until I got to the part where I'd stepped into the bathroom. "Brad was on the other side of the door, and I asked if he needed to get in the bathroom, and he said yes. So, I tried to move out of the way, but he ended up kissing me and pushing me back into the bathroom. I screamed and pushed him back," I mumbled, coughing in an attempt to clear the lump of emotions growing in my throat. "I told him to back off, and he told me he didn't think he would. I was able to kick him in the shin hard enough to get around him, but I couldn't get away fast enough, so he,"—I choked back a sob, feeling his hands on me, the horrifying memory haunting me as I talked—"grabbed me and carried me back into the bathroom and tried to kick the door shut. That was when Jesse grabbed him off me.

"By the time I realized Brad wasn't there, I saw Jesse chasing him down the stairs, and when I found them out in the backyard, Jesse was hitting him, yelling he shouldn't force himself on someone and he'd do more if Brad tried again." By the time I was done explaining, I was barely holding it together. Kaleb must have realized because he looked over his shoulder, nodding once. After a few moments, Kingston came in, shutting the door quickly behind him and kneeling next to me.

"Shh, Babydoll, he can't get you here," Kingston cooed, pulling me into his arms. As soon as I was wrapped in his arms, I couldn't hold back. The tears flowed, and my shoulders shook as I cried. The feeling of bugs crawling over my skin intensified as the sensation of Brad's lips and hands on me flared hauntingly close to the surface of my memories, making me uncomfortable and panicky.

"Did either of you have any previous interactions with him?" Kaleb asked quietly.

"He was working at the haunted house we went to the night before. Emma told me he made her uncomfortable when he was trying to talk to her. She had gone to the bathroom and was taking a while, so I went to check on her. She was scared, so we left, figuring we wouldn't see him outside of school."

"Any other times?" Kaleb continued. I mumbled a 'no' from my cocoon in Kingston's arms. "How about after that? Any incidents?"

"I ran into him on the way to the counselor's office," I murmured, pulling back enough to wipe my cheeks. "Actually, I think it was more 'he found me' because it was in the middle of class."

"When was that?" Kingston asked, his brows drawing down.

"Tuesday the twenty-sixth. The day before the issue with Mr. Derosa, remember?" I told him, a look of understanding washing over his face as he nodded.

"What did Brad say during that incident?" Kaleb's pen scrawled across the paper. I swallowed, trying to make the words form, but I couldn't seem to, and after a few minutes, Kaleb looked at me with a frown. "Do you need a moment?" Shaking my head, I closed my eyes and rattled off what was said when he had been cornered me.

"He kept trying to call me by the nicknames Kingston, Reid, and Jesse use. I told him to back off, or I'd scream, and he said, 'Maybe I want to hear you scream,'" I murmured. "That's when Ms. Rogers, my counselor,

intervened. She had me file a complaint for harassment."
Kingston's arms tensed, and his jaw was clenched in
anger, but he didn't say anything, letting me cuddle in his
embrace while answering the last of the questions Kaleb
had for me.

"Alright, Emma, I think that's it for now. If anything else
happens, I'll need to document it, okay?" I nodded, giving
him a thankful smile before standing up. "King, you can
take the rest of the night off and spend some time with
Emma. The files will be here tomorrow." Kingston just
nodded as he grabbed his coat and followed me outside.

"Are you okay?" I murmured, glancing at him out of the
corner of my eye. "You seem upset."

"I should be asking you that, Babydoll, you're the one
dealing with a fucking douche. I just want to punch him
in the face, really hard, with a chair," Kingston explained,
his shoulders finally deflating when I chuckled at his
statement. Sighing, I curled into his side, his arm going
around me once more as we reached our cars in the lot.

"I'm okay. Not all the time, but usually. You guys know
I'll tell you if I'm having trouble with anything to do with
him." Kingston nodded, giving me a quick kiss after we
made plans to hang out before we climbed into our cars.
As soon as I was alone, I felt that dark cloud descend over
me again.

Storms make trees take deeper roots. No matter how
much all of this sucked, no matter how frustrated, scared,
and worried I was, I'd just dig my roots in and take hold
as tightly as I could to what mattered most—my guys, my
friends, and making sure we can keep Jesse safe.

Let's see the storm knock me over then.

DECEMBER 10TH

If only Dad wanted to talk to me as much as Brad & Tyler do.
#Bradnet #DeadbeatDad #TurdtasticTyler #TickedOffTuesday

"Emma bean! Can you get the next customer?" I heard
Lyla holler, her head buried in one of the cabinets as she
finished cleaning up a bottle of syrup that had broken
when it fell off the cabinet shelf. Darting around the
counter from where I had been sweeping the floor, I
plastered on a smile and got settled behind the cash
register.

"What can I get for you?" I asked, looking at the man in
front of me and quickly recognizing him as the man I had
run into earlier that month.

"Just a black coffee, please," he ordered. I saw the
moment when he recognized who I was, his lips quirking
up slightly. "Glad neither of us had a collision this time
around."

"Yeah, sorry about that. Again," I cringed, readying his
order. "If it makes it any better, I haven't run into anyone
else since then," I tried to joke with a smile. The man
laughed, his voice booming and warm as he took his coffee
off the counter.

"That's good, then." He tipped his imaginary hat. "Nice
to see you again, Emma. I'm sure we'll run into each other
some other time. I love my coffee."

"Hopefully, not literally," I countered. I was answered
with another laugh as the man made his way outside.
Shaking my head at his friendly demeanor, I turned back
to watch Lyla finally crawl out from under the counter.

"If you two are good to go, you can head out. I'm going to be staying late to catalog everything, so I can handle any last-minute customers," Rick shared, his red hair poking out the door to the back. I perked up, untying my apron at the same time as Lyla.

"What're your plans for the evening?" Lyla asked, hanging her apron up in her locker and grabbing her bag.

"I was going to hit the mall. Want to join?" I asked, my words loud to my own ears as I was digging out my winter boots from the metal locker.

"Sure, let's go," she whooped excitedly. I rolled my eyes and laughed, happy at her enthusiasm.

I wonder if she snorts the ground coffee; otherwise, I have no idea how she is always so peppy.

"So," Lyla started as she glanced around, "what are we getting, Emma bean?"

"Well, I need to get Reid's birthday present for tomorrow, then the Christmas gifts for the guys and my mom."

"Alright, cool, we have approximately,"—she paused to look at her phone—"an hour and a half until the mall closes. Where do you want to hit first?"

"Let's hit that store over there. I want to get a collection of goofy and silly things for Reid's birthday. What he really wants to do is go to the planetarium, so I also got tickets for that, just need a good day to do it."

"Aww, that's adorable," Lyla cooed, hooking her arm through mine and walking me to the store. "How about some fun socks?"

"That'd be good, and this wallet is pretty awesome too." I held it up to show her. Lyla nodded her agreement, holding up different pairs of socks and letting me pick which ones I liked or thought would fit Reid the best.

"Seven pairs of funny socks and a wallet," Lyla counted. "That it for his birthday present, other than the tickets?"

"Yup," I stated, popping the 'p' at the end. "Now for Christmas gifts, or to at least look for a few of them. I might end up ordering them and having it shipped."

We wandered through the stores but ended up not picking anything up for the boys. It was nearing closing time when we finally decided to call it quits, figuring it'd be easier to order something online.

"Your phone has been blowing up all evening," Lyla laughed. "Those boys sure do talk a lot."

I chuckled, pulling out my phone to check it and groaned.

"What?"

"It wasn't just the boys," I grumbled, showing her my phone. "My ex is being annoying as heck. I haven't responded in a long time, but he's just so incessant."

She scrolled through the messages, her eyes widening as she shook her head.

"Block him if he continues, at least that's what I'd do," she offered, handing my phone back. "You don't have time for stage five clinger bullshit. Do your boys know?"

"Ugh, yes. They just wanted to text him themselves, but knowing how protective they can be and how much a dumb jerk Tyler is, I knew it wouldn't do anything other than cause a bunch of drama. They're all on edge, we all are, because of everything going on with Brad and the trial. Blocking, though, definitely a good idea. You have no idea how much I don't have time for it." I sighed, quickly making the decision to tell her everything going on in my life.

Other than the boys and Kaleb, I hadn't had a chance to talk to anyone who would see it from the outside with a fresh perspective on what I should do. *And honestly, sometimes there's just no replacement for girl talk, no matter how wonderful the guys are.* With that in mind, everything just tumbled out, Lyla's expression shifting from her usually smiling self to scowling in anger as I told her about Brad.

"You know what you need? A defense class," she told me. "They have ones specifically for women. I'll go with you because one can never be too prepared."

"Eh…" I hummed skeptically as I looked over at her. "I'm not too sure I could actually hit anyone."

"You kicked and pushed Brad, didn't you?" Lyla countered, nudging my shoulder. "I'm not saying you have to go, or you'd ever have to use it, but it's an option."

Thinking a bit longer, I realized she was right. *I don't ever want to feel weak or powerless like I did the night of the party.*

"Have I told you lately you're the best?" I gushed, wrapping my arm over her shoulders in a side hug. "I would love that, but you're not allowed to tell anyone how much I suck at it."

"Deal, but only as long as you don't tell Rick how terrible *I* am," Lyla countered, hugging me back as we neared our cars in the emptying lot.

"You got it. Say, what are you doing on Saturday? Working?" I asked over the hood of my car before she got into her truck.

"Nope, I work Sunday this week, why?"

"It's winter formal, and I was wondering if maybe you wanted to come over and help me get ready with Zoey and Aubrey." Lyla beamed, her smile only half visible as she nodded enthusiastically, her red hair flopping into her face. "Awesome, I'll let you know when we're getting together. Bye, Ly!"

"Ha, that rhymed," she countered with a laugh, getting into her own car. "Bye, Emma bean!"

Now I just need to dig out a formal dress... or buy one... Oops.

Guess I'm going back to the mall sometime this week.

CHAPTER 9

DECEMBER 11TH

Tried to get dress inspiration, and I fell down the rabbit hole of fashion trends. I can never unlearn that corsets used to be made from whale bones!
#SorryShamu #WhaleThatsAwkward #WeirdnessWednesday

"Good morning, Cali girl," Reid greeted, wrapping me in a tight hug before we headed into the building. Even though the truth of our odd relationship had been out for a while, we still got curious glances or hostile, judgmental sneers, but right now, I was too happy to care.

"Morning, babe," I murmured, kissing his scruff-covered jaw. "Happy birthday."

"Thanks, Cali girl." He smiled down at me, his olive cheeks tinted with a blush. "You know what I want to do today?"

"What?" I asked, smiling over at Kingston and Jesse, who had just joined us on our walk to the table.

"Spend time with my friends," Reid told me. I perked up with a sly smile, and as soon as Reid saw my grin, his eyes narrowed. "You have a plan, don't you?"

"Maybe,"—I shrugged with a smirk—"guess you'll have to wait and see, now won't you?"

"You are such a troublemaker, I love it," he whispered, nipping at my ear. The move was so unexpected, I couldn't contain the gasp that escaped, my core tightening as he snickered softly at my response. "Can't wait to see what other little sounds you make, Cali girl."

"Yeah?" I said lamely, my brain quickly melting into a puddle of hormones and need with thoughts of what we'd do if we could sneak off right now. *I definitely wouldn't complain about getting more time to explore him when we're* not *about to be interrupted.*

"Damn straight." He pulled back, standing upright. "But unfortunately, the bell's about to ring." My focus had been entirely on Reid, and at the reminder we were in the middle of a crowded cafeteria, my lust faded. In its wake were burning cheeks when I saw Kingston and Jesse watching with curious expressions. My body flared in a completely different way seeing the heat in my other boyfriends' faces, and that's when I knew.

Having fun in the future might get a bit interesting—in the best way.

"Almost done, Babydoll?" Kingston asked outside my bedroom door.

"Yup!" I called out, making sure I had Reid's present, and my slush-covered shoes were wiped clean and set out to dry. It had started snowing again right before school got out, meaning two things. First, I got my ankle booties wet, and second, I panicked almost the entire drive home. Thankfully, Kingston was driving us to where we were spending Reid's birthday.

"Can I know where we're going yet?" Reid whined as I came out, his lip poking out in a cute pout. Shaking my head, I started up the stairs, the guys following me.

"Hey, Mom, we're heading out for Reid's birthday. I'll be

back in a few hours," I called out. Reid pulled me into a hug, my back pressing into his hard chest as he continued to try to get where we were going out of me.

"Alright, let me know where you're headed or if you go anywhere else," Mom answered, her voice pulling me out of my laughter, her tone and raised brow at Reid's and my close proximity, making me immediately clam up.

"I will." She nodded, her eyes still glued on Reid's arms curled around my shoulders.

"Don't forget what I said the other day," she reminded, her eyes going to Kingston before returning to me, "about how others may feel."

"It's alright, Mrs. Clark. I don't mind," Kingston countered with a smile, clearly picking up on the very blatant point she was attempting to make. My mom just hummed skeptically before giving a wave and heading back to her office. Feeling uncomfortable being called out in front of them, I cursed myself for not telling her right then about all of us, but as soon as an opportunity presented itself, I couldn't.

"You okay, Em?" Jesse questioned, his honeyed voice pulling me from my quickly swirling thoughts. I mustered up a smile and nodded. "We're not upset, you know that, right? About you not being able to tell your mom."

"You sure?" I murmured, fiddling with the sleeve of my coat as I got into the front passenger seat of Kingston's car. "I just freeze up. I'm not ashamed of us, but I don't think she'd approve, and I don't want to worry about what she would say."

"Like we told you before, Cali girl," Reid reassured, leaning against the back of the driver's seat to look at me, "when you're ready, tell her. We're not going anywhere, just because one person doesn't know about us." His smile and soft tone helped ease my nerves, and Kingston and Jesse's agreement finally settled the last of my worries.

"You guys are amazing," I told them with a grateful smile. "Ready to know what we're doing for your birthday?" I asked Reid, who immediately started to bounce in his seat. "I'll give you a hint." Holding my hand up, I made a finger gun, 'pew-pewing' as I pretended to shoot him.

"Oh! The bowling alley and arcade!" Reid exclaimed in excitement, dancing in his seat. Nodding, I felt the butterflies soar. Despite his movements constricted by his seatbelt, his silliness was endearing, and I couldn't get enough. "Is it just us?"

"Nope, the others should be there already, getting a couple lanes," Kingston explained as he pulled onto the winding road that led to the bowling alley at the top of the hill.

"Bowling!" Reid shouted as soon as the car was parked, his voice echoing around the lot as he hopped out. The rest of us followed, shaking our heads at his antics before heading inside.

"They're over on lanes twelve and thirteen," Jesse pointed out, spotting our friends first, Zoey and Carter waving their hands all over the place. "You two head over, King and I will get shoes," he offered, kissing my cheek. When his fingers brushed over the curve of my butt, I felt my brows shoot up, thinking I may have imagined it, but at Jesse's soft laugh, I knew I hadn't.

Well, I guess I know what his favorite part is.
They're going to be the death of me.
Death by teasing.
Nasty way to go, in my opinion.

"Happy birthday!" Aubrey shouted, popping up and giving Reid and me a quick hug before sitting back down on the bench. A round of 'happy birthdays' went up around the group, each time making Reid's cheeks blush a bit redder.

So cute.

"Who wants to go first?" Brayden asked, his finger poised over the touch screen to enter in the names.

"Reid, it's his birthday," I said, bumping his shoulder playfully.

"Birthday boy, it is, then who?" Brayden continued to enter the names as people shouted them out, half of us on one lane, the other four on the second. Kingston and Jesse joined us as we finished figuring out the bowling order, Reid's and my shoes in hand before we all scattered to find a ball.

"So, who's excited for winter formal?" Zoey questioned as we got started. "We're still getting ready at your house, right, Emma?"

"Yup, Lyla said she'd come hang out with us too. Figured she could help."

"Anyone know who is supposed to win the king and queen thing?" Reid asked, plopping next to me on the couch, his arm going over my shoulder.

"Uh, I think the queen's going to be Natalie Grenlin, and the King was a tie between Forest Borsan and Brad Warland," Jason answered, lining up his shot and launching the ball down the aisle.

My blood ran cold, my chest constricting. *I can't go now. There won't be any way I can enjoy the dance, knowing he's there.* I hadn't even considered Brad would more than likely be attending the dance. Which was dumb, seeing as how he was one of the most popular guys in school.

How?

Don't ask me because I have no freaking idea.

"Oh, shit," Zoey gasped, looking at me. "I didn't think about him going."

"Who?" Jason asked, confused, walking back to his seat next to Aubrey. She scoffed, elbowing him in the side with a hushed whispered. "Oh, yeah." He flashed me a sympathetic smile that looked more like a grimace, his hand rubbing the back of his neck. "Sorry."

"It's alright. We have a lot going on with tests and crap to the point, I can barely remember my own name, so I freaking get it." Looking at Zoey and Aubry, I kept my smile as bright as I could. "I can still help you guys get ready."

"Does that mean you guys aren't going then?" Carter asked, glancing around at the guys. I noticed them glancing back and forth between each other, silent communication flowing as Zoey and Aubrey gave me sympathetic smiles.

"Nah, we'd rather hang with Cali girl, right?" Reid answered, the end of his statement directed at Kingston and Jesse, who immediately agreed. The tightness in my chest unwound, knowing I wasn't ruining our plans because of one stupid boy.

I hate Brad.

And his stupid boat shoes.

"Your turn, Babydoll," Kingston told me, nudging my leg. *Here goes nothing.* Hopping up, I grabbed my pink bowling ball from the return, lined up, and let the ball fly down the lane.

Strike.

"Yay!" I squealed, clapping my hands excitedly. "I did it!"

"Good job!" Brayden offered up a hand as I walked by for a high five.

"Let's grab drinks and snacks," Reid offered, "King, Jesse,

come help us. There's nine of us, and Cali girl and I only have two arms." We got everyone's orders and headed up to the counter. Thankfully, the place didn't seem to be too busy on Wednesday evenings, so we were able to quickly place our order.

"You *are* choosing to not go to winter formal, right, Cali girl?" Reid asked as soon as we were off to the side to wait for the drinks and two batches of fries to come up.

"Yeah, but if you guys want to—" I started.

"No, Em. Either you want to go, or you don't. This isn't about us, it's about you," Jesse countered. "We want you to feel safe and enjoy your night. So, we can do something else or just hang out and watch a movie. We're still getting to spend time with you, and that's all we want."

"You guys are too sweet," I murmured, sniffing back a wave of tears that threatened to spill.

"Why are you crying, Babydoll?" Kingston asked. His wide eyes and horrified expression only served to make me giggle, tears streaming down my cheeks as I struggled to take a breath.

"Happy tears," I huffed out between bouts of laugh crying. "You three treat me like a princess."

"Well, we'll just have to work on that, won't we, guys?" Reid stated. Finally getting control of my laughter, I wiped my tears before giving him a confused head tilt. "We don't want you to be treated like a princess."

"You don't?" I asked, surprised.

"Nope." Reid wrapped me into a hug, his gaze darting around my face. "We want to treat you like a queen."

They may be the death of me with all their teasing, but I will certainly die happy.

Chapter 10

DECEMBER 14TH

Today, I will enjoy my time with the girls, making memories and taking photos for my album. After that? Movie night with my boys
#AllTheSelfies #GirlsDay #StressFreeSaturday

"Emma." My mom's head poked into my room, her dark brown gaze centered on me sitting in the middle of my bed. "Can I come in?"

"Sure." Closing my textbook and notes, I scooted back enough for her to sit. "What's up?" Despite my calm appearance, my stomach constricted as she sat, my mind flaring with some of the most insane scenarios.

Divorce last time. What could it possibly be this time?
Another move?
She's getting married?
Alien Invasion?

"I know it isn't Christmas yet, and I wasn't sure what you and your friends had planned, but,"—she paused, holding out an unsealed envelope—"Merry Christmas."

Taking the envelope, I opened it carefully. Quickly reading the card before opening it, my jaw dropped at the present inside.

A plane ticket back to Cali.

"I figured you could spend the holidays with your dad

since it's been a few months since you've seen him," my mom offered with a small smile.

Unable to figure out what to say, I launched myself forward and hugged her fiercely.

"Thank you," I murmured. As much as I hadn't talked to my dad, I was ecstatic to see him again. I missed him more than I allowed myself to admit, so the thought of spending Christmas with him had my eyes watering.

"Of course, sweetie. I know he's excited to see you," she whispered, hugging me tightly, her hand rubbing soothing circles on my back. "Alright, I'll let you go back to studying. The girls still coming over to get ready?" I nodded. "What are your plans? I thought you were going to the dance?"

"The boys and I decided to stay in and watch movies. This week has been really stressful with finals," I explained, only half lying.

I mean, it had been stressful.

But not *just* because of finals.

"Okay, sweetie, as long as you have fun. Don't do anything you shouldn't," she warned with a stern look. "I'm going to be working, then probably taking it easy for a while before bed. If you need anything, I'll be upstairs."

"Okay, Mom. Thank you again for the present," I called out as she headed back up the stairs.

Ugh, back to studying.

So not fun.

"Who's ready to get pretty?" Lyla called out excitedly. Zoey and Aubrey laughed, shouting 'me' loudly from the basement. "What about you, Emma Bean?" I shook my head, and Lyla's brows dipped down in confusion.

That's right. I haven't updated her yet about the change

in plans.

"Why not? Did those boys back out? Do I need to go redhead crazy on them?" she huffed, puffing up her chest.

"Freaking Brad," I grumbled in irritation. I was happy to spend any time with my boys I could, but I had been excited about the dance, and knowing Brad would get to enjoy it, and I wouldn't put quite the damper on my mood.

"Ugh, screw that bastard," Lyla bit out. "Well, I'm still doing your makeup, so you'll just have to deal with it."

"She's still having a date night. Reid, Kingston, and Jesse are coming over for movie night," Zoey told her cheerfully. "Which I bet Emma is excited about." Zo waggled her brows at me, making me chuckle.

"Oooh, yeah, dark room, blankets, wandering hands," Lyla cooed in a sultry voice that made her sound like she had smoked cigarettes her whole life. Leaning in at the end of her statement, she walked her two fingers up my arm and shoulder with an exaggerated wink.

"I doubt that'll happen," I countered with a laugh. The three of them looked at me with skeptical gazes and an 'mm-hm.'

"How's that all going, anyway?" Lyla asked.

"How's what going? With the boys?" I asked, confused what she was referring to. *I thought it was pretty clear we were doing well.*

"The physical portion of it," Aubrey clarified for her, wiggling her eyebrows. Lyla pointed at her. "Bingo."

"Can't be easy, balancing three guys as friends, let alone three guys going hot and heavy. Hell, half the time, I want to punch Brayden, Carter, and Jason in the face, and we're not even dating," Aubrey explained.

"I mean, we haven't, uh," I stuttered, struggling to explain I was a virgin, and we hadn't done anything other than make out.

"Aww, look at that blush," Zoey teased with a grin. "Yeah, they're treatin' her right."

"Agreed," Lyla tacked on, looking at me with a mischievous glint in her eyes.

Huffing in exasperation at not being able to explain what I meant, I redirected the conversation. "How did I become the topic of conversation? You're the two with dates." I waved to Zoey and Aubrey.

"Tell us about them," Lyla prompted, pulling out makeup and sitting down on the coffee table in front of Zoey.

"I'm going with Brandon," Zoey exclaimed. Her excitement wasn't much of a surprise—she'd had a crush on Brandon since before I moved to the middle of nowhere, Nebraska—but it was the first time she'd been confident enough to talk to him.

"Uh, Jason," Audrey murmured under her breath. My eyes widened as Zoey's head whipped to face her.

"Like our friend Jason?" I asked in awe. Aubrey shrugged, her cheeks tinting red in a bashful blush.

"I've liked him for years, but it always seemed like he wasn't interested or saw me as just a friend, but then he asked me," Aubrey explained.

"That's adorable," Zo stated as Lyla aww-ed. "I'm glad he got his head out of his ass."

"Me too," Aubrey agreed, "I hope it goes well and doesn't get all weird between us if it doesn't work out."

"Don't worry about that, just enjoy your night. Nothing kills a potential relationship faster than worrying about what may or may not happen," Lyla murmured, her focus split between our girl talk and Zoey's eye makeup.

"Look at you, having all that adultier knowledge," I teased, picking up stuff to start on Aubrey's makeup.

"Well, I *am* the adult of the group, so I figured I would share my wisdom with the rest of you," she joked, making all of us laugh. "So, what's everyone doing for winter break? That's coming up, right?"

"My family and I are going to Colorado. We have extended family there, and my brothers and I love to ski," Aubrey stated, her eyes focused on the ceiling as I blended eyeliner on her bottom lash line. "Granted, my older brother is more of a cross-country skier, but my younger bro and I will be on the slopes."

"I plan on just hanging out, relaxing for approximately two days before my entire freaking family comes in for the holidays, then it's basically all family, all the time," Zoey groaned. "I love them, but there are so many of them. 'Oh Zoey, you're so big,' 'Zoey, what are you doing after graduation,' 'When you going to find a boyfriend, Zoey?'"

"Well, what are you doing after graduation? Having some babies?" Lyla asked before cackling, "Totally kidding. I couldn't even say that with a straight face."

"Ha ha," Zoey deadpanned before chuckling. "What about you, Emma? Any fun plans?"

"My mom actually got me a ticket back to Cali to visit my dad," I mumbled.

"The dad you haven't talked to much since moving?" Lyla questioned, looking over at me.

"Yup," I grumbled. "Like, I'm really excited because I've missed him so much, but at the same time... like, what if he doesn't want me there, and that's why he hasn't talked to me?" I shrugged, finally voicing the fears that had been rattling around in my mind, despite my refusal to acknowledge them since my mom gave me the tickets.

"I'm sure he wants you there, I mean, he's your dad," Zoey countered. "It might be weird at first, but I think it'll be good for you to go."

"I hope so. The whole running into my old friends thing is going to be weird, though. I've barely talked to them. All they wanted to do was gossip about their day. Which, don't get me wrong, I don't mind keeping up with things, but it just got tiring, ya know? With you guys and the boys, I feel like we talk about a lot more than that. I'm not sure how to describe it, but I feel happy with you guys, a stronger connection than just petty gossip."

"Aww, that was the sweetest thing ever, Emma Bean," Lyla teased, pretending to wipe tears away. "We love you, too." I rolled my eyes, my cheeks heating as we all laughed.

"Alright, you're all done, Aubs," I said, sitting back. "Just have to pick a lip color to go with your dress."

"Yay! Thank you, it looks awesome," Aubrey squealed, looking in the small mirror I held up. "I'm going to get my dress on! Coming, Zo?"

"Almost done, you go get started. Do you need us to touch up your curls?" Lyla asked, glancing between the two of them. Both shook their heads, the curls that framed their faces shifting with the movement.

I sank into the couch as Aubrey got up, grabbed her dress, and went into the bathroom. After a very loud squeal of excitement at her makeup, Zoey hopped up and darted into my room to change. Lyla chuckled as she scooted over to sit in front of me.

"You don't have to do—" I started.

"Nonsense! You're getting your makeup done, regardless of whether you're going to the dance," Lyla countered. "Now shush, I have to concentrate, or you'll look like a clown."

"Reid would probably find it funny," I murmured, trying hard to not move my face.

"Probably, but that's not what we're going for."

"Well, what are we going for then?"

"Sultry and seductive. You may not be glamming up in a dress or getting your hair done, but you'll still look hot as hell," she assured proudly. "Besides, I know how much you love taking photos for your album, so now you'll look amazing. Well, more amazing than you normally do. Wait... that didn't come out right. You know what I mean." By the time she was finished, we were both laughing our butts off, and thankfully, my eyes weren't watering, so all the work she had already done was spared.

"Okay, enough of that, don't want to risk ruining it." Lyla finished up my makeup with a sweep of mascara and a dab of lip color, forgoing blush at my request.

Because goodness knows, I don't need any when Reid, Kingston, and Jesse are around.

"Emma, Lyla, ready to see?" Zo called out.

"Yes," I squealed, turning so I could see Aubrey and Zoey's dresses. Aubs was wearing a muted purple dress, lace material from the hollow of her throat to her waist where the skirt flared and swooshed around her knees in a silky satin wave of lilac. The high halter top neckline showcased her thin neck and collarbones, and her chestnut hair was warm against the cool tone of her dress. Zoey was in a similar fall color, her dress a floor-length forest green. The fabric wasn't shiny, almost velvety, accentuating her dark curly hair and pale skin.

"Photo time!" Lyla held up their phones so they each could have pictures. "Alright, Emma Bean, get in there."

"Yeah, join us!" Aubrey bounced in excitement, the mood of the room making my cheeks hurt from constantly smiling. Climbing off the sofa, I stood between Zoey and Aubrey as Lyla took the pictures, several where I know we looked ridiculous because of Lyla's antics as she made funny faces at us.

"Lyla, you come stand with Emma, then we can get a few with all of us!" Zoey took the phones from Lyla, holding mine up to snap a picture of me and Lyla together. With Lyla being, well, Lyla, after the first normal photo, she wrapped her arms around my neck and hopped up into my arms. I barely had time to catch her in a cradle, thankfully, not dropping her in the process.

Ten minutes of funny picture taking later, the doorbell cut short our fun. Jason and Brandon stood on the other side, quickly followed by my boys climbing out of Reid's Jeep. After hugs and more photos of those attending the dance, everyone headed out save for my boys, leaving us in the basement, trying to figure out what movie to watch.

"It's the holidays, so we have to watch a holiday movie," I countered loudly at the boys who to groan. "You don't even know which Christmas movie I want to watch, so why are you all complaining?"

"Cause it'll probably be a sappy movie," Reid explained. "I'm all for sappy, but only on Christmas Eve or Christmas Day."

"So, this isn't what you had in mind? Because this is what I wanted to watch." I held up my movie, and the guys' jaws dropped. "Christmas doesn't start until I see Hans Gruber fall off of the Nakatomi Plaza tower."

"*Die Hard* isn't a Christmas movie, but I'm so down," Reid stated, taking the case from me and popping the DVD in the player.

"It totally counts as a Christmas movie," I scoffed. "There's a Christmas party in the movie, it's festive, and there's good family fun," I ticked off, putting a finger up for every point I made.

"I agree with her," Kingston added with a smile, "except maybe the family fun part, depending on how old the kids are."

"Psh!" Reid waved a hand at us dismissively.

"What about you?" Kingston asked Jesse, who shrugged.

"I don't have much of an opinion on it, I just like the movie," Jesse explained diplomatically.

"You're just full of surprises, Cali girl," Reid flashed me a smile as he plopped down onto the couch. I chuckled, getting situated in my spot, making room between Reid and Jesse. "You look really good, too, in case we didn't say anything." I beamed as I got settled.

"Thanks, babe, I'll tell Lyla you appreciate her hard work," I teased, turning to face the movie at Reid's chuckle.

Jesse's body was hot, his torso hard against my back as I leaned into him. My right leg was draped over Reid's lap, his hand resting on my knee while my left was planted firmly on the ground. Kingston was relaxed in the armchair off to the side, his body facing us, but his eyes were on the screen.

The movie had been playing for about a half hour when Jesse's fingers started to shift ever so slowly down my side to my hip. Thankfully, the backdoor shades were closed, the room was dark, and Jesse's movements were covered by a blanket Reid had tossed over me. My breath hitched, my heart galloping in my chest as his calloused fingers crept over the sliver of skin peeking out between the hem of my shirt and the band of my leggings.

Shifting, Jesse slouched into the couch further, his cheek pressing to the top of my head slowly moving his fingers under my pants. A rush of tingles spread over me, my veins on fire as the lightest touch ran along the top edge of my panties. I forced myself to sit still. My leg was still propped in Reid's lap, and I didn't want my wiggling to get his attention.

Going to be the death of me with this teasing.

Nibbling on my lip as discreetly as I could, my hearing filled with nothing but my breathing and erratic heartbeat. As Jesse's fingers ran over the front of my panties, I couldn't stop the slight jump, playing it off as I readjusted slightly when Reid glanced over at us.

Jesse's chuckle was so quiet, I barely heard it over the movie, the honeyed sound only making the surge of heat build between my thighs. Despite Reid nearly catching us, Jesse didn't stop, his fingers dipping below the cotton fabric to the slick entrance underneath. I nearly moaned as he tentatively pushed a finger into me, the angle restricting how far, but enough to make my breath whoosh from my lungs. Stars burst in front of my eyes at the overwhelming sensations that threatened to drown me.

It took all of my willpower not to move. I was held hostage by two desires—wanting Jesse to continue, but not wanting to let Reid or Kingston know what was going on right next to them. Jesse's erection was pressing into my lower back and hip, the hardened bulge only serving to make me hotter. When I thought I couldn't handle anymore, Kingston shifted to stand, breaking the bubble of teasing Jesse had created.

"Want us to pause it?" I asked, my voice cracking in the middle of my question, followed by Jesse soft grunt as I lightly elbowed him in the stomach to cut off his smothered laughter.

"If you could," Kingston agreed, smiling down at me as he moved around the couch and into the hallway to go to the bathroom.

"Anyone want snacks?" Jesse questioned, shifted

forward to stand, but not before thrusting his finger into me one final time. Closing my eyes, I took a deep breath and flopped back on the couch, spent from the swirling emotions that had my nerves on edge.

"I'll help you," Reid called out as Jesse headed up the stairs, shifting my leg off his lap before getting up. He stood there a moment, waiting until we were alone before he leaned down, his lips brushing the curve of my ear.

"Tsk tsk, naughty Emma, having fun in a room full of people," he whispered. I couldn't stop the shocked gasp that escaped as I felt the blood drain from my face. "Aww, don't look so scared, Cali girl, I like watching you squirm." With that, he kissed me quickly, pulling back to flash me a cocky smile that guaranteed he'd loved nearly giving me a heart attack, then headed up the stairs, leaving me to my racing thoughts.

The girls were right, wandering hands indeed.

Not that you'd hear me complaining, I can't wait for next time.

DECEMBER 21ST

Today, I'll do my best, and that will be more than good enough
#IAmGoodEnough #RockTheACT #StressFreeSaturday

"You did it," I reminded myself as I sank into my driver's seat. "You finished your practice ACT and didn't throw up. Gotta look on the bright side of things." I continued to tell myself little positive things like Jesse and Ms. Rogers' had told me to do if I was too anxious or worried to help set my mind on the right track. I even did some extra steps last night, to help start on the right foot today. After meditating, I went to bed early with my alarm set fifteen minutes before my usual alarm, so I could eat a nutritious breakfast.

Who said I couldn't be responsible?

Call me, Miss I-Freaking-Got-This.

Almost home, my stomach finally settled, but my body was drained of energy as the last of the anxiety faded. Getting out of the car, I headed inside.

"What the heck?" I murmured under my breath as I flipped the light switch.

Nothing.

Not even a flicker.

"Must have blown a fuse," I surmised, heading to the basement where I knew the breaker was, but when I scanned the line of switches, none were off. "Maybe there's an outage? Why am I still talking to myself?"

Shaking my head, I pulled up a new tab on my phone, searching for outages, but according to the website, everything was up and running. My blood turned to ice as I made my way upstairs, snatching up the mail from its pile on the counter on my way. When I found the energy bill, I opened it and immediately felt my jaw drop.

Overdue.

Final notice until payment.

Mom couldn't even be bothered to pay the damn bill, now? Storming to her office, I yanked out her password book, scanning until I found the login for the utility company. *Hopefully, they have online bill pay.* I pulled up the site on my phone and waited for it to load.

Note to self, set up auto-pay when I own a freaking house.

I gasped when I saw the bill, knowing I had enough to cover it but not without eating up a large chunk of my most recent paycheck. *Guess Lyla and my friends are getting handmade gifts this year.*

"Why did you have to go to the middle of the country with bad reception?" I asked my mom's office as if I expected her to be able to hear me.

She didn't.

Obviously.

As soon as the bill was paid, a notification popped up saying the power would be turned back on within the next few hours. A chill settled over me when I finally realized how cold it had gotten in the house, so I hurried downstairs and bundled up on the couch. I got lost in a book Jesse and I had been reading together, wanting to reread the first part of the book, so I was ready for our second reading date.

After an hour of reading, a pounding on the door startled me. Jumping at the abrupt noise, I hopped out of the warm cocoon I had made and headed upstairs.

"Cali girl, it's us, open up," Reid hollered from the other side. Unlocking and opening the door, I was greeted with worried gazes and thinned lips. "Oh, thank goodness."

"What?" I questioned, shifting out of the way to let them in, temporarily forgetting our house still had no power. "Why do you guys all look like you saw a ghost or something?"

"Your phone is shut off," Kingston explained, pointing to the device sticking up from my pocket.

"What? No, it isn't..." I trailed off, seeing the 'no service' in the corner. "It was working only an hour ago," I said under my breath as a sense of defeat washed over me.

"Why is it so cold in here?" Jesse asked, glancing around before pulling his coat back on.

"What's going on, Emma?" Reid demanded, his tone

hard as he looked at me. "First there's no food, now your utilities and phone are off—"

"I know," I yelled, slamming the front door shut. "Alright? I know. My mom's never home, work seems to have taken over her whole freaking life. I see my mom about as often as my dad talks to me. Okay?" I deflated, everything finally coming pouring out as a wall of wavering shapes filled my sight.

"I'm trying to keep on top of everything with school and work and this shit with Brad, but in the last couple months, it's becoming more and more me taking care of the house and bills and being the adult of my family, and I'm tired..." I choked out, no longer able to hold it all in. Reid stepped up, wrapping his arms around me until I was clutching the back of his coat as if he could keep me from drowning in my sobs.

"It's alright, Babydoll, we're here to help you," Kingston reassured softly, his hand rubbing my lower back. "Did you get the utilities figured out?"

"Yeah, should be turned back on soon. They said within a couple of hours, and that was about an hour ago," I explained through my sniffles. "But I don't think I'll have enough to cover the phone bill, and—"

"Let us worry about that, Cali girl," Reid cut me off, squeezing before leaning back, his handsome face filling my teary vision. "Do you know the login and stuff for the phone bill?"

"Uh, yeah," I stuttered, wiping my cheeks in a poor attempt to get my crying under control. "Let me grab it." Turning, I walked back up the stairs and into my mom's office for the second time. "Here you go." I passed the booklet over to Kingston and Reid, who stood right outside the doorway in the hall. "Where's Jesse?"

"He's downstairs," Kingston explained. There was a thread of something in his words that had my eyes narrowing, but I couldn't put my finger on it.

"I'll go check on him," I explained, going around them, but before walking away, I paused. "Thank you. Seriously, you guys don't have to do this, but I really appreciate it."

"We don't have to, but we want to, Cali girl. We want to know you're taken care of," Reid explained with a cocksure smile. "I mean, that's the knightly thing to do, isn't it?"

As much as I didn't want to laugh, his boisterous exclamation had me chuckling, already feeling lighter as I shook my head and headed to the basement.

"Jess?" I called out hesitantly. His back was to me, his arm propped on the door frame to the backyard as he stared through the glass. My steps slowed as I neared him, something about his tense shoulders worrying me. "Jesse?"

"Why didn't you tell us?" he murmured, still not turning to look at me. My heart squeezed at the hurt in his question.

"Because we already had enough to worry about, and I was hoping it was just a temporary thing. I never expected it to get this bad," I explained quietly. "I planned on telling you."

"When, Em?" Jesse finally turned to look over his shoulder at me, his lips curled down, and his eyes filled with hurt that made my heart crack.

"When everything else calmed down or when it got worse."

"Is there anything else that's been bothering you?" Jesse questioned. "We can't help you if we don't know what's going on. You're the one who said we need to communicate." Questions about his cuts, bruises, and family life flared on the tip of my tongue, but I bit them back because he was right, I had said that, and right now, we were discussing my problems, not his.

Oh, he's so going to get questioned about it.

Just not right now.

"Tyler won't leave me alone," I murmured. "I still don't respond or acknowledge his messages or calls. I actually had planned on talking to you guys about it again today since I'm flying back to Cali tomorrow, and I wouldn't be surprised if I ran into him."

"Would it be frowned upon if I punched him?" Reid's question startled me, not having heard them come down to the basement. Reid seemed irritated, but not necessarily with me, winking when I glanced at him. Kingston stood silently, his lips curling into a soft, reassuring smile, letting me know he wasn't upset either.

"I'm pretty sure it would be, and I can't handle another situation where I have to testify," I tried to joke. It fell flat, but Reid and Kingston gave a soft chuckle. Glancing back at Jesse, I nibbled on my lip.

"It might be frowned upon, but I can't say I disagree," Jesse mumbled, finally turning to face us fully. "Come here, Em." Jesse held his arms out. Taking a shuddering breath, I felt a few wayward tears leak out as I launched into his waiting hug. "I'm sorry, I didn't mean to make you think I was mad. I just want to make sure you're okay."

"That's what we said," Reid exclaimed. "See, Cali girl? We're here for you, even when shit gets hard."

"I know," I mumbled against Jesse's soft shirt. "I'm sorry."

"You don't have to apologize," Kingston explained. "We just hate not knowing what's bothering you. We want you to know we're here to help, even if we get a bit worked up like we have about Tyler."

"Yeah, you're our girl," Reid continued, "and it's hard not being able to help. Hell, we don't even have to help if you don't want us to. We're here for you to vent, rant, or cuddle."

"I know," I murmured, feeling worse the longer the conversation went on. "I'll work on it, okay?"

"Alright, Cali girl. We didn't say these things to hurt your feelings. We wanted you to see we can be open too and figured telling you how we felt would be good." Reid's sad smile filled my peripherals as he looked at me, and I realized I had a wayward tear rolling down my cheek.

"I think we could all work on the opening up part from here on out, though." I didn't have to look at Kingston to know the last comment was directed at Jesse, his body stiffening slightly as he held me.

"Yeah, but right now, we should help Em pack and figure out what she can do if she runs into Tyler on her trip," Jesse countered, effectively shutting down the topic of his life. Reid and Kingston sighed but didn't press the issue as they started toward my room. I pulled back, popped up on my toes, and kissed Jesse's stubbled cheek before I turned to follow

"Don't think I won't pester you for answers sooner or later, Jess," I whispered. His jaw ticked against my lips, but he didn't argue. He may not want to tell me now, but soon enough, he would.

Baby steps.

CHAPTER 11

DECEMBER 22ND

No words for what happened today. None.
#FML #OverIt #NOTSundayFunday

Thank you for flying with us, and we hope to see you on a future flight." The flight attendant's cheerful voice filtered through the crackly speakers as the rest of the passengers unbuckled and stood up once the seatbelt sign turned off. I followed at a slower pace, my body buzzing with a mixture of nervousness and excitement. *And cramps, because why wouldn't my period line up with something so nerve-wracking?* Rolling the dramatic thought away, I stepped out of my row of seats. This would be the first time I had seen my dad since the move, and as much as I missed him, I felt our reunion would be less than comfortable.

Well, that's what happens when you've only talked maybe ten times since moving away, I grumbled internally, pulling my duffel from the overhead bin when it was my turn to exit. As I disembarked, I was happy I didn't have to worry about getting a checked suitcase, my backpack and duffel holding everything I needed for my week trip. Following the signs, I headed to the exit from the concourse and into the main airport.

It was busy, being the holiday season as well as the weekend, so scanning the crowd was slow going, but after about ten minutes of searching, I gave up and dialed my dad's number.

One ring.

Two rings.

Three rings.

Voicemail.

"Uh, hey, Dad," I started after the beep. "I'm not sure if you're here in the airport or not, but I don't see you. I'll try the house and vineyard phones, and if I can't reach you, I'll take an Uber," I explained hesitantly, an odd sense of doom filling the pit of my stomach when the other two numbers went to voicemail as well.

Holding out hope for as long as my antsy anticipation would allow, I shuffled from one foot to the other until finally, after a half hour, I scheduled an Uber pickup, which thankfully, only took a few minutes to arrive. Climbing in, I gave the woman the address and tried to text my dad.

Emma: Hey, got an Uber, heading to the house now. See you soon.

I held off on the urge to put a 'hopefully' at the end, but just barely, my already gnawed and cracked lip finding its way between my teeth for what seemed like the tenth time in the last hour.

An hour and a half of traffic later, the Uber pulled up to the rounded drive and came to a stop. Paying quickly, I gave a forced smile and hopped out of the car. Staring at the two-story house that had once been my home—all my childhood memories, all the holidays, get-togethers with my friends—I should feel sad, but it only made my anxiety flare.

I was a stranger in my own home.

Taking a deep breath, I walked to the front door and rang the bell, fidgeting until I heard the locks turn. His black hair was graying ever so slightly at the temples, his face clean shaven, and his normal slacks and button-up shirt had been traded out for a pair of jeans and a long-sleeve shirt. Swallowing, I mustered up a smile, hoping it seemed genuine as I stared at the man who looked more like a stranger than my own father.

"Emma?" my dad asked in confusion, glancing between my bag in my hand and my face. "What are you doing here?"

"Mom got me tickets to visit this week, remember?" I squeaked out, trying hard to keep my quickly unraveling emotions in check. My dad checked his watch and groaned.

"I'm so sorry, sweetheart, I must have lost track of what day it was. Come on in." My dad stepped off to the side, reaching for my duffel in the process. "There's something you need to know, though, Emm—"

"Darling," a woman called from deeper in the house, and my heart dropped into my stomach. "Who is it? One of Ruby's or Tanner's friends?"

I gaped, shock rolling through me as I processed what was happening. The stomach-turning surprise quickly accompanied a painful ache in the center of my chest as I glanced at my dad. A grimace and a worried gaze looked back at me.

"Wow," I deadpanned, looking at my dad in a new light. "It all makes sense now," I bit out. Anger grew with each moment that passed, smothering the hurt and surprise until all I was felt was fury as I shook with the urge to scream.

"Sweetheart, I need to introduce you to Meredith and her two teenagers, Ruby and Tanner," my father started, but I shook my head.

"No. I don't want to meet your new family," I ground out through clenched teeth. Did he seriously think I would just *accept* this? His life where I seemingly didn't exist, eighteen years meaning nothing. Maybe before moving, I would have been too stunned to argue, to snap, to demand answers, but there had been too much going on in my life lately to waste my time, letting people walk all over me.

"Why the heck didn't you tell me? Oh, right, you wouldn't have ever had the chance in the total of twenty minutes we've talked in the last three and a half months." A woman with red curly hair came around the corner, concern on her face. She was petite and pretty in a pair of black pants and a light green sweater.

"Emma, this is Meredith. Meredith, this is my—" my father tried to introduce me, but I laughed so hard, tears of anger and heartbreak fell.

Oh, hell no.

He doesn't get to forget me and still expect me to be the perfect daughter.

That's not me... not anymore.

"You're really going to try this, aren't you?" I challenged. "You don't bother to talk to me, to even tell me you had a new freaking family! Why should I bother to play nice?" I snapped, glaring between the two of them.

"You didn't tell her?" my dad's girlfriend—fiancée, based on the giant rock on her hand—*Meredith*, murmured in surprise. "David—"

"I didn't want to interfere with your schooling," he tried to explain, but I just shook my head. Taking my bag from my dad's hand, I started toward the door. "Emma, wait!"

"If you're so willing to replace me, I don't need you as a dad," I hissed, running off the porch and across the drive.

Screw them, I've been doing just fine on my own for the last few months. Gripping my duffle, I trudged to the closest coffee shop two miles down the road.

Well, fine enough.

By the time I saw the coffee shop's familiar logo and neon colors, my feet were throbbing, and my back and shoulders were stiff and achy from carrying my bags. Thankfully, it only took a few more minutes before I was finally in the air-conditioned café, surrounded by the calming scent of coffee.

Thank goodness for empty seats.

As soon as I was seated, I sighed with relief, and after a brief moment to rest, I pulled out my phone and called the first of the boys I could find on my phone.

"Hey, Babydoll," Kingston greeted. "How's your dad?" At the reminder of what happened, I felt my eyes water and my jaw clench in anger.

"I'm coming home," I croaked quietly to not catch the attention of the other shop goers.

"What's wrong? Are you okay?" I heard Reid question, and the sounds of the three of them moving filled the phone, so Kingston must have put it on speaker.

"Turns out, he has a new family," I whispered, playing with the end of my sleeve. "A fiancée, and she has two teenagers." None of them spoke, stunned into silence.

"Wow," Jesse breathed, so softly, I wasn't sure he had realized he'd spoken aloud.

"So, yeah, I'm going to see if I can find a cheap ticket to fly home."

"We can do that. We're sitting at Kingston's laptop, anyway," Reid explained, the sound of typing filtering through the speaker.

"I'm not sure about what I'll do if the flight's tomorrow. I left my dad's and went to the coffee shop near my house..." I trailed off when my phone beeped, an incoming call from my dad I promptly ignored.

"So, uh, how's the cabin?" I redirected the conversation while they searched.

"It's not bad, just watching a movie until the game is on," Reid explained. "How are you, really, Cali girl?"

"Angry, upset, but in reality, it doesn't honestly surprise me. In a way, I'm actually glad to know why he's been so distant." I went to continue when I heard my name practically shouted by a familiar nasally voice. Glancing over, I spotted Kara's frizzy blond hair and bright smile.

"Who's that?" I heard Jesse ask, but Kara closed the distance between us before I could answer. I dropped the phone from my ear, but left the call connected, hoping she would get the memo that I really wasn't up for talking.

"Hey, Kara." I mustered up as much cheer as I could and flashed her a smile. Well, hopefully, it looked like a smile and not a grimace. "How's it going?"

"It's great! How are you? I didn't realize you were coming back into town for the holidays," she rattled on. "Staying with your dad? Oh, have you met Ruby or Tanner yet?" At the mention of my dad's new family, my smile fell. Kara must have realized something was wrong because her brows furrowed, and her head tilted slightly.

"I didn't know about Meredith or her kids until I showed up on my dad's doorstep today after he forgot I was flying in. So, no, I haven't met them," I deadpanned, growing irritated.

"Oh," Kara squeaked in surprise, "I thought you knew. I mean, if I knew you hadn't, I would have told you. Well, if you ever want a chance to meet them, they're both really cool. Tanner is a cutie to the max, and I'm actually hoping to score a date with him. Maybe when you see him, you could drop my name or something?"

"Uh, I doubt I'll be seeing him anytime soon. I'm heading home tonight," I explained, my brow cocked in disbelief she'd really just asked me that.

"Oh, well, in case you see him, or I don't know, get his number or something." Kara seemed unfazed by the awkwardness of the conversation and gave me a quick hug before fluttering away, but before she could make it out the door, I called out.

"You know, Kara, people aren't here just for you to use. I don't exist solely for you to get an 'in' with someone." Sighing, I shook my head and looked away. "Just something to think about."

She stood there stunned, but instead of saying anything real, she turned with a muttered 'whatever' and stormed out. Was that really what my friends and life were like? Shallow and self-absorbed? I mean, I'm all for wanting to get a chance with a boy I liked, but wow. My brain whirled until I finally remembered I had the boys on the phone and put it against my ear.

"There's this one? It's late, but it'll work," I heard Kingston say. "We can pick her up."

"I'm sure she doesn't want to field questions from her mom at almost one in the morning after going through the day from hell," Jesse countered.

"I meant we could bring her here, then take her home whenever she's ready. We're going to my house for Christmas Eve and Christmas day, anyway, and you know my mom will throw a fit if she doesn't come," Kingston explained.

My heart warmed, the vise-like grip around my chest, the shock of the day slowly easing.

"I would love that," I said. "I don't really want to talk to my mom or anyone. Not until I have some time to really process everything. I mean, if it's okay that I come to the cabin with you?" I tacked onto the end, my statement going up like a question.

"Of course, it is." Reid scoffed. "We think we found a flight, but it doesn't leave until later, so you need to find a place to chill until then or hang out at the airport for like five or six hours."

"I don't mind doing that—" I started, then felt someone's eyes on me. Looking back out over the shop, I found the one person I hadn't wanted to see on this trip.

Tyler.

"Oh, awesome," I murmured sarcastically as he started toward me.

"What?" Jesse asked, his voice low, picking up on my tone. Sighing, I started to collect my things, typing quickly on my phone to order a Uber. *Oh, of course, they wouldn't be here for at least five to ten minutes.* Deciding to grab a coffee, I put the phone back to my ear, pretending I didn't have time to talk.

I mean, I was actually doing something... not that he would listen, I'm sure.

"Emma?" Tyler's voice made my already frayed nerves jolt.

"Tyler," I greeted flatly. I heard Reid and Jesse grumbling on the line after figuring out what was happening.

"Kara said you were here," he explained, hitching a thumb over to nothing in particular. "I figured I could stop by and say hi."

"Ah, figures she did," I sighed. "I'm actually about to leave, but it was good to see you," I lied through my teeth. Turning, I ordered a cup to go, mentally chanting that Tyler would get the hint and leave me the heck alone.

But of course, no such luck.

Did I break a mirror? Walk under a ladder?

Why was karma being such a witch with a b lately?

"Because of your dad's fiancée and her kids?" Tyler asked after I finished my order.

"My, my, Kara is quite the jabbermouth," I mumbled under my breath.

"Babydoll, remember what we talked about."

Kingston's smooth, melodic voice was the life preserver among the anxiety, nerves, and blaring anger threatening to drown me. *Right.* I took a deep breath, remembering the boys' advice in my mind—shut down any unwanted conversation quickly, and if possible, leave the situation. I glanced at my phone. *Five minutes until my ride was here. I can totally make it for five minutes.*

Right?

"Uh, yeah," I finally answered Tyler, gratefully taking my cup from the barista and quickly grabbed my bags from the table. "My ride should be here soon, actually."

"I could give you a lift. I assume you probably can't get a flight for today, so if you need somewhere to stay, you know you can stay with me," he offered. I raised a brow at him.

"Last I checked, your parents didn't exactly like me," I challenged, but before I could tell him I did, in fact, have a flight home, he laughed.

"I have my own place now," Tyler explained, "you can stay tonight or however long you need, Emma."

"Oh, hell no," Reid snapped. "Give him the phone, Cali girl."

"No, Reid," I answered, listening to him grumble on the other end. Tyler's lips thinned, finally realizing I was on the phone.

"Reid, your *friend* from Nebraska?" Tyler asked, irritation littering his words.

"Boyfriend, actually," I stated simply. "Now, if you'll excuse me, Tyler, my ride is almost here."

"Emma, I miss you. Can we at least talk? Without your boyfriend listening?" Tyler huffed, following me out of the coffee shop into the sunny California weather.

I sighed, the urge to rub my eyes overwhelming. This was always the issue with Tyler—what I said went in one ear and out the other.

"No," I said firmly. "I told you months ago if you wanted to be friends, we could try, but all you've done is overwhelm me with messages and 'I miss yous.' I have boyfriends I'm happy with, Tyler, can't you respect that?"

"Give him the phone, Em," Jesse bit out.

"No, I'm not giving him the phone, Jesse," I countered. Tyler's brows shot up at the name, but he wisely kept his mouth shut. *First smart thing he's done since I've known him.* "Now, for the second time, if you'll excuse me, I need to get back to the airport," I ground out as a car pulled up next to us and stopped. Without giving him a chance to say anything else, I tossed my bag in the backseat of my Uber without a second glance.

Goodbye, California.

Several hours and a second flight within twenty-four hours later, I landed back in the middle of nowhere, tired and sore. My mood was completely tanked, but as soon as I saw my three boys hanging out in the hall, right outside security, I nearly cried.

Being a girl sucked sometimes—PMS is the devil.

"Come here, Cali girl." Reid pulled me into him as Jesse took my duffel, and Kingston took my backpack. Clutching him, I squeezed tightly as he dropped a kiss on my head. Stepping back, I didn't even wait for Jesse to hold his arms out, wedging myself in his embrace. His signature mint scent soothed my rampant emotions, but I didn't feel completely at ease until I was wrapped in Kingston's arms.

"Let's go home," I murmured against Kingston's flannel button-up. Three happy smiles greeted me when I stepped back.

Hello, Nebraska.

DECEMBER 23RD

'Be around people who are good for your soul' -Unknown
#NewMe #MyStoryChapterOne #MondayMotvitation

The sun rose slowly over the snow-covered ground, the icicles hanging from the roof sparkling in the pinks, purples, and oranges of sunrise. I hadn't been able to sleep after returning from the airport, my body too on edge from everything that had happened yesterday to relax. So, I finally gave up after several hours of trying and made some hot chocolate before I settled onto the plush couch in the sunroom under a fuzzy blanket. My mom had finally messaged me back this morning, apologizing for my dad and everything that happened. Thankfully, she didn't give me any crap for staying at the cabin with the guys, only saying she'd see me at Christmas brunch at the Bells.

"Babydoll?" Hearing Kingston call out was music to my ears as he popped his head into the space. "What are you doing awake already?"

"Couldn't sleep," I murmured. "Why are you up?"

"Was going to make breakfast for everyone," he explained, walking down the two steps into the sunroom, his bare feet plodding across the wood floor. "Want some company?"

"I'd love some." I held open the blanket as Kingston sank into the seat next to me, angling my legs until they were curled in his lap, and my head was lying on his shoulder. "It's peaceful out here."

"Yeah, it is. It's one of our favorite places to go during the winter, summer... basically any time. I hope to have a place like this someday. Large lot, middle of nowhere, able to enjoy the space away from the city and its stressors. Is this different from Cali?"

"Yeah. While we had land at the vineyard, we were still close to a city. There's really no land like this on the coast, and what there is, is extremely expensive."

"Think you could get used to somewhere like this?" King asked softly. I hesitated, remembering how I had felt when my mom and I first moved, but the rush of memories I had since then shone in my mind.

"I think I already have," I smiled, turning my head to look up at him. Kingston's molten chocolate eyes centered on my face, his bearded face smiling as he rubbed my back. "I expected to hate it here, in the middle of nowhere, but I think it made the people I've met so much sweeter. Can't avoid people, distracted with a hundred things to do or places to go."

"We're glad you like it here, Babydoll," Kingston chuckled, hugging me tighter. "So, you're happy, yeah?" The question was odd, so I glanced over at him with a scrunched brow, waiting for him to explain. "You say you like Nebraska, but that doesn't tell me how you feel about *us* and our relationship. What we have is unique, and I want to know you're happy with it."

"Oh, King," I murmured, my heart fluttering. "Yes, I'm happy in this relationship. It might be different, but I don't think I could ever pick between the three of you. You guys are all different but somehow fit together perfectly. To be honest, I don't think I've been as happy as I am now in a long time."

"Good," he whispered, pressing a kiss to my temple. "You're pretty perfect yourself, Babydoll. If I or one of the other guys ever do anything to piss you off or upset you—"

"I'll tell you guys, I promise," I finished for him, making him chuckle. "You three are the main reason I don't hate it here."

"Good. Wouldn't want you to run off back to Cali as soon as you graduate." Reid's teasing startled me since I hadn't heard him come into the sunroom, but I couldn't stop my laugh.

"Don't worry, I'm not going back to Cali. I'm ready to just live my life here. You know, not letting my parents or stupid people stop me from enjoying my life. I've spent my whole life going along with stuff even if I wasn't happy, but after everything with my mom and dad, Tyler, and freaking Brad, I'm tired of being walked over. So, now, it's me, the future, positivity, and all that jazz," I looked over to Reid, who had plopped down on my other side, Jesse silently sitting on the arm of the couch. "Ya know?"

"I think this is what people call a turning point, a

spiritual or personal awakening," Jesse said with a sly smile. "Or whatever they call it. An epiphany?"

"Regardless, we're happy you're here," Reid stated. "And we'll be here through everything, Cali girl, ups, downs, loop-de-loops, and all."

"You guys are going to make me cry," I murmured, my eyes watering at their sweetness. "Being so sweet when I haven't slept, makes me all emotional."

"How is that different from normal?" Reid joked. I elbowed him in the side, making sure the blow was soft enough, he knew I was joking.

"Come on, let's make some food, then maybe you'll be sleepy enough to get a nap in," Kingston offered, his hand coming down to help me off the couch.

"You let your mom know where you are?" Reid asked. Nodding, I followed King and Jesse into the kitchen, situating myself on one of the bar stools. "You know you're more than welcome to stay here over winter break. We're going back to Kingston's for Christmas, but other than that, we're hanging here."

"Really? I'd love that."

No dealing with the stress of my family for two weeks? Well, save for Christmas...

Heck, yes.

CHAPTER 12

DECEMBER 22ND

Do we really have to go back to the real world in a week?
#IJustWantCuddles #RealWorldGoAway #TickedOffTuesday

E m, love."
Jesse's honeyed voice pulling me from my sleepy state, my eyes cracked open as I looked over at him. The fuzzy blanket was warm, and the leather couch had molded to my body as I curled into the back cushions. I mumbled unintelligibly, wanting to go back to napping, but Jesse's chuckling had me opening my eyes fully.

"Want to exchange gifts?"

"Presents, you say?" I perked up, smiling when a mug of hot chocolate appeared in front of me as Reid reached over the back of the couch.

"Yup, present time." Jesse smiled, his hand resting on my knee, squeezing gently.

"My gifts for you guys are in the car—" I started until I saw Kingston coming through the front door with an armful of gift bags. "Well, they were in the car, but apparently, Kingston knew I put them in there before leaving."

"Here's yours, Babydoll." Kingston pointed to the small

stack of boxes and bags next to me on the coffee table. He busied himself, adding my presents to the boys' piles before sinking into his seat next to me on the overstuffed recliner. "Come on, dude, how long does it take to make cocoa?" Kingston called to Reid. At the mention of hot cocoa, I took a sip of mine, a wash of something different, hitting my tongue and making me shift my marshmallows around to see it was lighter than normal hot chocolate.

"Sorry, I wanted to make sure the powder and the Baileys were mixed together well," Reid explained, handing the last two mugs to Kingston and Jesse before reaching into the kitchen and picking his up off the counter.

"Oh, yum, this is good," I said, taking another sip, "I don't think I've ever had something like this. How much alcohol is in it?"

"Just a shot, maybe a little less," Reid explained. "There wasn't much left, but there was enough for one mug each. Now, how do we want to do this? A free-for-all?"

"I'm good with that," Kingston agreed as Jesse and I nodded. "Just save this one for last," he warned, pointing to the box wrapped in a sparkly red wrapping paper and an extravagant silver and green bow. Setting my mug down on the side table between Kingston and me, I got ready to dig into the others.

"Guess that means have at it?" I asked. With that, we leaned forward, grabbing one of our gifts from our piles.

The first one I grabbed was a bag, small despite the hefty rectangular box at the bottom. Pulling it out, my lips parted—another jewelry box, like the one from my birthday. There was no card inside of the tissue paper, so I opened the box, finding a handwritten note inside.

To my Em,

> *I know how much you love to match. Merry*
> *Christmas, love.*

xoxo, Jesse

A pink tourmaline heart pendant sparkled under the soft overhead lighting, the flickering flames from the fireplace showcasing all the facets of the gem. I squealed, launching into Jesse's side with a tight hug.

"It's beautiful," I murmured as I pulled back. "Will you help me put it on?"

"I'm glad you like it, Em." Jesse gave me a bashful smile, pulling the light silvery gold chain out of the velvet packaging. "Turn around," he instructed. I shifted, moving my hair out of the way as he hooked the dainty necklace that matched the pink earrings he got me for my birthday.

"It's gorgeous," Kingston stated, seeing the necklace. "Thank you, Babydoll. Fuzzy socks were exactly what I wanted." He held up two pairs of patterned socks, his grin growing to a bright smile as he looked at me.

"You're welcome," I said, my words almost covered by Reid's laughter. He held up his present, a funny shirt, in front of him as he read it.

"I love this, Cali girl. It's perfect." At the request from the others to read it out loud, Reid turned it—a square from the Periodic Table of Elements with an 'Ah!' followed by 'the element of surprise' printed in white on the front of the gray material. Turning back to my gifts, I opened the second one of the three I was allowed to open before the final present.

"Aww, King," I cooed, holding up the certificate. "Thank you! I've never been to a spa."

"You got her a ticket to go to the spa?" Reid huffed. "Well, you two just blew my present out of the water." With that, I pulled the big box toward me, tearing open the wrapping paper quickly. The soft sweater and hat I had been eyeing during our Black Friday shopping were tied in a neat stack with a ribbon, a small card with a doodled heart and 'love, Reid' attached to the bow.

"Don't pout, babe, I love your presents," I murmured, getting up to kiss him on the cheek. "I can't believe you got the things I wanted from our shopping trip."

"Of course, Cali girl. You said you weren't getting anything, but I saw how much you wanted them."

"You three are the sweetest. Now, open the rest of your presents before I open my last one," I instructed, kissing Jesse and Kingston on the cheek briefly before I sank back into my seat.

"Em, it's perfect," Jesse whispered, holding up the small set of paints and a pad of paper. After seeing how much he seemed to enjoy our impromptu painting date, I thought it would be perfect. "Thank you."

"Of course, but that's not all, keep going," I prompted excitedly, waiting for them to get to the next present so they could get to my final gift at the bottom of each of their bags. Their eyes lit up when they saw the leather braided bracelets I had made for them, each with their own unique metal charm tied in.

A book for Jesse.

The scales of truth for Kingston.

And a beaker for Reid.

After they slipped on the bracelets, they pulled out their final presents—a mini album with photos from our time together. I wanted them to know they each meant something special to me, despite our unconventional relationship, so half of each book was filled with pictures of all of us, the other half photos of just me and that specific guy, handwritten notes sprinkled between for each of them.

"Are you crying?" I asked, startled seeing Reid wipe his eyes quickly. "Why are you crying?"

"Happy tears, Cali girl. This is amazing," he explained with a smile.

"Perfect present, Babydoll," Kingston agreed, Jesse's hand coming to squeeze my leg as he nodded.

"Open yours," Jesse prompted before Reid could have another wave of happy tears take over. I snatched the small box from the table and carefully pulled the bow off before ripping into the paper.

"This is the sweetest thing ever, you guys," I exclaimed, flipping through the little booklet. They had made me a coupon book, ten coupons for each of them. I saw a back rub on a couple, my choice of a date with no complaints, even two where it was my choice of movie—sappy ones included—from Reid. "I can't wait to use them."

"Now, photo time." I jumped up to grab my camera and set it on the TV stand after setting the timer. My boys corralled onto the couch, Reid's arms open and waiting for me. Chuckling, I darted into the collection of guys. The shutter sounded, and I hopped back up to check the photo. "Perfect."

"Yes, you are," Reid piped in with an impish grin. My cheeks heated, the tingling of three sets of eyes on me quickly flaring over my skin as they moved back to their seats.

They wanted to treat me like a queen.

They're definitely succeeding.

DECEMBER 25TH

Not sure what it'll be like seeing Mom after all the chaos with Dad. Hopefully, the holiday cheer outweighs any of the themes of today's entry
#HereGoesNothing #ITotallyGotThis #WeirdnessWednesday

I was warm, nestled in Kingston's embrace as he curled around me. His arm shifted, leisurely rubbing soft circles over my stomach. I sighed happily as I felt his beard brushing against the back of my neck, his nose buried in my hair.

"Merry Christmas, Babydoll," he murmured, his musical voice making my toes curl and my blood surge as his fingers crept south.

"Merry Christmas, King," I whispered, a tiny gasp accompanying my greeting as his fingers slipped under the hem of my pajama shorts.

"Want another present?" he teased, my face pressing into the pillow to stop the moan wanting to escape. Nodding, I pressed my butt back into his hardening length, my body waking quickly as he kissed my neck.

"We have to be quick, we're supposed to leave in ten minutes," I mumbled, shaking my hips so he would keep going, my panties quickly wetting as he ran a finger over the edge of the lace.

Biting the puff of the pillow, I let go, letting Kingston's fingers slip under the fabric to unhurriedly tease me. A warm chuckle filled my ears as I bucked against his hand, his palm grinding onto the sensitive nub, a finger slipping inside me.

Holy crap, he's got quite the knack for this without any

experience.

I can't wait to see what else he's good at.

He peppered my neck and shoulder with lingering kisses and little nibbles, his pace picking up when he felt me panting. He slowed slightly as I shuddered, but when I reached down and nudging his hand, he continued. My skin was electrified, my blood pounding, my core tightening as he tentatively slipped in another finger. I was on the very edge of release when I reached down, guiding his hand until he was rubbing small circles with a calloused palm on my clit. As soon as he did that, I was lost, spasming in his arms as he made me come.

When I was finally able to think, I turned, his hand slipping out of my shorts and panties in the process. His gaze was hesitant, the skin around his eyes tightening as I shifted, but when I smiled, his tension eased. Leaning forward, I gave him a kiss, my own hand coming between his legs. He groaned, his body shivering as I ran my hand over his erection, my lips quirking up at the guttural sound. Wanting to give him a present too, I took a steeling breath and slipped my hand into his boxers.

It wasn't as though I hadn't given a hand job before, but this was the first time I had for any of my boys, and I couldn't help the surge of nerves that built in the pit of my stomach. Kingston's tensing jaw and soft moans pushed me onward, his hand coming to cup my jaw as our kisses turned more passionate.

"Babydoll," he groaned breathlessly, his hips bucking as I sped up my pace over his hardened length. "I'm so close."

Moving faster, it only took a few more pumps before he spasmed in my hand, his cum spurting onto my palm, his boxers, and skin. We were silent for a few moments, Kingston catching his breath, and my heart rate finally settling. His fingers traced my cheek, tucking my hair behind my ear.

"You didn't have to do that, Babydoll."

"No, but I wanted to give you a present, too," I murmured. "I know you said at my birthday party you hadn't gone farther than a kiss, so I wanted you to know I appreciate you letting me experience that with you first. You're the first I've done that with between you guys."

"Really?" Kingston perked up, his lip curling. I tried to enjoy the happiness in his eyes, but all I could focus on was the quickly cooling cum on my skin.

"Yes, but I'm covered in stuff, and it's sticky, so I'm going to go wash my hand." Kingston's laughter followed me as I rolled out of the warm bedding and stepped quickly to the door. I cracked it open and looked both ways. When I saw no one was in the hall, I darted into the bathroom, quickly rinsing my hand and grabbed a spare towel.

Definitely going to need to do laundry before this week is over if this is going to be a repeated thing with my boys.

I can't wait to see what else this holiday break has in store.

"Ready, Em?" Jesse asked me a few hours later, his fingers brushing against my arm. I took a steadying breath, staring at my mom's car in the Kingston's driveway. Nodding, I hopped out with the boys and started inside.

Have to talk to her at some point.

"Emma, boys! Come on in, how was the cabin?" Stella called out cheerfully. The scent of breakfast permeated the air—bacon, eggs, and pancakes, all swirling with the freshly brewed coffee. I had to stop myself from moaning at the heavenly smell, my stomach grumbling in anticipation for our Christmas brunch.

"Hi, Stella, Mr. Bell," I said, giving her a quick hug, chuckling at Kaleb's "three more times."

"Your mom is in the bathroom. If you want some time alone with her, you can head to the living room," Stella murmured in my ear. I gave her a grateful smile and nodded. "So, how was it? The boys perfect gentlemen?"

"Of course, Stella, when have you ever seen me be anything but?" Reid pushed, waving his hands in mock offense. She rolled her eyes and shook her head before looking at Jesse and Kingston.

"It's good, Mom," King stated, giving his mom a hug before doing the same to his dad. Jesse and Reid quickly followed as Stella made her way around the group. A movement in the corner of my eye caught my attention, pulling my focus from the guys.

"Merry Christmas, Mom," I murmured with a smile, stepping up to her as she walked into the living room.

"Merry Christmas, sweetie," she whispered, holding me tightly. "I'm sorry about everything with your dad."

"Honestly, it makes sense now, why he was so quiet or always busy," I explained, taking in her soft rose perfume.

"I didn't realize everything that was going on. I knew there was someone else," she choked out, squeezing me harder, "but I didn't realize it was like *that*."

We clung to each other, my fractured heart sewing itself further together, the longer we hugged. I understood now why my mom had chosen to move and leave everything behind. Well, I was sure there was more to their divorce, but for now, I was content to leave it as it was. My mom was here, no work distracting her, and I could finally spend more than a few tense moments together with her and my boys.

"Other than that, how was Cali? Run into any of your old friends?" she asked, trying to turn the depressing topic to something cheerful, but all it did was make my frown worse. "I always did like them and Tyler. Maybe one or two of them could come out and visit," she suggested.

Yeah, Mom's ability to "read the room" was never great.

"Uh, we're not really friends anymore," I tried to explain, shrugging. It had been so long since I had talked to her about anything other than menial day-to-day goings on, I wasn't sure how to anymore. "Kara was just trying to get me to drop her name to Tanner," I ground out the name. "Tyler and I broke up before we left Cali. We tried to be friends, but it didn't really work, ya know?" My mom nodded, her hand rubbing my back soothingly, but the doorbell ringing throughout the main floor pulled our focus to the main entryway hall.

"Oh, that should be your parents, Reid," Stella said from the kitchen, her voice carrying through the dining area and over the back of the couch to us in the living room. Figuring our conversation was over, my mom and I started toward the rest of the party. Making her away around the island, Stella glanced at Reid.

"Want to go get them with me?"

"Sure," Reid agreed. Hopping up, he accompanied King's mom into the entryway. The conversation at the front of the house filtered to the kitchen in a jumble as Reid and Stella greeted his parents. Pulling away, I grabbed one of the mugs of hot chocolate Kaleb held out for my mom and me, gave him a soft 'thank you,' and sank onto one of the open barstools.

"Erin, meet Faith and Micha, Reid's parents," Stella introduced. My mom stepped away from me, quickly launching into a conversation with Reid's parents and Stella while Kaleb focused on moving the finished food to the table, decorated to match the holiday theme. Jesse and Kingston assisted him as Reid came by, trying and failing to sneakily steal one of the marshmallows from my drink.

"Alright, brunch is ready to go," Kaleb called out. "Come and get it!"

We converged on the table, my mom to my right, and Kingston to my left. Jesse sat on the other side of Kingston with Reid and his parents across the table. Reid's foot brushed against my ankles, pretending he wasn't playing footsie. Killian came bursting into the room, his hair wet from a shower before he sank into the seat next to Stella near the right-hand end of the table.

"Glad you could join us," Kaleb teased.

"Sorry," Killian apologized with a grimace. "The water was hot, and I didn't want to get out."

"That's alright, you're here now," Stella said with a pat on his hand.

"Do you mind if we say grace?" Faith asked. "It's a family tradition for us."

My brow quirked slightly as I glanced at Reid, who gave an eye roll, unseen by his parents. We never really talked about religion, but I knew none of my boys were regular churchgoers, so finding out his parents were religious was a bit of a shock.

The more you know.

I bowed my head, holding my mom's and Kingston's hands to be courteous to Reid's parent's request, but I struggled to focus as she talked, my stomach growling at every scent that reached my nose. Finally, Faith finished her prayer, and we were able to dig in. The only sound filling the space was the soft sound of holiday music playing through the house speakers, all of us focused on dishing out what we wanted before passing the dish to the left. Kingston, being the sweet gentleman he was, served me, stopping each time I said when. My mom's lips quirked up at the gesture but—thankfully—kept her mouth shut.

Brunch was filled with conversation, mainly from our parents, talking about work or things they'd done that year. The boys, Killian, and I were content to scarf down our food and let them chat away, knowing we'd be opening presents and hanging out after we were done.

"So, Erin, Emma, how are you liking Nebraska?" Faith questioned. "It's certainly no California, I'm sure."

"It definitely isn't, but I find myself enjoying it. Work takes up a lot of my time, though. The firm is expanding, and while we're working on hiring more people for my team, my immediate supervisor and I are taking the brunt of the load," my mom explained. *Ah, so that explains why she's so much busier here than back in Cali.* "We're aiming to have my team finalized by late-January or early February, so hopefully, I can go back to somewhat normal work hours."

"That would be good. Do you enjoy working for the marketing firm?"

"Very much. My supervisor and I work well together, and we're able to smoothly, well as smoothly as any project can go, pull off the events. How about you, sweetie? Are you enjoying it here?" My mom turned to me, and it was the first time since moving, I saw the bright smile on her face, no longer forced or tired.

"Yeah, it's nice. Although driving in snow still isn't something on my list of skills," I stated with a laugh. "I'm not sure I'll ever get used to it."

"We'll help you, Cali girl," Reid exclaimed, his hand waving between Kingston, Jesse, and him. "We've had a lifetime of learning how, so soon enough, you'll be a true Nebraskan. Well, if only we can get you to say pop instead of soda."

"Not happening," I smarted with a smirk, shoveling another bite of hashbrowns into my mouth.

"Not yet," Reid practically yelled. "But it will, just you wait!"

"Reid, hon," Faith murmured, "you're shouting."

"Sorry, Ma," Reid said quietly, his cheeks tinting pink as he flashed her an apologetic smile.

"Everyone finished?" Stella asked, noting we were all slowing down. "If you guys are done, you can head into the living room. Kill, you can pass out the presents."

"Why do I have to?" Killian groaned, getting up and moving toward the living room.

"Because you're the baby," Kingston teased, patting him on the back before plopping onto the couch, which set them into a playful brotherly fight, making me laugh. Standing, I collected my plate and silverware, stacking it with my mom's and Kingston's.

"You go sit," Kaleb shooed me, trying to take the stack of dirty dishes from my hands as I turned to take it to the sink.

"But you cooked," I argued, turning so he couldn't get the dishes. "At least let me put the dirty dishes in the sink."

"You are the sweetest thing," Stella cooed, patting me on the back as I set the plates and silverware gently into the deep basin. "Kingston hit the jackpot with you. You tell him if he tries to break it off with you, he's not allowed." I couldn't hold back a laugh at her playful finger wag and ridiculous statement, shaking my head, at a loss for words.

"I can hear you, Mom!" Kingston hollered from the living room, still wrestling Killian on the floor. "Don't worry, though, I don't foresee that happening."

"Boys," Kaleb called out, his two sons stopping their playful fight. "Presents. Both of you."

"Ugh, fine," Kingston huffed, seeming unconcerned he was roped into helping hand out presents. They made quick work of passing out the pretty wrapped boxes and bags to the group as I made my way to sit on the floor next to the armchair my mom was sitting in.

"Here, Em," Jesse moved, tugging on my sweater sleeve. "There's plenty of room up here, you don't need to sit on the floor."

"It's not a problem, I don't want to take your spot," I countered, but Jesse just gave me a small smile, scooting closer to the arm of the love seat, so there was a space between Kingston and him. Sighing at his persistence, I got up and squished between the two of them, my lip curling at the sweet gesture.

Thankfully, knowing I wasn't ready to tell my mom about us yet, we were close enough, Jesse's leg pressing into mine didn't look unusual to anyone in the room, even though I knew it was his way of showing his affection. Everyone busied themselves, opening their gifts, excited gasps and emphatic thank yous filling the room as people worked their way through their small piles.

I finished up my last gift, smiling as I looked over the few gifts I had received. Since the boys and I had already exchanged presents, there were only three, one from each of our parents. Reid's parents had gotten me a gift card to Sephora and a pre-recorded card of Reid singing Jingle Bells while Stella and Kaleb had gifted me a big gift basket of self-care items. Looking through it, I couldn't wait to dig into it later that night, the whole cute pink tub calling my name. Lastly, was from my mom, an empty album, the front decorated with motivational quotes and a pink heart painted in the middle. It was a struggle to keep my rampant emotions at bay, but I managed.

Somehow.

As the present opening finished, Stella had our parents move back into the kitchen for homemade hot cocoa, mimosas, and mulled wine along with a few boozy desserts Kaleb had pulled from the garage refrigerator. The rest of us were given the go ahead to put a movie on or head to the basement to play games.

"What do you want to watch, Babydoll?" Kingston questioned, flipping through the channels. "Sappy? This is the only time we get sappy, so take it while you can," he teased with a smart-ass grin. I snatched the remote, quickly turning to the Hallmark channel. I had kept up with some of the new holiday movies they'd aired, but I had missed a good chunk, so I was damned if I would miss the ones on Christmas day.

Especially if it was the only time, I could get my boys to watch them with me.

Killian tried to grumble about the girly romance, but after Kingston threw balled up leftover wrapping paper at his head, he quieted. Surprisingly, all four of the boys were engrossed in the movie when I got up to get some hot cocoa a little while later. I kept my chuckle to myself as I stepped into the boisterous kitchen, Reid's mom telling a grand story about one of their flights for work, Micha content to stand silently next to his wife. Stella, Kaleb, and my mom's eyes were glued to Faith during her story, so they didn't see me come and go.

I happily settled between my boys, loving the homey

feel of the holiday, knowing in a few hours, we would be heading back to the cabin to bake cookies and decorate gingerbread houses. *Merry Christmas to me.* Smiling, I tuned back into the movie.

Couldn't have asked for a better day, even if I tried.

Chapter 13

I can't believe it's already the end of the year," Jesse stated, looking at the TV where the ball was hanging out at the top of the building for the countdown. "Where does the time go?"

"I can think of one reason time has passed so quickly," I started with a grin. "There are these three boys who hog all my attention. They're sweet and funny, and I can't get enough."

"Aww, look at Cali girl, getting all sappy," Reid teased leaning over the back of the couch and giving me a brief kiss. "Though I can't say I disagree. I wouldn't have it any other way. Now, who wants something to drink?"

"Beer for me, please," Kingston asked.

"Oh, we have alcohol? I mean, other than the Baileys," I perked up. "What all do we have?"

"Beer, champagne, and some girly drinks," Jesse called out, having gone into the kitchen as Reid was asking.

"Girly drink for me, please," I smirked, knowing more than likely I was why they had those drinks in the first place. "How'd you guys get the alcohol?"

"Always stocked here cause my parents come out pretty frequently when my dad has a free weekend. Rules are we're supposed to keep it to one or two drinks and absolutely no driving," Kingston explained.

"I can do that, especially seeing how I don't have a car here, and I just want a small glass of champagne in a bit when the ball drops." Jesse handed over the glass bottle, the bright pink liquid a stark contrast to the dark brown bottles of the guys' drinks.

"Anyone have any New Year's resolutions?" Kingston asked after taking a drink, everyone getting quickly settled back into their own spots.

"Graduate with honors, preferably top of the class," Jesse smiled, slouching in his seat. "Nothing like showing all our classmates who talk shit, I'm not who they say I am."

"Ms. Rogers said you were the valedictorian, at least when she recommended you for tutoring," I told him, his smile widening as his eyes glowed.

"Really?" he perked up. "I've been trying not to pester her about my standing, just focusing on grades until we get a bit closer."

"Yeah, she was very proud of you," I told him. "As for mine, I don't think I have that many, maybe just work on what I talked about after getting back from Cali—not letting people or things make me feel like what I want or deserve is secondary. I'm my own person, and just because I'm eighteen doesn't mean I want or need any less," I shrugged, trailing off when the boys were all staring. "What?"

"Even in the last four months we've seen you change, Cali girl," Reid murmured with a soft smile. "You're still you, but you're really growing into that 'take no shit' attitude we all knew you had in you."

"Is that a good thing?" I asked softly, my lip tucking between my teeth. As soon as my question was out, all three of them beamed at me, nodding fervently.

"Of course, it is. We want you to have the confidence in yourself, we all see inside you," Reid murmured, pulling my feet onto his lap and rubbing the balls of my feet in sweeping circles. "Mine is really to just enjoy life. Not let shit keep me down," he told us. "You know how I thrive on being the weirdo of the group, so the more laughs I get, the better I feel."

"Get into a good pre-law program," Kingston added, "and enjoy the rest of senior year with my best friends."

"Aww," Reid cooed, his hand pressing against his chest. "That's so sweet." Kingston laughed, rolling his eyes, then taking another pull from his beer.

"Oooh!" I exclaimed, "less than three minutes!" Reid and Kingston hopped up, going into the kitchen to open the champagne, leaving Jesse and me alone. Standing up, I shuffled over to Jesse in the armchair, sitting on his lap, and wrapped my arms around his shoulders.

"How's your winter break so far, Jess?"

"I couldn't ask for anything better than time with my best friends and my girlfriend," he murmured softly, his free hand tracing a figure eight on my thigh. "How about you, Em? Is the holiday what you were hoping for?"

"Better than I could have imagined," I whispered, leaning in for a kiss.

"Aww," Kingston cooed as Reid shouted, 'Say cheese.' The sound of a camera going off filled the space before we pulled apart. I threw a half-hearted glare at the two troublemakers but couldn't stop the curl of my lips at their broad smiles.

"Come on, Em, hop up." Jesse tapped my thigh, so I shifted and made my way over to where Reid and Kingston were standing with glasses full of golden bubbly alcohol.

"Goodbye, 2019," Reid toasted, holding up his glass as the last ten seconds counted down on TV. "Hello, New Year. Full of happiness and possibilities." As soon as the ball dropped and the countdown ended, we clinked glasses and took a sip. Right as I finished mine, Reid stepped forward, his sparkling hazel eyes centered on my face as he wrapped me in his arms. "Happy New Year, Cali girl."

"Happy New Year, babe," I whispered, smiling as he leaned down to press a soft kiss to my lips. The sweet, toe-curling kiss was over too soon, Reid moving out of the way to let Kingston step up next.

"I couldn't ask for anyone better to spend tonight with," Kingston murmured, his thumbs rubbing my lower back. His whiskers tickled my cheeks as he kissed me, his lips lingering on mine as I felt Jesse's warm fingers brush across my arm. Kingston didn't need a nudge, pulling away with a wink.

"Em," Jesse whispered, "you are absolutely the most amazing girl I have ever met, and I can't wait to see what this year has in store for us." I felt my heart skip a beat as he kissed me, his hands cupping my face gently.

"Photo time!" Reid hollered, corralling all of us into the frame. My cheeks were tinted pink, my smile bright as I stood, surrounded by my boys.

We spent the next couple hours playing board games and bingeing on soda and treats, like puppy chow and homemade dip, until Kingston and Jesse turned in, tired from the long day of playing in the snow.

"Come on, Cali girl," Reid took ahold of my hand, "let's go lie down."

"Tired already?" I asked, feeling good after the delicious food and all the laughter.

"Nah, I just want some alone time with you," he murmured, his lip curling up slightly as he glanced over his shoulder at me.

My body erupted in a flare of fire, very aware of his hand clutching mine. The way the rooms were set up in the cabin meant Reid and I were in two rooms on the opposite side of the house from the other two. My heart beat loudly in my ears, thinking about everything possible as Reid closed the door.

"Cali girl, please don't look so scared."

"I'm not," I whispered, wrapping my arms around his shoulders. "Nervous and excited? Yes. Scared? No."

"Excited, huh?" Reid's heated whisper filled my ears as he moved into my embrace. "About what? Maybe I just wanted to cuddle."

"Alright, then." I shrugged playfully, stepping back, but his arms tightened around my waist, stopping me.

"Kidding," he whispered, "well, I do want that, but after."

"After?" I asked, my blood roaring through my ears, my lower belly tingly as my core surged.

"Figured we don't get much alone time, thought maybe we could, I don't know, have some fun. If you're up for it? We don't have to do anything you're not comfortable with, Cali girl."

Instead of responding, I smiled, pressing my lips to his, reveling in the feeling of his five o'clock shadow skimming my cheeks. His curls were soft against the tips of my fingers as I ran them up the back of his neck, tangling them into the soft tresses as his tongue darted out. As he brushed across the seam of my lips, I felt him hardening against my hip and stomach. Opening, he swept in, tasting every piece of me, his hands slipping under my shirt until I felt his calloused fingers running over my goosebump-covered skin.

Overwhelming sensations pressed down on me—want, need, nerves, excitement, and anticipation—all rotating until I couldn't tell which way was up or down; there was just Reid. My cute clown whose fingers worked their way up to the cup of my bra as our tongues tangled together. Nudging me to the left, Reid led me to the edge of the bed, lowering me until I was nestled against the soft quilt that covered the mattress. Reid kept himself propped above me on one arm, the other still roving under my shirt until finally, he shifted it up and over my head.

My breath hitched when his half-lidded gaze fell on my torso, a sinful glint lighting the hazel depths as he kissed me once more. This time, our moves weren't leisurely, our hands wandering over each other's bodies, and when he cupped one of my boobs, I couldn't stop the whimper that escaped. I was on fire, completely and utterly burning from the inside out. We hadn't even gone very far... but at that moment?

I wanted more.

So much more.

With that in mind, I grabbed the end of his shirt and pulled it up, exposing his olive skin that dipped and shifted as he yanked it the rest of the way over his head. When he folded back over me, his skin was hot, his kisses peppering across my jaw and neck.

"Emma, if you want to stop or if I do something you don't want, just tell me, okay?" he murmured against my skin.

"I will, but I don't want to stop," I whispered, my heart jumping into my throat in excitement at Reid's smile.

"Oh, so this doesn't bother you?" he asked softly, rocking his hips forward. The pressure of his erection rubbing against my core through our jeans had me gasping, my eyes rolling back as a bolt of lightning shot through me.

"More," I moaned, my voice cracking under the onslaught of need flooding my system, "I want more."

"Your wish is my command, milady," he whispered. Nipping my collarbone, his hands quickly unhooked my bra. Calloused palms ran over my chest, my nipples pebbling against his skin. I pulled off the straps, tossing the bra to the side as Reid sucked one of the peaks into his mouth. I couldn't stop the groan that worked its way out of me, my hips bucking up as he nibbled the sensitive skin.

Holy crap. I moaned, his kisses and licks moving down my stomach until he reached my jeans. He unbuttoned and unzipped the denim, making quick work of the tight material, pulling them down my legs to toss over his shoulder. A wave of nerves washed over me when I was in nothing but my skimpy panties.

"What's wrong?" Reid picked up on my change in demeanor, his brows drawing down as he looked at me from between my legs, his hands coming to rest on the bed on either side of my hips. "Want to stop?"

"No, it's not that." I shook my head, my arm coming to cross over my stomach in an unconscious move to cover myself. "I just... I don't know. No one has seen me like this, and I'm..."

"Self-conscious?" I nodded slightly, happy he understood what I was trying to explain. "Emma Brooke, my sweet Cali girl, you are beautiful. I know I can't show you what I see, but you don't need to worry. If you want, we can stop for now until you feel more comfortable being naked in front of me."

"No, babe, I don't want to stop. I just... wanted to warn you if I'm weird, that's probably why," I explained, feeling the signature burn of a blush as he chuckled.

"I'm honored you'd be willing to show me first. I know I can be a bit much for a lot of people—"

"Reid, you're perfect, silliness and all," I reassured him, cutting off his statement. I took a deep breath, barely able to ask what was swirling around in my mind. "Would you... would you be willing to be my first?"

"Like, for sex?" he asked, his lip curling as his brow raised.

I nodded, feeling silly having to ask, but I didn't want to just assume that was where we were going, and I didn't want him to think I didn't want this each time I froze.

"Right now?" Another nod.

"If that's what you want," I muttered, realizing I might have been getting ahead of myself. Reid's smile brightened, and he nodded.

"I would love to be your first, Cali girl, but I want it to be special for you," he whispered before standing up and grabbing his phone, plugging it into the small speaker.

"It wasn't already special?" I teased, my heart warming as a soft but seductive song started to play, quickly realizing it was *My Eyes* by Blake Shelton and Gwen Sebastian. "Why are you so cute?"

"Only the best for milady" He gave a slight bow before smirking at me, coming to nestle between my legs. "I brought condoms, you know, just in case."

"Good." Feeling a boost of confidence, I pulled him down on top of me. Our lips and tongues battled as his fingers slipped under my panties. This time, I didn't feel nervous energy, only the heat and searing desire of how sexy he made me feel, filling me.

"Oh God," I moaned as he thrust two fingers into me, my entrance so wet, there was no resistance, my eyes rolling back as stars flared in front of my eyes. "Reid..."

"I could definitely get used to hearing you moan my name," he murmured between kisses that quickly moved down my chest and stomach. Withdrawing his hand, he pulled my panties down, tossing them over his shoulder to join my discarded jeans and sweater. Feeling his breath against the crest of my thighs, my breath hitched. One thing I hadn't told him was, I had never felt comfortable letting Tyler eat me out, so not only would Reid be my first for sex, but this as well.

And boy, was it worth the wait.

I groaned, my back arching as he placed the softest kiss to my slick skin. The briefest contact from his warm lips and I was already ready to explode, so when his tongue shot out, I couldn't stop the cry that erupted. Reid's arms wrapped around my legs, holding my hips in place so he could eat me out, the stubble on his cheek a sharp contrast to the wet circles of his tongue.

"I'm going..." I couldn't even finish my statement as I shuddered, coming hard, another wave of stars bursting in front of my eyes, my breaths coming out in pants. "Holy shit." My body continued to convulse, the searing heat flowing freely through me as I came down from my high.

"Oh, the cussing is coming out," Reid murmured a few moments later with a sinful smirk. "I'll take it I'm living up to expectations then."

"Past expectations," I whispered, my words barely audible as I still struggled to catch my breath. "Babe, you've already blown my mind." Taking a deep breath as my body finally started to calm, I glanced at him with a small curl to my lips. "You were my first for that, too, you know."

"Yeah?" he asked with a grin. "Good." Without further banter, he kissed me hard, his lips slick with my release. It was an odd sensation, feeling my cum on his mouth and tongue, the slight tang subtle, a hint of salty sweetness mixing in. Reid rocked his hips against me, only the thin material of his underwear between us, silencing my thoughts before I could get carried away. With that thought, anticipation made my stomach flip and my skin tingle.

Feeling a surge of confidence, I reached between us, my hand slipping its way between the fabric of his boxers to his hot skin. His hardened length was silky in my hand as I wrapped it around the base of his shaft. A soft groan rumbled through Reid's chest, the sound only serving to turn me on more. Tangling my other hand in his hair, I stroked him, loving the small buck his hips gave each time. Reid kissed the side of my neck, nibbling on my ear lobe before finally pulling back to sit on his knees.

"You're sure, Cali girl?" he asked, his thumbs hooked into the elastic of his underwear, hesitating to pull them off until I gave him a yes. As soon as my lips turned up and my head nodded, he slipped off the fabric, reaching into the side pocket of his duffle to grab the foil wrapper. Ripping it open with his teeth, he pulled the rubber circle out, sliding it down his erection, and nestled back between my thighs.

My heartbeat was galloping, my blood pounding, and I knew if I looked in the mirror, my cheeks would be bright pink, not only from seeing Reid in all of his glory but for what we were about to do. Nerves wracked my body, but I knew this was what I wanted. Some may say too soon, too young, too whatever, but right now, it was about my cute clown who wanted to treat me like a queen and *my choice*. The disregarding, bossy nature Tyler had treated me with melted away until Reid's half-lidded hazel gaze and sexy grin was all I saw.

Pressing forward, he nudged against my slick entrance, moving slowly and carefully, not pushing in too fast or too hard. There was no pain—at least not the kind they tell you about in sex-ed when the hymen breaks—just the slight burn of being stretched. I couldn't stop the breathy moan that came tumbling out as Reid rocked in and out.

When he was fully seated, I was burning from the inside out, my eyes rolling back as he pulled back smoothly before thrusting until our hips met. *Oh, fuck*. Moaning, I ran my nails up Reid's back and shoulders to tangle in his curls. The scratching made his pace falter, slamming home a moment later as he groaned. Gasping as he picked up his pace, I couldn't seem to catch my breath. Every rock, thrust, and movement took my breath away as my release neared. Finally, when it felt like I couldn't handle it any longer, the tingles that radiated throughout my body released, and I clamped around him in a wave of blissful pleasure.

"Reid," I whispered, his name barely audible as I came apart under him. He didn't speak, capturing my lips in a fierce kiss as his pace moved harder and faster, bringing me quickly up to another orgasm before I even had time to come down. There was no intense build up this time, no tingles or goosebumps, but the vision-darkening release felt just as amazing and had me clawing his back and the sheets. His body shook, and I felt him twitch inside me, his pace quickly slowing.

We were quiet, the soft music of "You Make It Easy"

by Jason Aldean and our panting the only sounds filling the room. When it seemed Reid got his breathing under control, he slipped out and smiled down at me, his thumbs brushing my temples.

"Thank you," he murmured, making my slow-to-thought brain confused. He chuckled at my furrowed brows and explained, "For giving me that. Letting me be your first."

"Thank you for making it special for me," I whispered, tracing the lightest of circles on his shoulder blades. "But now, I am actually tired." Both laughing, Reid got up to grab a towel from over the side of the hamper, making quick work of cleaning me before pulling off the condom. Only then did it occur to me that I'd had sex, without even considering Jesse or Kingston.

"What's wrong?" Reid picked up on my mood shift as he looked over me.

"What about King and Jesse?" I murmured, my body flooding with worry, but Reid shook his head and came to kneel in front of me.

"Emma, this was about what you wanted. They will understand, I promise," he reassured me. "We actually talked about this a while ago, just to see where we were with each other in the relationship, and we all agreed it was up to you." I couldn't drum up any anger at them talking about something like that when all I felt was a flood of relief. "You alright, Cali girl?"

"Yeah," I whispered, my body warming under his gaze as it dipped down to my still naked body. "Thank you for reassuring me." Leaning forward, I pecked him on the cheek.

"Cuddle time now, right?" he asked as he pulled back, tossing on his boxers and crawling into bed, forgoing a shirt as he held up the blankets for me. Chuckling, I pulled on my panties and shirt before crawling into his open arms, nestling against his chest.

Happy New Year's indeed.

Chapter 14

I 'll talk to you guys later," I hollered, hopping out of the Jeep and shouldering the bag Reid had gotten out to grab from the back. "Thanks, babe, I'll text you."

"Not if I text you first," he prodded with a cocksure grin. Chuckling, I rolled my eyes and headed inside. My stress levels had finally subsided after spending a week with my boys. Just watching television, movies, and eating home-cooked meals had done wonders for my mood, so I found myself practically skipping inside.

At least until I found my mom in the kitchen, standing with her arms crossed, a scowl curling her lip.

So much for that jolly attitude.

"Emma Brooke Clark," she snapped, "care to explain why you've been subpoenaed to testify in a criminal court case against Jesse?" My blood turned to ice as she held up the official paperwork calling me to testify on Jesse's behalf.

"Mom," I started, but she cut her hand through the air and shook her head.

"I don't want to hear any excuses. I want to know why

you thought it would be alright to not include me in on the fact *one* of your *three* boyfriends is being charged with assault. Yes, Emma, I know about the four of you. Stella explained it to me when I had questions about this criminal case. Why you would think it's okay to have three boyfriends?"

"Why does it matter if I have one or three as long as we're not hurting anyone?" I countered in exasperation. "As for testifying for Jesse, he beat up a kid who was trying to force himself on me at a party. So, I think it's pretty safe to say, I have no issues with what Jesse did."

"So, why didn't you tell me about it, then? Parties, sleeping around, dealing with the law," she rattled off, shaking her head. I expected each word to hurt, to cut into my already aching heart, but all it served to do was piss me off. "Now, I'm going to have to be more of a babysitter than a mother because you can't be trusted."

"Are you freaking kidding me right now?" I shouted, finally having enough. Everything that had been building over the last four months since our move raced out of my mouth at the insinuation she had to babysit me. "When the heck would I have a chance to tell you anything? In the few brief moments, I actually get to see you?"

"You know I've been working hard to support both of us," she tried to argue, but I laughed, appalled she would even try to go there.

Is she really that oblivious to the fact I've had to pay bills and buy food for us?

"You've been working, but you haven't been supporting us! I've had to buy food and groceries several times. Our electricity and utilities were turned off while you were away in the middle of freaking nowhere, followed quickly by our phones! Those three guys you seem to have such a problem with me seeing are the only reason we have heat and working phones, seeing how you're too caught up in whatever is so damned important at work. You can't babysit me when you've barely had time to be my mom!" By the time I was done, my cheeks were wet with tears I didn't even know were falling. Taking a shuddering breath, I turned on my heels and ran downstairs. I slammed the door behind me, quickly unpacking my backpack and duffel from my trips before shoving clean clothes and school items into my backpack.

"Where do you think you're going?" my mom demanded as I shouldered my bags. Her brow arched in silent challenge, the one that always had me biting my tongue and keeping whatever it was I was about to say or do to myself.

Not this time.

First, my boyfriend cheats on me.

My parents get divorced and forget I exist.

Then, I deal with the party from hell and all of Brad's shit.

Now, I am done being forgotten, mistreated, or talked down to.

"I'm going to Kingston's," I explained, walking around her and to the garage. "When I've calmed down, maybe I'll be home.

"You can't go without my permission, Emma Brooke, I am your mother," she snapped. I kept walking, throwing my bag into the back of my car as she followed me out.

"You stopped being able to tell me what to do when you left me to be the adult of the two of us," I deadpanned, staring right at her. "I think you forget I'm my own person and can make my own choices, choices you don't get to dictate." I got into my car and pulled away, leaving my mom gaping, standing in the garage.

Twenty minutes later, I pulled into Kingston's drive, my anger finally settling and leaving sickening nausea in the pit of my stomach. Getting out, I found Kingston standing on the porch, looking at me with a soft smile. I grimaced and walked up to him, realizing I had come over without much of a warning.

"Hey, Babydoll, you okay?" Kingston asked quietly, pulling me into a hug.

"How'd you know?" I mumbled against his shoulder, inhaling his orange and cinnamon scent.

"Your mom called my mom, something about wanting you to come home. I only got the basic gist of what happened," he explained.

"Does your mom want me to go home?" I asked, worried I had upset Stella and Kaleb by overstepping on my welcome.

"You can stay as long as you need, Emma darling. I remember what it was like to go through issues with my mom," Stella's voice filtered around Kingston's lean torso, making me breathe easier. "Come inside for goodness sakes, you two. You're going to have frostbite on your nose before you can say, 'Go Big Red.'"

Chuckling, I followed her inside, the heat of their house flowing over me as the scent of cookies permeated the air. Did Stella ever *not* have some kind of baked goods in the oven or on the counter?

Not that I'm complaining.

"Hello, Emma," Kaleb called out.

"Hi, Mr. Bell," I hollered back, following Kingston up the stairs.

"Two more times!" Kaleb shouted, my lips curling up at the fact he was keeping track.

"Keep the door cracked, you two!"

"Okay, Mom!" Kingston responded, his melodic voice making me curl my toes as the smooth notes filled my ears. "Come on, Babydoll, we can watch TV up here. I have to get my bag ready for tomorrow, anyway."

I placed my bag on the floor near the door, kicking off my shoes and flopping onto the futon. Kingston busied himself, digging through his notebooks, making sure he had everything for our first day back to school, before glancing over at me.

"You want to talk about it?" he asked softly.

"Not really," I grumbled, the residual anger simmering in the back of my mind as I sat there. "My mom knows about all of us, and that I have to testify at Jesse's trial."

"How'd she find that out? I thought the police weren't contacting your parents because you're over the legal age?"

"Subpoena came in the mail, so she called your mom and found out that way. Tried to say she has to babysit me now because I 'can't be trusted,'" I ground out, anger resurfacing.

"I'm sorry, Babydoll. At least we had fun over the break," he stated with a knowing smile.

My heart leapt into my throat as I realized what he was talking about, worrying he and Jesse may be upset I slept with Reid.

"Emma, it's okay, breathe," he reassured me, coming to crouch in front of me.

"So, you know?" I barely got the question out, the words sounding squeaky to my own ears.

"Reid told us, but Babydoll, we had already talked about it. After you agreed to date us, we didn't want something like that to cause any issues with all of us, so we chatted. Came to the agreement that whoever went first wouldn't affect the others. To be honest, I was worried you'd pick me to be first," he murmured.

I couldn't find myself to be mad at them, despite it being a major discussion to have without me, but right now, all I could find was relief they had handled it.

Lord knows, I have way too much to worry about already.

"Why's that?" I asked, my brows drawing down at his last statement.

"I haven't done that before, and I didn't want your first time to be awkward fumbling as we both tried to figure it out," he explained with a chuckle. "I wanted it to be special for you."

"You're seriously one of the sweetest guys I've ever met, King," I murmured, leaning forward and pressing a soft kiss to his lips. "Thank you for telling me." Smiling, his eyes brightened.

"Of course, Babydoll—" His phone ringing cut off the rest of his statement, his brows furrowing as he answered it. "Hey, Reid..." he trailed off at whatever Reid was telling him, his eyes darting to me briefly. "Alright, I'll be down shortly." Kingston hung up quickly, jumping up from his crouched position and starting toward the door before turning back to me. "I need you to stay here," he murmured, "just for a bit."

"What's going on?" I asked, getting up.

"You'll find out in just a bit, okay? Trust me, please," he nearly pleaded. Grinding my teeth, I nodded, watching him sigh with relief before nearly sprinting down the stairs.

I waited, walking back and forth as I heard Stella and Kaleb greet Reid, asking if Jesse was with him. My stomach tightened as I heard a few pained groans. My worried pacing stopped as I saw Kingston open the door, Reid and Jesse behind him, gasping when I saw Jesse.

Beaten and bloodied, he hung onto Reid as he limped into the room. As soon as Jesse and Reid's eyes fell on me, the tension climbed to new heights, all of us standing in a silent staredown.

"What the heck happened?" I whispered, finally coming out of my stupor. "Jeez, Jesse, you need to be taken to the hospital."

"No, no hospital," Jesse bit out, limping the rest of the way to the futon with Reid's help. I stared at him, my mouth open. He did *not* just say that.

"Why the heck not? You're bleeding again, and you're clearly injured." I sighed, my face falling into my palms in a muffled scream. "Okay, fine. We're going to get you cleaned up, then I want answers."

"Here, I'll help grab the supplies," Reid offered, glancing at Kingston to make sure he was good with that. When Kingston sank next to Jesse, helping get his shirt up over his head, Reid got up and directed me into the bathroom. He didn't talk as he pulled the first aid supplies from the back of the linen closet, but after a few moments of me staring at the side of his face with crossed arms, he finally looked at me.

"I'm sorry, Cali girl. Jesse didn't want us to tell you," he whispered, his hazel eyes wide with worry. "Are you upset with us?"

"Reid," I huffed quietly, waving my hand toward the door. "Jesse is hurt, for the goodness knows what number time since I've moved here. I don't really care right now you didn't tell me, but why the hell didn't you tell Kingston's parents, or your parents, or even a teacher?"

"Because it's not that simple," he started, but I shook my head.

"Don't, Reid, please. It kills me to see any of you hurt,

so all I want to do right now is get Jesse cleaned up and figure out whatever the hell is going on," I grumbled, taking some of the supplies. Reid smiled slightly, looking at me with a little mischievous glint in his eyes. "What?"

"You only cuss when you're pissed off or... It's adorable," he explained, holding the bedroom door open. I gave him a half-hearted glare, knowing he was purposely trying to distract me, but I didn't have it in me to counter him.

"Holy shit," I breathed, my already puffy eyes stinging from the buildup of tears, when I saw a cluster of long welts and cuts on his chest, back, and arm. I sank to my knees, working as quickly as I could, ignoring Jesse's eyes on my face. He hissed when I placed the antiseptic pad against his cuts but didn't pull away thanks to Kingston and Reid holding him in place. "Sorry," I muttered, feeling terrible I was making the pain worse.

Ten minutes later, his chest was cleaned and bandaged. His face was bruised, but surprisingly, nothing had bled except his lip. Reid hopped up, taking the bin of first aid materials back to the bathroom and tossing the trash into a grocery sack on his way. Sitting back on my heels, my hands shook as the adrenaline from today's events faded. As soon as Reid was back in the room, I looked to Jesse with a raised brow and waited. Jesse, of course, was looking anywhere but my face, his jaw clenched as he ignored my attempt to get him to talk.

"Jesse, please." I reached out, taking his uninjured hand and interlacing our fingers. Rubbing his thumb across the back of my hand, he sighed, deflating.

"My dad has anger issues," he muttered, barely loud enough for me to hear him. "Normally, I can stay out of the house long enough, that by the time I get back, he's passed out drunk. It's usually after my mom is doped up on her opiates or whatever drug she can get her hands on. When the alcohol is flowing, and she's laid out in a drug-induced haze, that's when I have to be careful."

My throat burned, the urge to throw up building, the longer he talked. I knew whatever Jesse was going through was bad, but hearing him explain it as if that was just how life was, and there was nothing he could do about it was heart wrenching.

"So, when I found you back in October..." I trailed off, unsure of how to ask what was on my mind. Jesse nodded as he shifted forward with a pained grunt, his free hand wiping away the tears that leaked out despite trying to keep them contained.

"Yeah, he had started drinking super early that morning and got me before I had a chance to sneak out. Pretty sure he smashed my phone in the process, but it was in the living room, and I wasn't going to risk grabbing it before hopping out of the window."

"How many times has it happened since I've been here?" I choked out, glancing between the three of them. "How many times, Jesse?" I bit out when they didn't answer me.

"I don't know, like nine, ten times?" he muttered, shrugging. "Em, please..."

I sobbed, my shoulders shaking as I buried my face in my free hand. My heart shattered, knowing this had been happening, but I hadn't pushed, I hadn't demanded to know. I hadn't helped.

What kind of girlfriend am I?

"Em," Jesse's voice cracked, his hand cupping my jaw, nudging until he could press his lips to my forehead. "I'm sorry I didn't tell you, I just... it's just how my life is, and I was afraid if you knew you'd, I don't know, leave, and I couldn't risk you being in danger. My dad isn't a good guy, and the guys know that first hand."

"Why couldn't you let me make that choice?" I whispered between my crying. "I wouldn't have left then, and I'm not leaving now. I want you safe."

"I'm staying as safe as I can, Em," Jesse tried, but I shook my head.

"No, you're not. Tell Kingston's parents, stay somewhere safe. Permanently," I challenged. I may not have pushed earlier when I should have, but like hell was I going to let him walk back into that house now that I knew.

"I can't," Jesse countered.

"He's only seventeen, and even if he was old enough to move out without legal repercussions, the legal age of majority in Nebraska is nineteen," Kingston explained softly.

"Meaning he can't sign a contract or anything for an apartment," Reid continued. I glanced between them, my brain whirling with anything I could do to convince Jesse to tell someone.

"Emancipation," I murmured, "get emancipated. I knew a couple of people at my old school who did it. With your dad's help," I looked to Kingston as I talked, "I don't see why it would be an issue."

"Where would I live, Em?" Jesse sighed. It was at that moment I saw Reid and Kingston smirk, glancing at each other.

"Here," Kingston offered, "like we've told you before."

"Not again, guys," Jesse huffed in exasperation before he finally looked at me again. The skin around his eyes tightened when he saw my face. *Nothing like being red and puffy in front of your three boyfriends. Again.* As soon as I poked out my bottom lip ever so slightly, Jesse groaned in defeat. "I don't"—he cleared his throat—"I don't know if I could tell your parents."

"Why, dude?" Kingston asked softly. "You know they'll do anything to keep you from having to deal with that."

"Because I've known them since I was little. How do you think they'll react to learning this was going on, but I didn't tell them?"

We sat in silence, contemplating what Jesse said, but finally, after I saw the doubt starting to creep back onto their faces, I shook my head.

"Nope, I don't care how they react, Jesse. You're going to tell them, or I will," I demanded. His eyes locked with mine, curiosity and fear brimming in the near black depths, but I saw something else—the smallest hint of hope. "Please," I whispered. Jesse deflated, nodding his agreement.

"Come on, either we do this now, or it'll never happen," Jesse stated, struggling to get off the couch. Reid jumped up, assisting him to stand. We filed down the stairs, Jesse pausing with a gulp right outside the kitchen where I could hear Stella and Kaleb bustling around. Grabbing his hand, I squeezed, giving one last boost of confidence. It was enough for him to take the last few steps into the room.

"Mr. and Mrs. Bell?" he murmured. "Can I talk to you guys?"

"Of course," Stella said, then gasped when she saw the bandages across his torso.

I stayed out of sight while Jesse talked to them with Reid and Kingston. After a few minutes, I finally reached a breaking point, unable to just stand and listen, so I turned and tried to make my way back to Kingston's room. Before I could get more than two steps, Stella came around the corner and wrapped me in a tight hug.

"Thank you," she whispered, her thin frame shaking as she inhaled, "for convincing him to tell us."

"I just want him safe," I murmured, my own tears starting to leak out again.

I'm so freaking tired of crying.

You'd think I would have run out of tears at this point.

She squeezed one last time before stepping back, explaining what would happen next.

"You, Kingston, and Reid go try to enjoy your night. Kaleb and I will get everything from Jesse. When we have all the information we need, we'll send him back up. He'll be staying here from now on."

"Thank you." I tried to smile, but it was brittle as I looked at her. Patting my shoulder, she returned a fragile smile and left as Kingston and Reid came around the corner.

"Come on, Cali girl," Reid whispered, curling me under his arm. "Thank you."

"For what?" I asked, confused why he was thanking me. I didn't do anything.

"Finally convincing him. We've tried for years, and no matter what, nothing we said or did worked. Then you waltz your pretty face in and give a little pout and boom, convinced. Why couldn't we have gotten you before this year?" Reid explained, laughing with Kingston. Underneath the cheer, they sounded emotional, strangled under the gravity of what was about to change.

"At least you have me now," I countered. "Now, Jesse can be safe, and I can go to sleep without having to worry. Right now, I feel like I'm about to collapse."

They didn't say anything, focusing on putting something lighthearted on the TV in Kingston's room as I got changed and ready for bed. I knew I should have gone home and tried to level-headedly talk to my mom, but after everything since leaving the house, I couldn't bring myself to care. Curled in a fuzzy blanket on the bed, sandwiched between Kingston and Reid, I drifted to sleep, where not even the emotional toll of the last twenty-four hours could reach me.

CHAPTER 15

"S lut."

"Not wanted by her family."

"They're both living with Kingston."

The gossip about Jesse and me wouldn't stop, swirling around us as we walked the halls and cafeteria. My lips were permanently downturned in a harsh scowl as the darkened cloud descended on me, the weight on my shoulders only growing with each whispered rumor.

"Well, if it isn't the slut!" Dylan called out, stepping in front of me with a cruel smirk on his reddened face. I glared, not even bothering to counter his remark.

"Now, now, Dylan," a familiar voice responded, my blood turning to ice as the one person I wanted to punch most stepped in front of me. "My girl isn't a slut, she's a virgin who's playing hard to get."

Freaking Brad.

Yup, still rocking the stupid boat shoes and buttoned-up polo.

I tried to step around him, but he quickly blocked me,

Dylan following until they were shoulder-to-shoulder in front of me.

"Virgin, huh? Sounds like she'll be one of the best, then," Dylan sneered, winking at me. I shuddered, barely keeping it contained at his creepy smile.

"Move," I bit out. The warning bell rang overhead, but it didn't deter the crowd from watching what was happening. Of course, no one stepped up to help, everyone content to watch and laugh.

"Why should we?" Brad challenged. Steeling myself, I curved around him, shouldering into him as hard as I could. He grunted but made no other move to stop me, only calling out as I stormed away, "Aww, she's got some backbone in her after all."

"Freaking douche," I hissed under my breath as I stormed into the locker room, cursing that Jesse had to stay late to talk to our chemistry teacher and couldn't walk with me.

"Hey," a girl called out as I shoved my bag into my locker. "You're the one dating Jesse Parker, right?" I sighed, tired and irritable, but I nodded, hoping she didn't have anything stupid to say. "Is it true he's got trial coming up, you know, for attempted murder?"

"Not really your business," I snapped. "But it's for assault against Brad Warland." I tried to counter the rumor, not even caring how it got so out of control.

"Brad? Why'd he do that?" she questioned, her face scrunched. Her skin held an overly orange tan, she had stick straight strawberry blonde hair, and she was wearing a short skirt and skintight top despite it being winter.

No idea how she doesn't freeze in that.

"Everyone likes Brad."

"Ha," I deadpanned, utterly over the day at that point.

"Not *everyone* likes Brad, especially me, seeing as how he tried to force himself on me at a party. Jesse saved me. So maybe next time you want to gossip, you can get the facts correct."

"Brad wouldn't do that," she tried to counter, but I waved my hand through the air, cutting her off.

"Save it, I don't want to freaking hear it. You can believe whatever the heck you want, but I know what happened, and I'm the one with nightmares every night about his unwanted wandering hands and creepy smile," I snapped before turning to leave the locker room, the girl's wide eyes and slack jaw seared in my brain as I headed into dance class.

If people wanted to know about what happened, I'd gladly tell them. Then maybe they'd shut up about it.

Sometimes, high school really sucked.

My sucky luck continued after school, finding my mom's car parked in the driveway when I pulled up. Groaning, I dropped my head against the steering wheel.

"Well, might as well just get this over with. Grounding here I come," I ground out, climbing out of my car.

Yup, called it. I stewed in my anger as I made my way to my room thirty minutes later. Grounded for two weeks except for work.

The part that angered me the most was I wasn't allowed to see the boys except at school. I wasn't sure if that carried over after my grounding or not, but for right now, I wasn't going to push it since she let me keep my phone for work purposes. I had gotten a couple weeks off from work, but now that I was back, I had shifts on my schedule. If there were any shift changes or emergency shifts to fill, they had to be able to reach me, which my mom seemed to get after about twenty minutes of convincing.

If there were any extra shifts, I was freaking taking them.

Sinking onto my bed, I felt the weight of the day pressing down on me. I wanted to talk to my mom, I wanted her to listen to me, *really* listen to everything I was dealing with, but she was still too angry and busy working to not be all judgmental. I didn't know how much time passed as I spaced out, my thoughts whirling. It was only when my phone started to buzz, I was pulled from my stupor. Glancing at the caller ID, I saw my dad's face pop up, and I was reminded all over again about what happened when I visited. I waited until it finished ringing to text Lyla back from our current conversation, but a voicemail notification popped up, stopping me.

"Well, might as well listen to it since it's one of the few he's left since last month," I muttered, clicking on the notification.

Little did I know, it would only serve to completely shatter my world.

"Hey, sweetheart. It's me," he started, before sighing. "I'm sorry again. I know I owe you a thousand apologies for what happened when you came to visit, and I know I shouldn't have kept it a secret from you. With everything, I realized I don't want any more secrets between us, Emma. I wish I could have told you this in person."

My brows dipped down as he paused, and my stomach clenched in worry as he took a shuddering breath.

"When your mom and I divorced, it wasn't just because I had found someone I was actually happy with. It turns out, I'm not your biological father. It was such a shock, but I still love you as if you were my daughter. I know our relationship is strained, but I would like to work on that. It's my fault for pulling away when I thought you would be better off without me because I was angry and upset, but I realize how stupid that was. Seeing you crying because of me broke my heart, and I don't ever want to see that expression on your face again, sweetheart, especially because of me. When you're ready, I'll be here for you. I'll try texting or calling tomorrow. Love you, sweetheart."

Holy.

Freaking.

Shit.

My vision tunneled as my hand dropped to my lap. Struggling to process what he said, I sat there, stone still until finally, my brain seemed to understand.

My dad isn't my dad.

I reached over, yanking one of my photo albums off the shelf, flipping to a picture of me and my dad. Only when I saw the two of us, smiling together did my mind process, and tears started to flow. Wayward tears fell as I stared at the photo before growing to an uncontrollable river, my mind finally seeing all the differences between the man I thought was my dad and me.

His black hair was the only similarity, his facial structure, eye color, hell, even the way he smiled was different. I always just assumed I looked more like my mom, but when I looked over to the picture of the three of us, I realized that wasn't true either. A rush of anger so strong filled me, and I started to shake. I slammed the album shut, throwing the hard-covered book across the room, hearing it smack the wall and floor with a thump.

Standing up, I started up the stairs, ready to demand answers, but when I neared the top, I hesitated. Something held me back as I heard my mom angrily typing on her computer, and no matter what I told myself to convince my feet to move, I couldn't. I wasn't sure if it was fear, anger, worry, or the urge to run back to my room and curl under the blanket that held me captive at the top of the stairs, but whatever it was, it had me turning on my heel and walking back to my room with a vow to bring it up when she wasn't so angry, and I'd had more time to process. Dropping my phone on the nightstand, I curled under my blanket, content to hide and cry away the feelings, but one thought swirled in my head no matter how much I tried to push it away.

My dad isn't my dad.

JANUARY 9TH

Not only did I wind up with three exceptional boyfriends, but I have the best coworker and friend I could have asked for. #ThankGodForGirlTalk #Venting #SafePlace #ThankfulThursday

---

My shift was slow. The way the wind blew the quickly falling snow in whips of white flakes, made our customer flow almost nonexistent. Lyla was finishing up the last chapter in the book she was reading, but as soon as she did, she looked at me with narrowed eyes.

"Okay, Emma Bean. What's up? You've been quiet and frowny since you walked in. So, tell Doctor Lyla what's been going on," she instructed, propping her chin in her hand.

I could barely manage a smile at her antics. My mood had been dour the last four days—rock bottom where not even the rumors and sneers from my classmates could affect me. Thankfully, the guys thought my negative mood was because of the whispers.

"A lot has happened, Ly," I started tiredly. "Let's start with the shittiest of the news. Found out why my parents divorced."

"Not because your dad is engaged to someone else?" she asked with a head tilt. I laughed, the sound tired and cold.

"Turns out he's not my biological dad. Didn't know until the divorce. Called to say he wished he could have told me in person, but after all that happened in Cali, he didn't want any more secrets. He wants to try to fix our relationship. I haven't even brought it up to my mom yet cause of some other shit that's come up," I muttered. Lyla's expression would have been comical if I wasn't in such an utterly horrible mood.

"Holy shit," she exclaimed. "Okay, two questions. One, how did the guys react? And two, are you going to? Try to fix the relationship, I mean."

"I think so, I mean, he's my dad. Well, he's the only dad I know," I stumbled over my explanation, still feeling weird about having to make that distinction in my head. "As for the guys, I haven't told them yet. We're dealing with a lot of crap from other students. Brad is spreading rumors, and it's wearing on all of us with Jesse's trial and our relationship. Which leads me to my next problem. My mom found out. About the trial and that I'm dating all three of them."

"Safe to say she's upset?" Lyla took over. I huffed out a single laugh.

"Upset is an understatement," I proceeded to run through everything that had gone down since I got home from the cabin. Lyla's brows seemed to be permanently attached to her hairline, the more I explained. "So yeah. Here I am, grounded and not allowed to see them outside of school. On top of the rumors and the news about my dad-who's-not-actually-my-dad."

"Wow," she murmured in surprise. "That's intense. Is there any good news?"

"I may havelostmyvirginityoverbreak," I muttered.

"I'm sorry, what was that? Emma Bean popped her cherry?" she teased, her smile growing as my cheeks reddened. "Which one?"

"Reid."

She whooped, clapping excitedly.

"I'm so proud, I mean... bad Emma, sex before marriage is bad," she scolded with a finger wave but couldn't control her laughter. "You guys were safe, though, right?" I nodded. "Good. But now I get why you've seemed so upset. That's a lot of shit all at once." She opened her mouth to say more, but the bell above the door cut her off.

"Hey, Cali girl," Reid greeted cheerfully. His bright smile and hazel gaze warmed my chest, the butterflies erupting at the glint I saw in his eyes. "Hi, Lyla."

"Well, hello there," she stated with a grand wave of her arm. "It is nice to see you treated my girl right." I blanched, choking on nothing at Reid's pink cheeks and her blatant admission I'd told her we had sex. "You're so adorable when you get uncomfortable," she teased me. "Want to take your break? You guys can have coffee together since you're grounded outside of school and work hours."

"Thanks." I gave her a grateful smile, walking around the counter to follow Reid to one of the tables in the corner. "So, how are you, babe?"

"I came to ask *you* that, Cali girl," he stated with a cocked brow. I nibbled on my lip, saved for a little while by Lyla placing our two coffees on our table. "You're not happy, and I can't see that little light in your eyes anymore. Are you okay with us… me… I mean, after everything from break?" My heart cracked at his soft, unsure tone. "I didn't fuck anything up, right?"

"Babe, I swear I'm good with you and us and our group. It's been a tough few days, and I've learned some stuff earlier this week, but I wouldn't have changed a thing about what we did," I reassured him, intertwining our fingers together. I took a deep breath, then everything tumbled out.

"Holy shit," he exclaimed. "Yeah, okay, I see why you've been so quiet lately. Is there anything we can do?" I smiled at his use of 'we' even though Kingston was at the law firm, and Jesse was tutoring one of his students at the library tonight.

"Just be there like you guys have been. I'll call and let them know when I get off tonight," I told him. "I just need some more time, I think, before I bring it up to my mom. Going to try to get through the trial and this grounding, and hopefully, find out I passed my practice ACT and do well on the actual one. You know, normal teenager things," I grinned, already feeling lighter than I had all week.

It's nice to be reminded I'm not alone.

I had Lyla, Zo, Aubs, and my friends. I had my boys. Most importantly, though, I had confidence we could totally make it through this.

I think.

CHAPTER 16

We ate lunch quickly, having spent the first half of
the period goofing off and telling terrible jokes to
each other. While we stuffed our faces, I realized why I
felt off. Everything was going smoothly, too smoothly. My
grounding was officially over when school ended today,
and I still hadn't heard from the Warland's lawyer about
being questioned. I wasn't going to hold my breath that
it would keep going as well as it had, but I couldn't stop
the gratefulness that filled me, knowing I had about two
weeks of a relatively normal life.

Relative being the key word.

"Emma!" Zoey hollered, nearly barreling into me as she
and Aubrey ran up to the table.

"Oh, jeez, hi," I sputtered, trying to save the last bit of my
pizza before it fell out of my hand.

"What are you doing tonight? You're off lockdown,
right?" Aubrey asked, her eyes glowing with excitement.
"Cause we're having a girls' night, and we want you to
come. Figured we can do nails, face masks, and watch rom

coms."

"I'd love to. I don't work tonight, and my grounding is over when the bell rings at the end of school. I just need to tell her where I'm going and how long I'll be there because, apparently, I need a babysitter," I groaned, rolling my eyes.

"We're going to be at my house," Zoey stated. "I'm good to have people over until nine and figured we can get two or three movies in before then. We'll meet you out front, and we can drive over to my house after school." After I got the okay from my mom, I texted Zoey since they'd run back to their table with Brandon, Jason, Carter, and Brayden after inviting me. Shaking my head when I heard Zoey's and Aub's whoops from nearly ten tables over, I put my phone away, turning back to my smiling guys.

"What?"

"We love that you enjoy your friends here," Kingston explained.

"We like seeing you happy," Jesse tacked on.

"You're also gorgeous, so it's hard for us to look away," Reid teased.

I rolled my eyes but couldn't stop the eruption of butterflies in my stomach.

Whoever associated butterflies with butter must surely have been drunk.

"Which first?" Zoey held up some movies. I shrugged, not really caring, I was just happy to be able to spend time with my friends outside of school for the first time in two weeks. "Aubs, pick something. Emma, pick out your nail color."

"So bossy!" I teased but did as she asked. The tinkling

of the glass bottles hitting each other as I ran through the rows of colors filled the air while Aubrey hemmed and hawed about the movie before finally settling on *13 Going on 30*.

"Masked Monday," I called out after deciding to go with plain black nail color. "Sounds like superheroes," I laughed.

"I usually do 'self-care Sunday,' but I was busy yesterday hanging with Brandon, so I figured with everything going on with you and stuff, we could have a self-care party. Nothing helps me feel better than a couple stress-free hours with a soothing mask on and pretty nails," Zoey explained as she scanned through the nail colors quickly, settling on an icy blue while Aubrey decided on a sparkly red-orange.

"Same. I may take a bath when I get home, depending on how I feel. Those are the fastest ways to calm me, but I do love me some sheet masks and rom-coms, especially because the boys don't watch anything sappy with me. Unless it's Christmas, apparently," I added with a chuckle. "Okay, do either of you hate putting these things on, or is it just me? I always feel super clumsy doing it."

"Ugh, yes, I usually do mud mask style, but I ran out over the break, trying to make sure my skin wouldn't crack off from being so dry in the mountains," Aubrey murmured, her words muffled as she maneuvered the thin essence-soaked sheet onto her face. "I look ridiculous."

"That's okay, we can all look ridiculous together," I told her as I got the mask settled, pressing down on the edges of the eye, mouth, and nose holes to make sure it was secured—well, as secure as a slippery piece of material could be.

"Amen to that," Zo added. "Gotta get a picture for Emma's photo album."

"Did Reid tell you about that?" I laughed, my mouth unable to open very much because of the mask, so my words were slurred.

"Yeah, but we love the idea. It's easier than scrapbooking, but you're still able to keep memories in an easy-to-see place," Aubrey mumbled. "Okay, photo time. The movie's about to start." We crowded together, looking absolutely ridiculous with the translucent masks and strained half-smiles, but right now, I wouldn't change it for anything because of these two. They were pretty freaking amazing. I left later that night feeling relaxed and ready to handle the next day.

Nothing can dim my happy mood.

JANUARY 21ST

'Kill the Lawyer!' -Rufio
#Hook #MovieReference #DontActuallyMurder
#TickedoffTuesday

I spoke too soon.

A police officer closed the distance between us, weaving his way through the students who were trying to make it from lunch to their next class. My body was immediately set on edge as his narrowed gaze centered on me. Thankfully, I had been talking to Ms. Rogers before the bell rang, and she intercepted the cop, stepping in front of me.

"Can I help you?" Ms. Rogers questioned coolly, her arms crossing in front of her chest as the cop half glared at her.

"I've been instructed to bring Miss Clark to the Corsian Law Firm for questioning," he stated, his tone tired but hard. My teeth ground together, knowing the Warlands were behind this. How dare they have a police officer come get me from school in the middle of lunch when they knew it would be busy! I didn't have to turn to know the eyes I felt on my back were Brad's. The goosebumps that erupted over my skin told me more about my *admirer* than looking back ever would.

"Can I ask why this needs to be done in the middle of the school day?" Ms. Rogers snapped. "Emma has classes she needs to attend."

"Ms. Rogers," I heard a familiar voice ground out. My jaw was starting to ache from how hard I was grinding my teeth. Mr. Derosa stepped up to our little group, his hard eyes on my counselor before falling on me. His lip curled into a disgusted sneer briefly before smoothing out.

Yeah, well, I don't like you either jerkface.

"Mr. Derosa—" she started.

"Miss Clark is an adult in the eyes of the legal system," the assistant principal cut her off, "and this an important legal matter. We don't want any issues with police here in school, so I suggest she goes with him." I stepped around Ms. Rogers, not wanting her to get in trouble with Mr. Derosa because of me. I knew what I needed to do, remembering Kaleb's warnings and urgings when I talked to him.

"I'll go with you," I told the officer, "but I would like my lawyer to meet us there."

"You'll have to take that up with the lawyer when we get there," the officer bit out, seemingly irritated he was required to escort a teenager instead of doing his actual job.

"Are you sure, Emma? Do you need me to call your mom?" Ms. Rogers questioned quietly. I shook my head with what I hoped was a reassuring smile.

"It'll be alright, I know what I'm supposed to do," I whispered before turning and following the cop through the crowd that had formed to watch us. Taking a steeling breath, I held my head high and walked through the crowd as it parted.

I didn't do anything wrong, and I won't cower or be treated like a criminal.

The car ride was quiet, and the hard plastic of the back of the cruiser was uncomfortable, but I didn't complain because I knew the cop was just doing what he was asked to. He wasn't purposely out to inconvenience me, so I didn't want to make his day any harder than it was. When we finally reached the law office twenty minutes later, he gave me a grin and a small 'thank you' for being cooperative.

"Miss Clark," a smarmy man with greased back black hair and a pinstripe suit greeted me at the front door. I smashed my lips shut, trying hard to not make a sassy comment that he looked like a used car salesman or he'd just walked off the set of an old film noir shoot. "Please, come with me."

I followed him, silent and fuming as we made our way through the elegant and sleek building. If I hadn't been so danged angry, I probably would have appreciated the way the decor and modern elements mixed with the more unique architecture, but at that moment, all I could focus on was wanting to tell them I needed my lawyer.

They may have embarrassed me and made me miss classes, but I wasn't going to be dumb enough to believe they had my best interest at heart, so first chance I got, I told the man I wanted to call my lawyer.

"Miss Clark, there's no need for that," he tried to convince me in his most "charming" voice. "I just want to get the facts for the trial, and what better way to do that than to go to the source?"

"I want my lawyer," I repeated. "I'm not answering anything until Kaleb Bell is here."

"Can you tell me what happened the night of the party?" asked the man, who hadn't even bothered telling me his name. I sat silently, staring at him as I crossed my arms.

If this is how he wants to play it, so be it.

I might talk a lot, but I could play the silent game just as well as the next person.

After the eighth question, the man sighed, the noise irritated as his eyes narrowed on me. He got up, excusing himself, and walked out of the room. As soon as the door was shut, I dug out my phone, quickly texting Kingston to have him call his dad, followed by a quick explanation of what was going on. Not wanting to catch the attention of any cameras or anyone possibly watching through the mirror on the wall to my left, I put my phone away and continued to wait.

And wait, I did. After an hour, I finally heard a commotion on the other side of the door, shouting filtering through the thick wood. I was startled when the door flung open, revealing Kaleb's angry scowl on the other side of the threshold.

"Sir, you can't just barge in," a measley man tried to say, but Kaleb glared over his shoulder, stopping his statement.

"She is my client, and she has been here for over an hour after clearly stating she wanted a lawyer. I know because she had my son contact me after she was escorted by police from school. All of which was completely unnecessary, and if you try to tell me I'm not allowed back here one more time, I will take my client with me, and you can have the judge schedule a time to question her. Am I understood?"

My brows shot up, my lips parting in surprise. I'd never once heard Kaleb raise his voice or snap at anyone. Even when King or Killian were acting up, he would talk to them calmly. Kaleb turned and stepped into the room, slamming the door closed in the man's face before sinking into the chair next to me.

"Are you alright, Emma? I'm sorry if that scared you." He waved at the door to the interrogation room.

"It didn't, it was just different to see, that's all," I explained. "I'm tired, any idea how long this is going to take?"

"Hopefully, not long," Kaleb reassured.

As soon as he said that, the door opened again, showing the city's prosecutor talking to an older man and woman, dressed in nice clothes—the man in a black classic suit with a gray tie, and the woman standing next to him was wearing a soft sweater and slacks, a strand of pearls around her neck, and a large gaudy ring on her finger— anger prevalent on their faces, narrowed eyes and lips thinned into a tight line.

I instinctively knew who they were, their cold icy gaze on me as sneers curled their lips—Brad's parents.

They're as creepy as their son.

"Alright, Miss Clark, now that your lawyer is here, we can *finally* begin," Brad's lawyer bit out, placing a heavy emphasis on the fact he had to wait for Kaleb to show up.

This better not take long.

Not long, my ass. An hour later, we finally left the building. I was pissed, so angry, in fact, I could tell I was storming down the sidewalk to Kaleb's car since he had, thankfully, offered me a ride to my car.

"Are you okay?" Kaleb asked as we finally reached his car, the rumble of it starting the only sound as we sank into our seats. Huffing, I buckled my seatbelt and crossed my arms.

"I want him in jail. I don't want him or his family to do this to anyone else. I didn't do anything wrong, and I don't appreciate being made to feel like this was my fault," I ground out, remembering all the little snide comments the lawyer—Steve Corsian—made during his questioning about my behavior at the party and what I was wearing, hinting I wanted Brad to hit on me and I was leading him on.

Assholes.

"What?" I questioned when I noticed Kaleb hadn't said anything, just looked over at me with a little grin.

"I'm proud of you, Emma, for standing up for yourself and for anyone else who could be in this situation against the Warlands." His tone conveyed how pleased he was, and with his statement, my anger fizzled, my lips curling as we settled into our drive.

At least one adult in my life is proud of me.

JANUARY 22ND

I found out today, it's a myth that erotic, steamy books are only for desperate housewives. Holy BJ, Batman! #JesseReadingSmutIsSexy #FirstBJEver #WeirdnessWednesday

---

"Meh," I grumbled, my head flopping onto the open booklet in front of me. "Finally, to the end," I huffed, my words muffled by the paper.

"Yes, Em, all done," Jesse chuckled. I could hear him shuffling around next to me, so I sat back and looked at him.

"Now what?" I asked. "We're done earlier than normal, and I don't have to be home until nine. Not that it really matters since my mom will at work late tonight with for international call," I rambled.

"Want to read our book?" My heart fluttered as he dug out the paperback we had picked out to read together, loving the tradition we had started.

"Yeah, but since my mom's not going to be home for a while, want to head there? I think it'd be comfier than these wooden seats and table." I tapped the tabletop for emphasis. Don't get me wrong, I loved Coffee Grounds, but it wasn't the most conducive location for cuddling up to read together. Jesse agreed, and we made quick work of packing up our study supplies before we were in my car, heading to my broken home.

The only thing keeping the oppressive silence at bay in the house my mom and I rented was the sound of Jesse's movements as he followed me to the basement. As he settled into the corner of the couch, I pulled up one of the music channels I had taken to listening to when it was too quiet. Jesse reading out loud would help keep the loneliness at bay, but I still wanted something familiar.

"Come here, Em," he murmured, holding up the blanket he had draped over his legs extended on the chaise of the couch.

Smiling, I made my way over, curling into his chest, my head nestling against his muscled shoulder as I looked at the book. Jesse started to read, his honeyed voice soft and gentle, relaxing me. The book's epic storyline sucked me in, its fantasy world playing like a movie in my head as he made his way through the chapter. It had been all about action and adventure, but it quickly started to shift into a steamier scene, and with Jesse reading it aloud, I couldn't stop fidgeting.

"Are you okay?" Jesse finally questioned after what seemed like the tenth time I fidgeted. "Do you want me to skip this part?" Rolling further onto him, so I could look at him, I opened my mouth to tell him everything was fine, but instead, I came in contact with Jesse's hard-on.

It seems I'm not the only one turned on by the book.

"Are you okay?" I teased softly, shifting my leg up, so my thigh could rub against him. His eyes slammed shut, and he groaned, his head pressing back into the cushion.

"Em," he ground out. Feeling confident, I just smiled at him, continuing to tease. Jesse had his turn to tease me during our movie night last month—now it was my turn.

His gaze heated, his eyes melting into two obsidian pools as I dragged a finger down his chest and stomach. Pushing away from his chest, I sat back on my heels, straddling his right thigh. Without hesitating, knowing I might have chickened out, I reached out and cupped his erection.

His jeans were rough against my palm, but I reveled in the feeling as I rubbed him. My body burned, fueled by Jesse's clenched jaw and fists, so I unbuttoned and unzipped his pants, freeing him from the tight confines. He was thick, his silky skin shifting over the hardened steel as I stroked. Counting quickly to three in my head, building the last of the nerve to do something I hadn't done before, I bent over and wrapped my lips around him. A low groan mixed with a hiss emanated from Jesse as I tentatively brushed my tongue over the bulbous head.

"Em," Jesse breathed, "have you ever done this before?"

A rush of heat flooded my cheeks that had nothing to do with how wet my panties were or that my lips were wrapped around Jesse. Pulling off of him, I shook my head as I looked up at him from under my lashes.

"You don't have to..." he started.

"I want to," I whispered. "Will you... will you teach me?" Jesse's lip curled up, his hand brushing my hair away from my face.

"If that's what you want." When I nodded, Jesse's fingers brushed through my hair again, this time holding my head and hair, nudging me down, guiding me.

Not that it's rocket science, but still, this isn't about me right now, and I want Jesse to feel good.

He had a unique flavor, slightly salty, but for the most part, my attention was focused on adjusting to his size. Jesse was careful to not push my head down too far to the point where I'd gag, and my fist curled around the base of his shaft to keep me from choking.

When I heard him moan, the deep sound rumbling through his chest, I glanced up. His eyes were shut, his lips parting as his head fell back against the cushions. Shifting my head faster, Jesse's free hand wrapped around mine, guiding me to stroke him in time with my bobbing. Feeling curious, pressing my tongue against the bottom of his length, his hips jerked, and he started to pant. I knew he was near his release when he let go of my head and hand, allowing me to take over.

I didn't have time to pull back before he came, his cum coating my tongue in a mix of salty and sweet. Panicking slightly, I swallowed as a natural reaction to having something in my mouth.

"Holy fucking shit, Em," Jesse exclaimed breathlessly. "Come here." Reaching down, he pulled me up to him until I was sprawled out on his chest. "That was amazing... wait... did you swallow?"

"Uh, yeah," I dragged the word out with an awkward smile. He chuckled, shaking his head at me.

"You could have pulled away or spit it out, love," he explained. "Sorry I didn't warn you, I got too wrapped up in it all." I shrugged, figuring while it was odd at first, it wasn't all that bad.

"Did you know the skin inside our mouths is the same skin in vaginas?" I rambled before taking a deep breath to calm my racing mind. "So, how'd I do for my first time?" I asked softly. "Decent, I hope."

"Perfect, Em, absolutely perfect. I think I should return the favor now," he said, trying to reach down. Giggling, I rolled away from him, my chuckling growing to full laughter when I saw him staring at me with an open mouth.

"That was to get you back for movie night," I stated with a brow raise. "Maybe next time, we can both have fun, but for now, I just want to listen to you read. That was a lot more work than I anticipated."

Jesse laughed, letting it go as he tucked himself away in his pants.

"Alright, alright. I'll continue to read to you," he agreed with open arms, but once I settled in, he whispered, "But don't think I won't take the first chance I get, Em."

Good.

.

Chapter 17

January 23rd

I did it once, I can do it again! Go me!
#PracticeACT #IDidIt #ThanksJesse #ThankfulThursday

Nerves rattling, my eyes darted around the hall as I made my way to Ms. Rogers' office, worried I would run into Brad again. Thankfully, he was nowhere to be seen, but much to my surprise, Ms. Rogers was waiting outside the office door for me.

"I wanted to make sure what happened last time didn't happen again," she explained, reading the confusion on my face. "Come on in, Emma, I have your practice ACT results."

"And?" I asked as she opened her door, sinking into my usual seat.

"You got a thirty," she said.

Holy crap!

"Are you serious?" I breathed, my jaw dropping, unable to believe my score. She nodded excitely. "Now, I just have to do that during the actual test," I explained.

"I have you scheduled for this Saturday, January twenty-fifth; is that still good?" she asked, looking through her notes. "That way, we have one, possibly two more chances to make the cutoff date." My mouth dried up. "Emma? Are you alright?"

"Uh," I stuttered, "yeah, that's just two days before I have to testify for Jesse's court case."

"Do you want to reschedule? I don't want you to be too overwhelmed. I know you wanted to have a cushion between the official test and the deadline for the universities."

"No, I'll do it, I'll just do some extra studying that week beforehand to help. Maybe some extra relaxation meditations or something," I explained softly, taking a deep breath to calm my racing thoughts.

"Do you want to talk about it? You don't have to, but you're more than welcome to have this be a safe place for you," Ms. Rogers offered with a soft smile.

I went back and forth, the worries weighing on my mind starting to overwhelm me, and I didn't have much of anyone to talk to. Well, I had my friends and Kingston's parents, but no one who was a neutral third-party, not necessarily already involved in everything going on.

"Uh, Brad tried to force himself on me at a party," I mumbled, my eyes glued to the fake wood tabletop, "and Jesse saved me, but he ended up beating the heck out of him, so Brad's family is pressing assault charges. Wanting to have him charged as an adult and send him to jail. Prison. I don't really get the difference," I rambled. "But yeah, that's really it. Kingston's dad, who's Jesse's lawyer, and mine too, I guess, wants to charge Brad with attempted sexual assault."

"Oh, Emma, I'm so sorry. I knew the gist since the school has to be informed about anything with the students who are minors and facing legal trouble," she explained. "I have a question. Do you feel safe here in the school?" she questioned, worried. I shrugged, swallowing the lump in my throat.

"As long as Brad stays away from me or I'm surrounded by my friends and uh, boyfriends," I coughed the end, not wanting to see the judgment in her eyes, but all I saw was a small head tilt with a scrunched brow. Sighing, the rest of the explanation came tumbling out, "I'm dating Reid, Jesse, and Kingston, so whenever I'm with them, I feel okay. When I'm not—which isn't often—I don't feel safe. It's like I just know when he's nearby, and I can feel his creepy gaze on me." I shuddered, feeling the sliver of ice trail down my spine causing me to shiver.

"Here, how about we do this. We can look at his schedule and compare it to yours, then figure out ways you can go to class and avoid seeing him. I'll discuss with the Principal about having him specifically stay away from certain areas at certain times. How does that sound? Try to eliminate the number of times you see him throughout the day," she stated, pulling out a school map and quickly digging through one of the drawers in her filing cabinet until she had two pieces of paper.

By the time our meeting was over, I felt better about telling Ms. Rogers what happened. The worried voice in my head was silenced, knowing I had someone on the faculty who would look out for me here at school.

Now to get through the next couple of weeks.
I can totally do this.
I think.

JANUARY 24TH

Just read a few facts about frogs... they were ribbiting lol
#lol #RibbitRibbit #FunnyFriday

"Hey, Cali girl," Reid murmured, nudging me as we went through the line. "What are you doing tonight?"

"As of right now? Nothing, why?" I glanced at him with a narrowed gaze, knowing he was up to something based on the twitch in his lips. He had just opened his mouth as we walked to the table when Mr. Derosa stepped in front of us.

"Miss Clark, Mr. Hughes," he practically sneered, glancing between the two of us with disdain. "I thought you were supposed to be staying at least a certain distance from Mr. Warland?" I felt my face pale, my stomach dropping as he made his statement loud enough for the tables around us to hear him. "Yet here you are, not doing that. Is that because you think only he should be required to stay away from you?"

"What Ms. Rogers and I discussed was something private," I ground out, rage burning my throat as I controlled the urge to both yell and throw up at the increasing number of eyes I felt on us.

"It's also the only place we're allowed to eat lunch in the school," Reid countered loudly. "If you would give us other options, such as the hallway, outside, or go out to eat lunch, maybe Emma wouldn't have to see her attempted rapist at lunch every fucking day."

"That's enough, Mr. Hughes! To my office, now. As for you, Miss Clark, I suggest you stay out of trouble," Mr. Derosa bit out before marching Reid, who had dropped his tray on a random table, forcefully to his office. I stood frozen, nearly the entire cafeteria staring at me, whispers floating through the crowd as I started to tremble.

"Come on, Emma." Zoey and Aubrey appeared right as Kingston and Jesse showed up in front of us. "Let's go." They hooked their arms through mine, propelling me forward until I was seated between Kingston and Jesse at our usual table. With a quick hug and murmured reassurances, Aubs and Zo headed back to their own table.

"How? How is he able to treat me and Reid like that?" I hissed, absently waving a head in the direction the assistant principal and my boyfriend went. "That's confidential shit he just decided to yell around the room, and if a teacher or faculty member did that back in Cali, they'd be fired."

"That's how they are here, Em," Jesse murmured with a shrug. "The school and the ones in charge care more about their rep to the public and government than their students." Kingston stayed silent, his worried gaze focused on me as he reached across the table, rubbing circles over the back of my hand as we fell into a tense silence. My eyes were glued to the office door, waiting for Reid to come out, but by the time the bell rang, he had yet to appear.

"He'll be alright, Babydoll. He'll text us when he knows what's going on." Kingston continued murmuring reassurances as we walked to trig, but for the rest of the day, I couldn't focus on anything any of my teachers were saying.

Hopefully, none of what I missed would be on a test any time soon.

Reid still hadn't messaged by the time I was home, and the silence had my anxiety flaring at what punishment he was facing for standing up for me. *Probably grounded and his phone taken away,* I surmised, trying to calm my worry. Rubbing my eyes, a thud of a headache quickly forming after the terrible day I had, I walked into the house and upstairs for something to drink and discovered the headache was the least of my problems.

Tyler.

"What the heck?" I asked, my gaze darting between my ex-boyfriend, seated on the couch, and my mom, who had just walked from the kitchen. "Why is he here?"

"I thought it might be good for you to reconnect with someone from California, back before you were surrounded by bad influences and trouble. Someone I actually approve of," she explained coolly. My jaw dropped, and my brain refused to process the fact my mom had invited my clingy ex to Nebraska.

"Why don't you come sit, Emma?" Tyler tried to catch my attention, his hand patting the seat beside him. My mom smiled at his attempt, but I didn't move.

"Well, I'll leave you two to chat," my mom said happily, seeming quite proud of herself, but all I felt was appalled.

"No," I stated, "I don't want to reconnect with Tyler. Which I told you multitude times," I directed at him, before glaring at my mom. "He cheated on me, in case you're wondering why we broke up in the first place. I would rather be surrounded by my so called 'bad influences' of boyfriends than be with someone who disregards my worth. And the fact you did this behind my back when you know I'm dealing with getting ready for ACT and colleges, testifying at Jesse's trial, and building a case against Brad is... insane," I stumbled over the end of my rant, unable to formulate a decent response.

"Emma, I didn't say you had to date him, but I would rather have you be friends with someone I know I can trust," my mother countered with a thread of ice in her words.

"You might be able to trust him, but I can't. I confided in you at Christmas how everything went when I went back!

Did you even hear anything I said, or did it just go in one ear and out the other? Because right now, it seems like all you care about is what *you* see and what *you* want. But you know what, Mom? This isn't your life, it's mine. When he's back on a plane to Cali, I'll come home, but I'm not staying here, knowing you'd completely disregard what I need as your daughter." For the second time in a month, I turned, darting down the stairs and grabbing my duffel.

"Emma, wait," Tyler tried to stop me as I stuffed my bag full of clothes and toiletries.

I really need to start leaving things at Kingston's at this rate.

"No, Tyler." I yanked my arm back, shouldering my stuff and starting toward the garage. Ignoring what he was trying to say, I pulled out and turned onto the street, my mom standing there on the porch, scowling as I saw Tyler run to the rental car parked on the street. Noticing him following me about halfway to my destination, I dug out my phone and dialed Kingston.

"Hey, Babydoll, what's up?" he greeted.

"I'm on my way, I'm staying again. Unfortunately, this time around, I have a guest who won't leave me the hell alone," I ground out, watching him tail me.

"Wait, what?" I heard Reid bite out in the background.

"I'm almost there," I stated simply, hanging up and pulling onto the Kingston's street. By the time I pulled into the drive next to Reid's Jeep, my boys were on the porch, watching with narrowed eyes and harsh frowns. It didn't escape my notice that Stella and Kaleb were watching from the entry hall behind the glass storm door.

At least I'm not alone dealing with him this time.

"Emma, wait," Tyler called out, getting out of the rental car.

"I don't want to talk to you, and I don't have to talk to you, regardless of what my mom says, Tyler. I'm tired of having this same conversation over and over again. You blew your chance at being my friend when you didn't listen to me," I exclaimed, walking to the porch.

"You're being ridiculous, babe," he huffed, making me stop in my tracks. I spun to face him and dropped my bag on the ground.

"How dare you tell me what I feel or what I want is ridiculous. What's ridiculous is your expectation that I should have to talk to you or give you another chance or that you don't understand the concept of NO!" I shouted, and his eyes widened, darting between me and the guys on the wooden steps.

"I only cheated because you were such a prude. You wore all those frilly skirts all the time, and I complimented you about them, and still, *nothing*. No blow jobs, no giving it up like you should have," he snapped.

"That's enough," Kaleb barked. "I suggest you get off our property and leave Emma be, or she will be filing a restraining order for harassment."

"Emma wouldn't do that," Tyler scoffed. "She's too much of a people pleaser. Isn't that right, babe? That's why you have three boyfriends. Although last I knew, you were a timid virgin. Kudos to the guys who could bring out the slut in you."

I balked at the crude statement, barely stopping Reid in time before he went after Tyler.

"You have three seconds," Stella threatened, holding a phone in her hand, her thumb hovering over the call button. "I don't believe your parents would appreciate you being arrested, but I have no such qualms."

"That's alright, I don't want someone's sloppy seconds,"

Tyler sneered, "or thirds or fourths." With that, he turned and strode away, slamming the car door before peeling out down the street.

"Fucking ass," Kingston bit out.

"Language, son, though I have to agree," Kaleb reprimanded with a glare at the car that turned out of sight. "You alright, Emma?"

I took a shuddering breath, nodding. Despite the anger that filled me, I couldn't help being relieved, knowing this was going to be the last time Tyler spoke to me.

Hopefully.

"Yeah, thanks, Mr. Bell," I murmured with a grin, waiting for his usual response.

"One more time," he chimed with a chuckle. "Now, you're just doing that on purpose."

"Of course, she is. She's a little troublemaker, fitting in perfectly with these three," Stella teased with a smile. "Inside now, it's cold, and I don't want to deal with any hospital visits for frostbite."

We had just stepped inside when I noticed another duffel on the side of the entry hall. Glancing around, I noticed Reid's red-ringed eyes and tear-tracked face.

"What's wrong? What happened?"

"Uh," he sniffled, my heart racing as he looked at Stella and Kaleb. "My dad kicked me out. Disowned me for dating you while you're with King and Jesse. Said he wouldn't let me live in their house while I was living in sin."

"Holy crap," I breathed, stunned. "What'd your mom say?" Surely she wouldn't let that happen; she seemed to love her son too much for such extreme measures.

"Didn't say anything," Reid mumbled with a dejected shrug. "Mr. Derosa told them when he called to tell them I had been suspended for three days. Which I guess works since I'm going to the trial on Monday. Don't want you two to have to tackle that on your own." He directed his statement to Jesse and me, his forced attempt to smile more of a grimace.

"Welcome to the Bell household, sweetheart," Stella rubbed his back. "You're more than welcome to bunk in the spare room in the basement or up with Kingston."

"Thanks, Stella." Reid gave her a watery smile, and she pulled him into for a tight hug, glancing at Kaleb, who patted him on the back in an attempt to comfort him.

At least one of us has a decent family.

I wrapped my arms around Reid when Stella stepped back, pulling Kaleb down the hall to leave us alone.

"I'm sorry, babe, I didn't know that would happen," I whispered, my emotions slowly starting to numb. Too much had happened in recent weeks, and my body couldn't handle any more. Reid inhaled deeply, trying to keep his crying contained, his stubbled cheek pressing into my neck and shoulder.

"It's okay, Cali girl. If they can't accept what I want in life, I'll live it with people who love me for who I am and who I choose to be," he murmured, rubbing my back.

"Got that right," Kingston stated proudly. "You're stuck with us." The adamant statement made us chuckle, bringing us out of the sullen moment.

"I wouldn't have it any other way," Reid said simply, kissing me passionately before wrapping Kingston and Jesse in a hug. "Now, let's get some food. I never had lunch, and I'm starving." As soon as his statement left his mouth, my stomach growled loud enough for everyone to chuckle.

I couldn't agree more.

At least, my stomach certainly can't.

JANUARY 25TH

Stress free? Do I even remember what that feels like? #INeedABubbleBath #OrAFaceMask #OrANewIdentity #StressFreeSaturday

Nerves rattled, my body's capability to handle all the stress lately was growing thinner and thinner each day, but I left the official ACT, feeling more confident than I had about a test in years.

Positive thoughts.

Sinking into the driver's seat, I carefully drove from the school to Coffee Grounds, ready to start my shift in twenty minutes. I was glad Rick had scheduled me a bit later than usual, giving me enough time, not only to take the test but to change into my uniform beforehand without rushing.

I had just put my bag and outfit from the morning in the locker, shutting the metal door when Rick knocked on the girls' locker room door.

"Emma, when you're done, can you come into the office?" he called out. His tone didn't give away anything, but my heart galloped as a lead weight formed in my stomach.

"Yeah, I'll be there in just a moment," I hollered back, taking a deep breath and tying my apron around my waist. Though, depending on what he was about to say, it could be completely useless.

You're about to get fired.

Grinding my teeth, I pushed the negative thought away and left the locker room. I knocked on the door frame, not wanting to walk right into Rick's office, even though the door was open, and his red hair poked up from behind the desk.

"Ah, Emma! Perfect timing," he exclaimed. He didn't *seem* like he was about to fire me with his wide, toothy smile, but that didn't stop the rampant anxiety constricting my chest. "Do you know why I've called you in here today?" I shook my head, unable to say anything, my tongue fused to the roof of my mouth. "Ah, I'm surprised my cousin didn't spoil the surprise."

"Surprise?" I croaked out, my brows dipping down. That definitely didn't sound like I was getting fired, especially if Lyla knew. She would have told me.

"Yup! You, Miss Clark, are getting a raise," he stated in excitement. "I know you've been going through a lot, and I wanted to reward you for your professionalism and hard work, despite everything on your plate. I remember being a teenager and every little thing piling up, so I know it's not easy."

"So, you're not firing me?" I asked, just needing to be sure. He laughed, shaking his head.

"Nope, sorry if I scared you. I'll keep that in mind for the future when I get the idea to surprise you. But you're now at ten dollars and fifty cents an hour."

My jaw dropped. *A dollar fifty raise.* While it wasn't much in the grand scheme of things since I was only part time, I was thankful for a little positivity right now.

"Thank you!" I squeaked, my gaping turning into a bright smile.

"Of course. We want to make sure our hard-working employees are treated well," Rick assured. "That's it for right now if you want to head out to the front. I think I've tortured Lyla, making her run the busy front alone long enough."

With a chuckle, I nearly skipped to the front, my frown

turned into a smile for more than ten minutes at a time for the first time in weeks.

See, Emma? You've totally got this.

Now to just get through Jesse's trial.

Chapter 18

I read once that flying dreams mean you're doing the right thing with your life.
#GuessWhatIdreamedLastNight #UpUpandAway
#MotivationMonday

Everyone ready to go?" Kaleb called out, his voice echoing up the stairs. I stood in Kingston's bathroom, frozen in place, knowing today was the day.

Jesse's future depended on me and what I had to say on the stand.

Holy crap, I think I may throw up.

"Em?" Jesse's soft voice reached me, his slight frown pulling my attention from mindlessly staring at the sink to where he stood in the door frame. "Ready?"

"As ready as I'll ever be," I mumbled, my shaky voice betraying how I truly felt.

"We'll be alright, Em. I promise. No matter what happens, okay?" Jesse tried to convince me.

I mustered up a smile as best I could, but as we walked down the stairs to where Kingston and Reid were waiting in their dress shirts, pants, and ties with Kaleb and Stella, who both wore sleek suits, I felt my slight confidence falter.

"Alright, kids, into the SUV," Stella prompted, trying

to keep the positivity going strong with her smile and peppy words, but I could see the tension around her eyes and the worried glint in her gaze. We piled into the Bell family vehicle, Jesse and me in the middle two seats with Kingston and Reid in the backseat.

We were quiet as we drove to the courthouse, the tension thick enough, I could have cut it with a knife. Jesse's hand gripping mine was the only anchor in the sea of anxiety and 'what ifs' filtering through my mind, threatening to drown me in the possible negative outcomes of today.

I stumbled slightly as I exited the car, Stella catching me as my weak knees gave out, steadying me until I could get my feet righted again. Rubbing soothing circles on my back, she helped calm me enough, I could walk without falling on my face.

No one needs to see that right now. I can embarrass myself another time.

"Alright, Kingston, Reid, head in with Stell. I need to talk to Jesse and Emma before the proceedings start," Kaleb instructed quietly. Before walking off, Stella wrapped us both in a tight hug, lingering slightly before pulling back.

"It'll be okay," Kingston assured, hugging Jesse quickly before me, placing a soft kiss on the top of my head before following Stella into the courtroom.

"We'll be here the whole time," Reid murmured, doing the same, then made his way into the courtroom.

And just like that, there were only three.

"Just a quick rundown of what will happen," Kaleb murmured quietly. "Opening statements first, prosecution, then me. You, Emma, will be sitting with Stella and the boys while you, Jesse, are with me at the desk in front of the judge. Since we're going through the emancipation process, the judge was made aware of your current home situation and didn't contact your parents.

"Next will be testimonies and cross-examination. Emma, unfortunately, when Jesse and Brad are called to testify and be cross examined, you can't be in the room, in case it affects your testimony, so you'll wait out here with Stella.

"When it's your turn, the bailiff will come get you and bring you to the stand. You'll be sworn in like we talked about before, then you'll answer questions. If, at any point, you're worried or struggling, look at me, okay? Don't look at Brad, don't look at the people in attendance, just me. I'll help you get through the questions, okay?"

"Yeah," I mumbled, already overwhelmed with everything about to happen, and the trial hadn't even started yet. I opened my mouth to ask a question, but a group of people entering the front doors down at the end of the hall caught my attention. As soon as I felt my skin prickle, I knew who it was.

Brad.

And the whole freaking Warland family, it would seem.

"Emma, Jesse, look at me," Kaleb commanded softly. I dragged my gaze away from the group of well-dressed men and one woman, recognizing Brad's parents from the law firm. "Jess," Kaleb urged. Finally, after another tense moment, Jesse turned from the Warlands and focused on Kaleb. "Don't acknowledge them, don't listen to what they have to say, just pretend they don't exist. We're here to prove to the judge that while Jesse did assault Brad, there was a legitimate reason. That's it."

"What's after cross-examination?" I croaked, wanting to be aware of every step throughout the trial.

"Closing arguments," Kaleb answered. "You'll be allowed back in with the crowd at that point, Emma. Then the judge will adjourn to deliberate his verdict and announce his ruling as well as the punishment for Jesse."

"Oh God," I muttered, my stomach already turning at the thought of how this could go. "I think I may throw up before the end of this."

"If you think you need to, Stella has some extra bags in her purse just in case," Kaleb told me, his lip quirking up. "But I know you guys can do this. We'll get through this, together, alright?"

After we both nodded, we headed into the courtroom, but as soon as I was through the door, I stopped dead. Not because it was real, or I felt Brad's icy eyes on me, or my mom was sitting in the back row with her signature scowl on her face, but because my friends were there. Zoey, Aubrey, Jason, Carter, and Brayden sat in a row, Lyla on the end with Stella, a space between her and Reid. And when they all gave us encouraging smiles or thumbs ups, I nearly cried.

They're here, and they care about us.
This is what friendship is about.
Nebraska is definitely not so bad.

"Come on, Jesse," Kaleb directed, giving me a tiny nod to let me know I was good to sit. Ignoring my mom's scowl, the Warlands' scowls, and Brad's lingering gaze, I made my way to the place they had saved for me.

"Hey there, Emma Bean," Lyla murmured, grabbing my hand with a squeeze. "We got this. I can go out in the hall with you when you're supposed to leave if you want. Mrs. Bell gave us a rundown of what we should expect."

I gave her a grateful smile and a nod, unable to say yes through the lump of emotions that had built in my throat. Reid's arm wrapped around me, his fingers tracing circles on my shoulder. Kingston reached across Reid's lap, snatching my other hand before pressing a kiss to my knuckles. Kingston didn't let go, letting our entwined hands rest on Reid's legs. As soon as I felt both of my boys, my whirling thoughts settled, and I could finally take a deep breath.

I can totally do this.

"All rise," the bailiff called out, the door behind the judge's bench opening to reveal an older man with graying hair and a wrinkled face, his black robes billowing as he walked to his seat. He waved for us to sit back down as he sank into a chair I couldn't see.

"We are here to hear the case, Parker vs. State," the judge started, his voice strong as it resonated through the room. "Defendant, Mr. Jesse Parker, is charged with aggravated assault against the victim, Mr. Brad Warland, with the plea of not guilty, is this correct?"

"Yes, Your Honor," Kaleb stated, standing as he addressed the judge.

"Alright then, we will begin with opening statements. Mr. Corsian, you have the floor."

I don't know if it was because my nerves and anxiety had taken over or because it was Brad's lawyer talking, but my mind shut down, and my eyes glazed over, not hearing anything that came out of his mouth. As soon as he was finished, sounds started to reach me—Kaleb addressing the judge, stating the facts quickly and professionally.

"...going to prove, while my client laid hands on Mr. Warland, it wasn't without just cause. Brad Warland had been forcing himself on a mutual classmate, Miss Emma Clark, during the party. The advance was unwanted, and Miss Clark attempted to fight off her attacker but was unable to do so until my client forced Mr. Warland off her.

This is why I am pushing for charges against my client to be dropped."

"Thank you, counselor," the judge dipped his head as he addressed Kaleb. "We will move on to testimonies. If Miss Clark would please exit the room." My throat closed up, my body refusing to work until Lyla nudged me, and Reid gave my cheek a soft kiss. Shakily, I stood, exiting behind Stella, Lyla quickly on my heels as we made our way out of the courtroom. My vision tunneled, Stella's cream blazer the only thing in my sight as we walked out of the room.

"Emma, darling," Stella's voice pulled me back to myself, my eyes finally able to process what was around me as she and Lyla directed me to one of the wooden benches at the side of the hall. "Take a deep breath."

"Yeah, don't want you passing out on me. I'm smaller than you, remember? I'd drop you if you fainted," Lyla teased. A slightly hysterical laugh bubbled out, the sound helping ground me.

"You doing alright? Need a bag?" Stella questioned, holding up her purse.

I shook my head, my inhale shaky as I relaxed into the seat. Well, relaxed as much as I could be, wound up tight with anxiety.

"Nervous," I said simply. "This is downright terrifying, having to go in there and recount everything that happened to a room full of people *and* my mom, who's clearly not in a good mood."

"I thought that was her," Lyla mumbled. "She looks like the stick up her ass could be loosened."

"Oh, gross," I groaned, my lips curling despite the picture she had created. "Oh, by the way, Stella, this is Lyla. She works with me at Coffee Grounds. Lyla, this is Kingston's mom."

"Nice to meet you, Lyla. Thank you for being here today for them." Stella's hand came out, shaking Lyla's.

"No problem. Can't let Emma Bean navigate all this nonsense alone. Well, not alone exactly, seeing as how she has her boyfriends..." she trailed off, realizing she'd let that slip, but I waved away her worry.

"It's okay, she knows," I reassured her. She exhaled in an exaggerated 'phew,' her hand miming wiping away sweat off her forehead dramatically. I appreciated to the moon and back that she was trying to help keep my mind off everything.

"Miss Clark," the bailiff's voice pulled me from our little bubble, his call and the opening of the door shattering the cushion I had created by pretending I didn't have to testify. Taking a deep breath, I stood. My legs were shaky, but I didn't lose my footing this time around. With that positive thought, I followed the man to the front of the courtroom.

"Raise your right hand up," the bailiff instructed when I stepped into the witness booth. "Do you solemnly swear that the testimony you are about to give for this hearing shall be the truth, and nothing but the truth, under penalty of perjury?"

"I swear," I stated, forcing the words to be steady despite my hand shaking like a leaf in the air.

"Please have a seat, Miss Clark." The judge waved a hand to the seat, his head dipping as he gave me a small smile.

Well, at least he doesn't seem to be super judgmental.

What an oxymoron, seeing as how he's a judge.

"Miss Clark," Steve Corsian started, stepping around the prosecutor's table and into the space between the stand and the rest of the courtroom. "Can you tell us what happened the night of the party in question?"

I looked to Kaleb, and his head nodded slightly, his gaze

giving me strength. Taking a breath, I told what happened as well worded as I could, struggling to keep my emotions at bay. No one interrupted or questioned as I talked, letting me get through the entire explanation before Brad's lawyer started in.

"So, is it true the defendant, Jesse Parker, attacked Brad Warland?"

"Objection, asked and answered with original testimony and admitted during the official plea," Kaleb called out.

"Sustained," the judge responded. My brain whirled at the quick-paced calls between the lawyers, my body buzzing with overwhelming emotions.

"Did you, or did you not," Steve started again, "run into Mr. Warland the night before at his place of employment and have a private conversation with him?"

"I had just come out of the bathroom and accidentally ran into him. He introduced himself, followed by me introducing myself, but he wouldn't let go of my upper arms when I tried to move around him," I explained, fidgeting in my seat.

"If Mr. Warland wanted to force himself on you, why wouldn't he have done it then? It was dark, away from other people."

"My friend, Kingston, came up, interrupting something Brad was going to say, giving me a chance to leave," I stated. I could see the tic in Steve's jaw at my answer. It was small, and from anywhere else in the room, I don't think I would have seen it.

The move put me on edge.

Well, more so than I already freaking was.

Man, do I want to spout some random facts right now.

"Is it true there was drinking at the party?" Steve redirected the questions. "And that you were drinking?"

"Yes, to both," I murmured, my cheeks heated, admitting in the middle of a court case I had broken the law.

"So, couldn't it have been that, in an intoxicated state, you misinterpreted the situation?"

"Objection," Kaleb countered. "Speculation on level of intoxication."

"Sustained," the judge agreed, looking to Brad's lawyer. "Counselor, stay on topic."

"Of course, Your Honor," Steve answered, dipping his head in apology. "Miss Clark, was Mr. Warland injured after the defendant Mr. Parker physically attacked him?"

"Uh, I don't know, it was dark," I mumbled. "I was still trying to process what had happened upstairs."

"No further questions, Your Honor," Steve bit out. His eyes narrowed on me, and his lips twitched at my answer, clearly irritated I hadn't helped his case at all.

"Counselor Bell, the witness is yours for cross-examination," the judge instructed. Kaleb nodded, getting up from his seat, and stepped up to the witness box.

"Miss Clark, did you, in any way, give Mr. Warland permission for his advances?"

"No," I stated clearly, my head shaking in response.

"Just to clarify, you did not verbally or non-verbally signal to Mr. Warland, you were okay with him placing his hands on you or kissing you?"

"No, I didn't."

"You did, though, try to push him away and tell him to stop, correct?"

"Objection, leading," Steve called.

"Overruled, used as clarification of previous testimony," the judge countered.

"That's correct," I said when the judge and Kaleb indicated for me to answer.

"No further questions, Your Honor," Kaleb stated, giving me a small smile.

"Would you like to re-examine the witness, counselor?"

"No, Your Honor," Steve stated, a sleazy smile widening as he glanced at me. The smile didn't fool me; I saw the fire his gaze was spitting at me. "I think everything was covered."

"You can go take a seat, Miss Clark."

"Thank you," I murmured with a forced smile, hopping up as fast as my tingling legs would work, focusing on walking back to my seat between Reid and Lyla without tripping.

"Closing Arguments," the judge instructed, but at that point, my hearing fuzzed over as if I had been wrapped in a noise-canceling bubble. It was an odd experience, the rush of relief my testimony was over, all while the anxiety that continued to flood my system whirled in my veins. I watched both lawyers conclude their final statements, feeling a disconnect to the room around me.

"Cali girl," Reid stated, his words muddled as he nudged my shoulders. "Emma, Judge called a recess." The longer he talked, the more the sounds of what was happening around me caught up to my brain. "We can go see Jesse. Want to go give him a big hug?" Nodding, I got up, but my movements were sluggish.

This day could not be over freaking fast enough.

"You did very well, Emma," Kaleb praised as soon as we were congregated outside the room, Jesse surrounded by our friends who were giving him reassurances and pats on the back. As soon as our eyes met, he waded his way through the group and wrapped me in a tight hug.

"Em, love, this may be the worst fucking time to say this, but I love you. Thank you for going up there, for being with me and us. I don't think I'd have survived this long without the three of you," he whispered, his honeyed words warming me from the inside out, thawing the coldness that had started to take over and dulling the worries.

"Wait... you love me?" I pulled back, my brain finally processing what he said. When he nodded, my heart skipped a beat, and I couldn't hold back the giant smile that split across my face.

"I love you too, Jess," I murmured, hugging him tightly before pressing my lips to his. "And you don't have to thank me. You three are my world, and I'll do whatever I have to, to make sure it stays that way."

"Mr. Bell," the bailiff called, "Judge Tursen would like to see you in his chambers."

"Okay, kids, stay with Stell until I get back," Kaleb instructed, waving Reid and Kingston over to where Jesse and I stood apart from the group. "Don't talk to anyone outside of your friends, alright?"

"Of course, Dad," Kingston agreed, the rest of us nodding before he followed the officer. "Probably a shitty question, but how are you guys feeling?"

"Ha, sick," Jesse huffed, his lips curling despite the worry in his eyes.

"Same. That was utterly terrifying, and if I don't have to go through that ever again, it'll be too soon," I muttered in irritation. "Can it be after graduation already, and we're on our flight to Hawaii to do all the things on our bucket list like we talked about?"

"Soon, Cali girl, soon," Reid agreed with a nod.

Not soon enough.

Twenty minutes passed painfully slow, but when the court was called, I found myself holding a barf bag.

You know, just in case.

"Alright, in the case of Mr. Jesse Parker vs. the State of Nebraska," the judge stated. "I find the defendant guilty of juvenile misdemeanor assault with the punishment of two hundred community service hours to be completed in the next six months. If you fail to complete the punishment within the allotted time, you will face up to a year in jail. Understood?" Jesse dipped his head with a "Yes, Your Honor," as the crowd gasped, either from surprise at the lenient punishment or what the judge said next.

"There are also new charges against Mr. Brad Warland for attempted first-degree sexual assault and harassment. Bailiff, if you would, escort Mr. Warland to Booking and Intake for processing." Brad scoffed, but was agitated, glancing at his parents who were outraged based on their bright red faces and near snarls.

Holy shit.

Brad just got arrested.

As soon as Brad had been removed from the room in handcuffs, somewhat forcefully by the bailiff, the judge banged his gavel.

"Court is adjourned."

Our friends jumped up in excitement, hugging Jesse as he came around the barrier separating the defense table from the gallery, but all I could think was, it was finally over.

Well, for now.

I'll deal with that bridge when we get to it.

"Is that why the judge asked to talk to you?" I asked when Kaleb came over to where I sat, still unable to move.

"Yes. He wanted to know if we were pursuing charges

against Brad, and when I said yes, he nodded. I hadn't expected him to have him arrested immediately, but I am grateful he did," Kaleb explained, holding his hand out to help me up. My mom stood stoically off to the side of the room, her lips still curled into a scowl, but it wasn't as harsh.

At least, I didn't think it was.

Might just be the intense relief flowing through me right now.

"We did it, Em," Jesse stated quietly, his smile full of relief as his shoulders drooped.

"Told you everything would work out," Reid exclaimed. "Now, who's up for some pizza or dessert? Some sort of food because now that my stomach has settled, I'm starving."

I had just opened my mouth to agree when Brad's parents stepped in front of me, cutting off my path out of the building. His parents glared at me, his mom's brow rising sharply as his father stepped closer.

Now I see where freaking Brad learned it from.

"Don't think this is over, *Miss Clark*," he sneered. "By the end of this, you'll be ruined for coming after our family." My blood ran ice-cold as they turned on their heel and stormed away.

"That won't happen, Babydoll," Kingston stated.

"Yeah, Cali girl," Reid agreed, "we're here."

"You're not alone," Jesse finished out the round of promises, and as much as I loved their reassurances, I couldn't stop the lead weight that formed in my stomach.

One trial down, one to go.

Awesome.

EPILOGUE

Anonymous

How little she notices, almost as if she's taunting me, trying to make this easy for me.

She shuffled through the cold winter weather into the shop, her head bowed. My lip curled, the urge to sneer growing as I watched her move behind the counter and into the employees' only hallway. My fists flexed, the unconscious movement betraying the adrenaline that ran through me at the thought of what I could do once I had her.

The way her skin would bloom a fresh bruise, all the more startling against her fairness. Coils of her hair would twist around my fist. Imagining the way she would gasp with each gratifying tug, the urge to sneak into the back became a persistent itch I was dying to scratch. *It would be so easy to just go through with it now...* I shoved the thought away, settling into my seat as I prepared for a long night of watching and waiting.

But when it's time?

I'll break the ungrateful brat for good.

Chaps & Cappuccinos

Book 3 of the High School Clowns & Coffee Grounds Series

Coming Spring 2020

ACKNOWLEDGEMENTS

Jake, my amazing husband, who supported me and cheered me on even when I doubted myself!

To Jaresif for being the best friend I could ever ask for as well as Cas and Ash who have been behind me through this book's rough journey

My beta readers-Michelle, Jessica, and Cassie—you guys are awesome and are the best, forever #AJsAlphabets!

Finally, for all of my readers, this wouldn't be possible without you.

ALSO BY A.J. MACEY

Best Wishes Series:
Book 1: Smoke and Wishes
Book 2: Smoke and Survival
Book 3: Smoke and Mistletoe
Supplemental Point-of-View Stories: Between the Wishes

FSID Agents Series (Spin-Off to Best Wishes):
Book 1: Whisper of Spirits

The Aces Series:
Book 1: Rival
Book 2: Adversary
Book 3: Enemy
Supplemental Point-of-View Stories: Making the Cut

High School Clowns & Coffee Grounds Series:
Book 1: Lads & Lattes
Book 2: Misters & Mochas
Book 3: Chaps & Cappuccinos
Supplemental Point-of-View Stories: Behind the Grind

Vega City Vigilantes Series:
Book 1: Masked by Vengeance

Not Your Basic Witch co-write with Jarica James:
Book 1: Witch, Please
Book 2: Resting Witch Face
Book 3: Witches be Crazy

Standalone co-write with Lucy Smoke:
Sweet Possession

About Author

A.J. Macey has a B.S. in Criminology and Criminal Justice, and previous coursework in Forensic Science, Behavioral Psychology, and Cybersecurity. Before becoming an author, A.J. worked as a Correctional Officer in a jail where she met her husband. She has a daughter and two cats named Thor and Loki, and an addiction to coffee and swearing. Sucks at adulting and talking to people, so she'll frequently be lost in a book or running away with her imagination.

Stay Connected

Join the Readers' Group for exclusive content, teasers and sneaks, giveaways, and more at A.J. Macey's Minions on Facebook and sign-up for the 'Tuesday Newsday' newsletter at www.authorajmacey.com

Made in the USA
Coppell, TX
26 February 2020

16211925R00154